CW00926614

Also by Stephen Grant

A Moment More Sublime: A Novel

★

Upper West Side Philosophers, Inc. provides a publication
venue for original philosophical thinking steeped in lived life,
in line with our motto: *philosophical living & lived philosophy*.

Stephen Grant

Spanish Light

A Novel

Upper West Side Philosophers, Inc.
New York

Published by Upper West Side Philosophers, Inc.
P. O. Box 250645, New York, NY 10025, USA
www.westside-philosophers.com / www.yogaforthemind.us

Yoga for the Mind®

Design: UWSP
Cover Art: © Rolffimages (Dreamstime.com, Photo ID: 30953951)

Library of Congress Cataloging-in-Publication Data

Names: Grant, Stephen, 1963- author.
Title: Spanish light : a novel / Stephen Grant.
Description: New York : Upper West Side Philosophers, Inc., [2018]
Identifiers: LCCN 2017015855 | ISBN 9781935830504 (softcover : acid-free
  paper)
Subjects: LCSH: Global Financial Crisis, 2008-2009--Fiction. | Wall Street
  (New York, N.Y.)--Fiction. | Emigration and immigration--Fiction. | Labor
  laws and legislation--Fiction. | European Union--Fiction. |
  Adoption--Fiction. | Ethics--Fiction. | GSAFD: Love stories.
Classification: LCC PR6107.R376 S68 2017 | DDC 823/.92--dc23
LC record available at https://lccn.loc.gov/2017015855

For Jana

"Every civilization carries the seeds of its own destruction"
—Mark Twain

PART ONE

———

LONDON

Chapter One

He takes a small sip of the excellent red. He retains the few drops on his tongue and slowly draws in some air. There is the soft, instant taste of blackcurrant, and moments later he is aware of the spice. He drinks some more and leans back. He overpaid for it from a specialist on 19th Street. A hipster with a flowing red beard and multiple rings in each ear talked him through the history of the château and the controversial production methods. Reverse osmosis to extract more water from the grape, almost two years in oak barrels, ten years before you should drink it. The two hundred dollars would normally be a restaurant price, but not there. He didn't even charge it to expenses, although he easily could have. He could have picked up a couple of bottles at ten times the price, and no one would have queried the claim.

*

Joe had called him in. "I don't understand what they are. Just find out what they are and tell me why everyone is buying them. Go to New York and find out what they are." So he is signed up for a conference with a name of such opacity that he is unclear what he will hear about. The initial talks are about performance. These products have seen this yield over this time. But what are they? More and more sophisticated versions are now being developed that offer potentially greater returns. The pitch relies upon simple principles. We are offering something many people have bought over the last two years, and they have seen huge profits. The basic model is built upon such indestructible foundations that future versions can only increase in value as they are improved by the architects who have designed them, the world's most creative and mathematically advanced people. It is a simple inductive argument aiming to remove the need for any clear understanding of what the object is. Since profit is the sole point of interest, action requires only an awareness of the profitable effect rather than the mechanics of the cause. Those who have devised the object have understood what the causal chain must be, and the smart move is to defer to theorists whose work is now proven in the real world. After all, how many people who turn on a light understand the generation of electricity?

By late morning Mat has sat through two presentations and is already growing weary. The third speaker is an MIT graduate from Hong Kong, the kind of mathematician major institutions have been hiring in ever greater numbers because such individuals hint at the elimination of doubt. He finishes and fields a series of forecasting questions that allow him to set out further statistical data to enhance the case he has already made *ad nauseam*. But the final question is different. The tone is aggressive, and the accent is not one polished over the course of an Ivy League MBA. Numbers are presented to counter the story of inevitable growth, only to be met with a further set of figures intended to undercut any doubt. But now there is a problem for Mat. He feels something may be wrong with the calculations. He is suspicious of finance's growing infatuation with mathematics, too many people seeing it as some divine force capable of conquering chance. He doesn't like the smugness of the response. Yet beyond all of this is a simple disquiet about the fact that he just doesn't know what he would be buying.

Lunch is a sumptuous buffet in a gleaming hall. Marble floors, fake crystal chandeliers and white-coated staff. He chooses from the four different forms of ethnic cuisine on offer and then scans the room. There are several groups following the CNN announcement that Obama will run, but the questioner is predictably on his own, and Mat asks if he can sit. The man looks up and motions with his head, not a word. Mat looks at the name badge. Ricardo Gomez, Devon Capital. He has never heard of it, which means nothing. Ricardo's plate is stacked high, but each pile is carefully separated from the others. The dessert cutlery is placed precisely above the plate with his main course, and the dessert itself is set neatly to the side, more as if a waiter had arranged it for him. There is no attempt to engage in conversation, but Mat wants something from this man. "I believe Devon is one of the new hedge funds."

Ricardo looks up at him, wipes his mouth with his napkin and glances at the name. "Fieldings. London?"

"Yes. We're interested in CDOs, and this seemed like a good opportunity to identify the best ones."

Ricardo smiles. There is an annoying condescension to his look, which goes well with the sharp tone of voice. Mat also realises the man is wearing an ordinary high-street suit, and there is a ridiculous comb-over to conceal the balding head. Whoever he is, he cannot be with any major fund, and he considers giving up. What could someone like this know? But before the eye contact ends, Ricardo fixes him. "What do you know about CDOs?

"Enough to recognise a lot of major institutions are attracted by them."

Ricardo is still smiling. "It's all shit."

"What do you mean? You mean all CDOs are shit?"

"Yes, all CDOs are shit. Some are worse than others, but all of them are going to be worthless within the next three years." He can see Mat is unconvinced, but the hook is in. Here is a small-timer at the same table as a major investor. "Tell me honestly if you understand exactly what they are."

"Securities backed by home loans. The loans are repaid each month and the security pays out on the basis of that income."

"Very good." Still the condescension, but also the sense this man knows something. "Now tell me the exact composition of the different types of home loan in any CDO."

Mat is caught off guard, and Ricardo treats the silence as an opportunity to continue. "Look, imagine some thirty-five-year-old called Marlene who lives in some shitty suburb outside of Atlanta. She has two kids and hasn't seen a cent from the father since he took off after Dwayne was born. She flips burgers at the local Wendy and clears nine hundred bucks a month after tax. Half of this goes on the rent for a two-room apartment where the boys sleep on a fold-up bed and she's on the couch. Then Consuela on fries tells her she's moving into her own condo, and she gives Marlene the business card for the broker who fixed up the loan. Next day she calls him and he's such a stand-up guy he's ready to come over that afternoon if Marlene's free. So Lyle pulls up in his used X3 and flashes his cheap white caps. He tells her president Bush says that she's allowed to have her share of the dream, and there are loans available to decent, hard-working people like her. Then he drives her over to a couple of the places she could have, and she imagines her boys kicking their ball around in the front yard as she rocks on the porch, and when they're tired they'll all go sleep in their own rooms. She's so choked up she starts crying, and when Lyle's seen her last two pay slips he pulls out just the sort of contract that is right for her. She signs, then she tears up again because for the first time in her life she's got the same chances others have always had.

"So now the company that issued the loans takes Marlene's, and those of all her little friends, and they put them together with some loans from people like you, and they sell them to investment banks who think they're buying this rock solid twenty-year stream of income, so how can they lose? And they sell them to other banks, and then the CDOs get more exotic, with more complex names. Now you buy a synthetic, and it's so amazing it must be even more profitable. And so everyone's happy, except that there is only one thing that Marlene has in common with everyone in this room except me. She doesn't have the first fucking idea what she's signed up to. The institutions selling this stuff wheel out Jackie Chan up there to tell us that even if Marlene doesn't keep up her payments she can always sell because property prices always rise. But when Marlene defaults, so will everyone else, and her cute little house won't be worth shit."

This speech is so obviously rehearsed that Mat has lost interest well before the punch line. He is used to technical presentations steeped in data and prosaic argument. He is sure this man is like others he has occasionally come across, someone making his way in penny stocks and day trading, tempting the odd amateur investor with spectacular claims on his cheap website. Forty thousand dollars would be a stellar year, and now he is ready to pronounce on all the world's leading financial institutions. Mat finds it reminiscent of arguments with evangelicals at university, where no evidence would sway them, and he is curious to know how impermeable the man's commitment is. "So your pessimism relies upon the view that all these borrowers will default simultaneously. You don't think this is rather unlikely?"

"It's inevitable."

Mat is now amused, but still curious about the impossible premise. "And why is that?"

"Because every subprime borrower spends the first year or two paying at an introductory rate, and this rate doubles when that period expires. None of them knew this when they signed, so they start out paying four hundred a month from their thousand take-home, and when it doubles they won't be able to pay. All the horseshit about house prices rising is a fantasy, because they can't rise fast enough to help the poor sons of bitches who bought them, and when Marlene and her friends start defaulting the whole housing market will collapse on top of them."

Now Mat is silent. It remains implausible that such fundamental errors can go so widely unnoticed. Ricardo sees the continuing doubt and raises a finger. "All right, so you still don't believe me." He then turns to the four sitting at the next table, presumably one of the specialty finance teams who dominate the conference. Immaculate suits and hair, each Blackberry handily placed, talking to one another with minimal focus as they glance down and message repeatedly. Ricardo calls over to them. "Guys, can you settle a dispute between my friend and me? The hundred per cent floating-rate, negative-amortising mortgage-backed CDOs. That means the client has paid ten per cent of the value of the home up front, right?"

The four look at one another and smile. The oldest of the group starts nodding. "That sounds right. I definitely remember reading about exactly that sort of security." Ricardo smiles back at him. "Thank you, my friend. You have just won me a bottle of champagne." Laughs all round. "Glad to help you."

Ricardo now looks at Mat and lowers his voice to ensure they cannot be heard by their new friends. "That type of loan means the borrower just defers a repayment any time he can't make one and where you don't even need to show proof of income. I could take one of the catering staff out of here and get him a three-hundred-thousand-dollar loan in the next couple of hours. Even if he's earning below minimum wage, there's a place in southern California he can move into next week. He lives his dream for a couple of years without paying a cent, and eventually he just defaults. The broker doesn't care cos he's got his commission. The seller doesn't care cos he's got his money, and the originator of the loans doesn't care because he's sold them all to these assholes who don't know what they're buying."

It's not possible. It's just not possible. The oldest and simplest of the rules is that you don't bet against the market. The best returns come from what the market tells you to buy, and the modern world has vastly augmented this collective wisdom by globalising who can buy anything. It's not safety in numbers, it's a scientifically reliable method. It's too absurd that someone like this can overturn the expertise of even those in this room, let alone all the others who have invested so heavily in such products. "You say all those with the subprime loans will default. There must be some record of the loans, and of which loans are related to which CDOs."

"Give me your business card. I'll email you the contracts for the specific ones I'm interested in. See for yourself."

"How have you selected those you're interested in?"

"The CDOs backed by the highest number of bad loans have the most potential."

"I'm not with you." The words are out before Mat has time to check himself. He is acknowledging for the first time that he is sitting with someone who understands more than he does, who can ignore the conventional sales pitch because he may have found something no one else has. "How do you actually work this?"

"You want the short or the long answer?" There is something oddly liberating about the straightforward rudeness, and Mat is so intrigued that he no longer feels the need to pretend to have any real understanding of what he is falling into. "Give me the short answer."

"Insurance."

"I buy bad CDOs and then insure them against under-performance?"

"No. You just buy the insurance."

"I can't insure something I don't own."

"Impressive, isn't it. I'll send you the contracts for a couple of those, too. Oh, and there's one more thing you're going to come across when you start looking into this. A lot of the shit you're going to be looking at is triple-A rated. That's because the only guy who works for a ratings agency is one who can't hold down a job as a trader. So you have guys earning seventy K a year taking calls from the biggest dicks at Goldman who offer them a fat fee for the correct rating of their newest product. They look at hundreds of different products, so no one can reasonably expect the kind of loser who works there to understand the terrain that even the specialists in the major banks don't know how to decipher. Just look at the fucking contracts, and look at the rate of defaults for the last six months. Don't look at the ratings, and don't look at the advertising. Just look at the real world."

Delegates are now filing back into the auditorium. The senior manager from the next table smiles as he walks by, and Mat sees Deutsche Bank written under the WASPish name. A year from now his bank will own every tenth home in Cleveland, many of them an empty rotting heap whose owners have been evicted. The manager will make twelve million dollars between now and then. Mat looks over at Ricardo. "How long will it take to get me copies of the contracts?"

"Fifteen minutes."

"I'll read them this afternoon. I assume I can find the conditions for investing in your fund on the website."

"Six-month lock-in. After that, immediate payout on request."

Mat nods. Ricardo offers a hand, and they shake. He then moves in the direction of the hotel's business centre, from where he will doubtless email the documents. Mat will see him once more, but not in New York, and not in a cheap suit.

★

He drinks again. There is a curious set of rules about the tasting of wine. Look for the separate flavours. Consider balance, luminosity, bouquet. But there is then the distinct question of whether you like it. It is as if the properties of the object being assessed are entirely separate from its quality. It seems logically possible that one could like a wine which fails against all the criteria set down for analysing it. Mat believes this to be inextricably linked to the absurdity of the industry as a whole. The aging process opens up the possibility of identifying a new property for someone sufficiently trained to recognise it. When this is combined with effective marketing, it becomes practical to charge more to those for whom self-affirmation comes with the sense of their money lifting them into a world high above that of others. It is good to pay two hundred dollars for a bottle of wine because this adds immeasurably to a fulfilling life. What is the reality? The wine is perhaps fractionally better than one for which he could have paid twenty dollars, and had he been drinking it with friends, their appreciation would have been forgotten after the first sip. He drinks some more.

★

On returning to London, he senses having stumbled on something that is too big. He had skipped the afternoon sessions of the New York conference, and worked his way through the official documents outlining the content of two different CDOs. He then laboured through two more on credit default swaps, the insurance policies Ricardo had spoken about. The achingly dull legal style revealed exactly what he had been told, and the form of the documents seemed to provide further evidence of what this oddball had said. The opaque titles were explained in language used only by lawyers, and it was difficult to believe that traders accustomed to acting on instinct would have trudged through the hideous legal jargon. It seemed ever more likely that everyone was simply jumping because really smart people said it was a good idea. The first CDO he looked at was backed by a range of different loans, many of which would be entirely safe. But even here, a high proportion were risky. The second was for a security backed entirely by loans to people on low incomes, where the risk was far greater. Ricardo had found triple-A rated CDOs like the second one, and wanted Mat to invest in his fund, which would pay out when the insurance came through.

The question now becomes what he should do. His own analysis is that all the CDOs will collapse. He could simply recommend buying the insurance without going through Devon Capital, and Ricardo must have known of this danger when he explained matters. But the unspoken understanding was that Ricardo's insight was vastly superior, and this was a form of expertise worth paying for. He already knew exactly which CDOs were weakest and which insurance was therefore most attractive. It may take months to generate a picture that will be less reliable than the one on offer.

So his recommendation to Joe is twofold. He argues that the profits from CDOs over the last two years have been so impressive, and that the momentum behind them is so great, there is good reason to invest. They put forty million pounds into six different schemes, each of which strikes Mat as having the least number of poor loans behind them. There is no rational reason for Mat to suggest this beyond a fear of betting against the market, and a residual faith in its general wisdom.

Mat also speaks of potential instability, and the second strategy is to invest five million in Devon Capital. They assume Ricardo will bank everything in a single CDS that will pay out if the riskiest CDO collapses. This leads to the theoretical conclusion that they cannot lose. If the CDOs continue to increase in value, the profits will be immense, and they can withdraw their money from Devon in six months. If Ricardo is right, however, the payout will be so vast that they needn't worry about the losses on the CDOs. Mat submits his report four days after returning from New York. Joe meets him two days later and agrees with the conclusion. The money goes out the next day.

Writing his report is a curious experience. It contains no lies, and it expresses doubts that will give him the status of a prophet. Yet the careful understatement is somehow a greater lie. The impression of balance hides his fear of fully committing to what he knows must happen, and this is not his only act of concealment. The day after he gets back, he calls his financial advisor and asks her about the option of increasing his loan against the apartment.

"How much?"

"A hundred thousand."

"How soon?"

"Immediately."

"Means a higher rate."

"I'll pay."

Only four days later, the money hits his account. He has waited until he has it before submitting the report to Joe. He knows that opening the sort of account he needs is straightforward, but it also brings with it a painfully obvious risk. He searches for the best options for new offshore accounts but must then find a means of ensuring that his money won't disappear into some beautifully presented Russian scam. He studies some business sites for their recommendations but finally hits upon a source he believes must be unimpeachable. He scours a site devoted to the exposure of tax evasion and finds an entry on just how easy it is. The supporters of the site include prominent trade unionists and left-wing Labour MPs. He cross checks the advice from the business sites against some of the articles on the pressure group's site, and identifies five possible banks in three former colonies. He sees no great advantage to any one over the others but ultimately selects the International Bank of Credit and Commerce because it's located on an island called Prickly Pear, and he is amused that for each of the thirty thousand or so who live on the Virgin Islands there are around twenty-five different companies.

It takes him around two hours to complete the tediously detailed process, but as soon as the confirmation comes that his virtual office is now set up he transfers the money from his London account to his new company. He calls it Chapelle, after the 19th Street wine, also hoping a French name will disguise him a little more from Ricardo. Nothing illegal in what he's doing. No insider information, just outsider information that none of the insiders bothered to read. Still, no need to advertise what he's up to. He puts the full hundred thousand into Devon. A tiny drop in the wider world but plenty for a fund run by a small-timer like Ricardo. He is pretty sure he will know where it's come from, and as soon as Fieldings' five million comes in he will know exactly what is going on. So what? Worst-case scenario, the fund goes bust and he loses it all. That's bad but affordable. Best case? "Jesus," he thinks. "What a case!"

*

So he waits. It is easy to watch the news and see an analogy with the opening scenes of a post-apocalypse film. Items here and there hint at some increasing danger that starts in a particular location and seems to spread unchecked. IMF warnings. Bond issues to cover losses. Interest rates lower. Institutions with immense stature sold off like scrap. There is a sense of politicians struggling to use primitive tools to confront a disease transmitted with lightning efficiency to all corners. Month after month of increasing concern, and then pandemic. At eleven forty-three, on a warm Sunday evening, Lehman files. They have spent the entire weekend trying to sell themselves, but no bank will buy them, and no government will help them. The politicians think this will stop everyone panicking on Monday morning because you can't run from a bank that doesn't exist, and the neocons love the purity of the market sifting the weak from the strong. Instead, they produce paranoia. Who else is sick? Who is next? And so the lending stops, because exposure is unavoidable in a time of effortless, digital contact.

On the Monday, Mat sees a world where the possibility of orientation is lost. No one to sell to because they cannot find the money to buy. No one to buy from because they cannot borrow to fund any further deals. Now there is simply debt without income, and each day will see the debt increase. He is called to an emergency meeting with senior management just before ten. There is analysis of Lehman, and then questions about Fieldings' investment in

CDOs. Joe turns to him, not even a word. Mat explains that they are hedged in such a way that the complete loss on their CDO investments will be theoretically covered by the default swaps. He is unsure what reaction to expect, and when silence follows, he realises that no one in the room is sure what to make of this. The CFO shows him a printout from the Bloomberg website. AIG has issued a statement saying that it may face short-term difficulties in honouring the contracts from its credit default swaps portfolio. Mat then instantly grasps a series of quite distinct conclusions. It is AIG where Ricardo must be investing, and AIG is on the verge of bankruptcy. He will lose his entire investment, as will Fieldings. If companies of the magnitude of Lehman and AIG are going under, then there is no financial institution that is capable of survival. He is days or even hours from complete financial ruin. His breath grows short, and he realises he is on the verge of throwing up.

The Chief Executive looks over at him. "You're sitting in the conference room of an investment bank, not leaping out of a helicopter in Helmand. Just control yourself." He focuses on breathing regularly, and the conversation carries on around him without anyone addressing him again. It is perversely reassuring that his own advice has had no serious influence even on his own bank. The nature of the problem is so unimaginably broad that no possible action he could have taken would have had any impact.

He doesn't sleep, just watches TV screens, laptop monitors, Blackberry messages. Everything goes down as everyone tries to run. Even Goldman and Morgan Stanley drop ten per cent in a couple of days. Every bank is going to go bust in a world that will then be unable to function because people won't be able to withdraw money from a cashpoint machine to buy food. He divides his reflection between the personal horror of losing all he has, and the general catastrophe of returning to some pre-modern age of bartering. He recalls seeing a documentary on life in Zimbabwe under Mugabe, where money was so paradoxically without value that people would swap food for petrol. There is also an odd sense of his own stupidity at having been given an insight into the absurdity of what the banks were doing, but having failed to see what the full effect would be. He loses weight between Monday morning and Tuesday night, and the two days at work are a descent to the world of those who live without any certainty or security. Within a few hours, a future of endless material comfort is replaced with the prospect of one filled only with the cost of past excess. Now homes and cars and every manner of designer product are a burden for which he has no means of paying.

It is when he sees only disaster that there is a spark of hope. He is watching CNBC at two on Wednesday morning when AIG announces it will receive eighty-five billion from the Fed. This is from Hank Paulson, who had previously worked at Goldman and allowed the fall of his former nemeses at Lehman. Mat searches every website and discovers the money will be in return for stock. Bush is nationalising. The contempt for government alters seamlessly into the unconditional need for a saviour, and by Thursday morning there are rumours of a plan. Now the market surges back at mere talk of a cure. All governments move to stop anyone shorting, so now there will be no one who can cash in if the giants fall. Then the Fed starts guaranteeing funds, and then it says it will just buy all the shit the banks have, at least it tries to until the House says no. So now more panic, as the politicians won't pay to save the banks. Too many people would just rather see them die from their own decadence even if everyone goes with them. So now Paulson goes away and comes back with more. Except it's really less, because the government doesn't even get any assets or stock. He just gives them money. Mat has to read the figure twice because he can't take it in the first time. The Fed just gives them seven hundred billion so everyone will calm down and they have enough money to keep going. No one ever calculates how much the banks actually need to cover losses in the real world, as this is all simply a question of giving them so much that they will feel comfortable enough to start borrowing and lending again. Done. Saved. Now the masters are back where they belong.

It takes seven weeks before his own bank derives the full benefit. AIG simply passes out all the money to pay for the default swaps, and Devon Capital pays its investors, including Fieldings.

They make seventy-four million. Mat is the genius who has made this possible, and there is a narrative that now emerges. His vision and judgement have resulted in an extraordinary return, and he will see the full two hundred thousand bonus on top of the hundred and twenty basic. How impressive to have been able to make such decisions in the midst of the complexity and chaos of what was happening. It is a tribute to the talent this City employs, and it explains why so much must be paid to attract and retain it.

★

He pours the last of the wine into his glass. He has tried to maintain focus on its quality instead of drifting off into other thoughts after the initial taste. When he wrapped it in a towel to bring it back to London there was no unswerving belief that he really would be able to drink it in response to this sort of moment, but it seemed like a nice gesture. There is some sediment that accompanies the final drops, and he must wait for this to fall before he drinks. Such a perfect balance. In the hour before he opened it, he paid off his enormous mortgage and ordered a case of the same wine. He did this because even after the immense payment for the apartment he has over two million sitting in a bank on Prickly Pear.

Chapter Two

When he looks back, it will strike him how absurdly trivial the key event was.

His mother sends him a link to an article from the *Bristol Courier*. Such messages usually lead him to news from the village to which his parents have now moved. It might be a former school friend who is getting married, or swimming the Avon for cancer research, or founding a sanctuary for abandoned cats. Each article reminds him of why he left, because it reveals a world in which such events are the most interesting ones to read about. Not this time. This is an interview with Pete Spelling, the man who taught him *Gatsby*. He had a kind of geek chic, with designer tee shirts and the square, Joe Ninety glasses. He would walk around the class with such animation that it became difficult to follow the passages he was reading, but the passion for the text and his offbeat humour made him a merciful alternative to other, more technical subjects.

Mat assumes the article will be one about Pete being elevated to some position in senior management, or winning one of the golf tournaments he used to tell them about. Instead it's an interview about the impact of losing your job when you're a middle-aged teacher with a large mortgage and two children. It is classic local journalism, with dramatic quotes lighting up the simple narrative. "Complete shock … Funding cuts … Taught at the college for twenty-two years … On the dust heap … Difficult to find another job at my age …" But the final line is one which unleashes a stream of unwelcome thoughts. "Seems unfair that I should pay the price for the actions of the banks."

Mat's initial reaction is one of resentment that he personally is being blamed for someone he used to know losing his job, but this is unsustainable. There are too many brute facts that cannot be rationalized. Austerity is biting everywhere, public services are being savaged, there are immense job losses, and all this to fund the bailouts. Yet it is not just the truth that moves him but also the attitudes he perceives and what he feels complicit in. He was initially amused by some of the stories that started to emerge after the chaos calmed down. All the guys at AIG who had sold the credit default swaps kept their jobs with the same salaries. But the delicious touch was that they all received their full bonuses. Mat found the public outrage understandable but was disappointed that no one asked some of the questions to which he was curious to know the answers. What was the job description? What were the criteria for earning the bonuses? One might assume that theoretically destroying not merely one of the world's largest companies but also the entire global financial system may fall into the category of underperformance, yet around seventy of them picked up over a million that year. When it was suggested the Fed should put an end to this, Ed Liddy came out and said he couldn't run the company if the government was interfering. He needed to pay good salaries to retain the top people, which amused Mat still more. Wouldn't the company be better off with a group of morons bereft of ideas? If you're just bearing the cost of their salaries while they do nothing, it would be a lot more profitable than paying really smart people to cleverly destroy you.

Mat has a growing sense of something more than absurdity, despite not feeling personally responsible for what has happened. He did not create the CDOs or the default swaps, and his buying them didn't directly cause anyone to lose a job. He also worked on deals in a London bank, and the profits from those deals incurred British tax, so why should he feel culpable? This troubling process of introspection gathers pace when he catches a clip of Bob Diamond in front of a select committee. He explains that the time for remorse is now over, and Mat looks at him in disbelief. Even if you think the bailouts had to happen, you might recognise it will take a generation before others have paid for them, and that would appear to be the shortest period of time contrition should last. Mat follows the matter-of-fact delivery and the first thought that strikes him is how obvious it is that the public apologies are no more than the transparent recommendations of Barclays' PR division.

When he reads the interview with Pete Spelling shortly afterwards, he fully appreciates for the first time why he has felt so uneasy over recent months. A single thought now pursues him, and it is made so much more powerful by the fact that it is so obvious and that he has spent so much time evading it. It wasn't the banks who paid him, it was the teachers. Not just them. He also got it from nurses and social workers and firefighters and anyone else who worked in a public service. He didn't take it from them directly, but he took it nonetheless.

This is not a straightforward process of guilt. He still feels oddly distant from the direct act of causing what has happened, and none of his colleagues appear to think like Diamond. Yet he somehow feels a part of what now appalls him, and it is a rapid journey to the conclusion that he must get out. He reaches this view sipping single malt on his balcony, the evening surprisingly warm for one so early in the summer.   When he wakes up the next morning, the force of the decision is undiminished.

Exit is astonishingly simple. His prescience before the crisis ensures periodic offers from other City institutions, and he simply tells Joe he has been offered a position with a Canadian hedge fund. There is an immediate round of pay negotiation, but he makes it clear he is leaving, and the conflict of interest ensures he must go straight away. He walks into Joe's office at eight fifteen and leaves the building at ten. He has not lied as such but simply chose not to reveal that he has no intention of taking up the Canadians' offer. He will still be paid for the three months' notice he won't be working off, and there is a possibility Fieldings may find out that he never took up the post.   But the City rarely spends time chasing people who screw them around. The sums involved are so pitiful that it would be purely a question of principle, and who is interested in paying for that? The constant danger of bad publicity is a far higher priority, and any story that may potentially hook a journalist needs to be avoided.

So he's gone. Eighteen years in the City now brought to an end in less than a couple of hours. There is an element of fear when he walks across the marble lobby, but he is able to dismiss it as nervousness at a major change. He knows that he is absolutely secure and that he wants out. Back at the apartment, he makes himself an Americano and calls one of the upper-end estate agents. She almost simpers at the sight of the high spec granite surfaces, and the Italian slate. "The view from Battersea over the river is just what so many investors are looking for today."

"How much?"

"At least one-point-four, but I suggest putting it on at one-point-six."

"How long?"

"I will put together the brochure as soon as I get back to the office, but the time difference will mean the clients I have in mind probably won't respond before tomorrow."

"Time difference?"

"Moscow, Shanghai, Brunei."

"The best bet is people who have to fly in to view it?"

"Oh they won't view it. The market is so buoyant they just buy and leave it empty. It will appreciate so fast it's a better return than any fund they can invest in and so much safer. After all, who would trust a bank these days?" She laughs at this little in-joke. The fact that Mat is seeing her in the middle of a weekday and is dressed in shorts and a tee doubtless leads her to think his money is inherited.

"How long?"

"For something like this. Mmmm ... Three days."

He likes the efficiency, but it also requires him to think immediately as to where he will go. "Any areas that are a little more modest and where there is plenty available? I mean, still in London."

"The fastest rises recently have been in parts of southwest London. Balham, Streatham Hill, around there."

"Do you have a list of places?"

"I'm afraid Executive Properties doesn't have an office there. I suggest looking on Rightmove or Zoopla. I believe they have an excellent range."

There is a slight shift in tone, and he realises she has the impression he is selling because he needs to. He considers thanking her and calling someone else, but then stops. Who cares what she thinks, and after all, she wasn't so far from the truth. "All right. Let me think about it. What's your commission?"

"We ask for a fee of three per cent of the sale price, sir. This isn't payable until the sale is complete."

"Three per cent?" He injects a tone of mock surprise. "Thank you. I'll call you back if I decide to go with you."

She is now visibly uncomfortable. A moment earlier she was looking at her share of thirty thousand for emailing out a brochure it would take her half an hour to edit together. "If the commission is an issue, we could look at two-and-three-quarters."

"What do you mean 'look at'?"

"I mean I can offer that."

He nods. "All right, you can have sole rights for two-and-a-half."

She smiles. "Great. I'll send you a copy of the brochure this afternoon, and we'll notify you of any interest. I am sure this will go very quickly."

Such a worthless exchange. What does he care how she thinks of him? Why worry about someone whom he could see flirting with some bloated fund manager to get the business? Yet it irritated him that this parasite thought she could look down on him, and if that tone cost her a couple of thousand then so much the better.

So now he has to find somewhere else to go, and there can be no question of slogging from one place to another. He searches for two bedroom flats with no upper price limit and looks only at the first page of results. He rules out contemporary ones because he wishes to get away from the floor to ceiling glass and the immaculate lines of the one he is selling. Having picked out three Victorian conversions, he manages to get an appointment to see the first the next day. He has already decided to offer over the asking price if necessary, but doesn't like the place. It is vacant and has been cleverly converted by a developer, but he can hear the bass from the flat above and he dislikes the cheaply laid decking in the miniscule garden. After he leaves, he takes a call from another agent and arranges to meet her that evening. He is early and he likes the fact that she is there before him. She's young, maybe twenty-five, black. The hair is straightened with burgundy highlights, and she wears a formal business suit, citing key facts in the formal tone that reminds him of confidant graduate trainees from Fieldings. The building is a glorious red-brick Victorian converted into two flats. The first of them takes up the lower two floors, and the one Mat is viewing includes what was originally the top floor, but now with stairs leading up into the former loft, where he likes the sloping, exposed beams of the master bedroom, and the reasonable ensuite. There is a small balcony off the kitchen, and this looks out over a tennis club that is surrounded by other similar houses.

The agent is silent after the initial play, waiting for him to speak. "How much again?"

"It's on at four hundred and fifty, but they have already found another property and the woman is pregnant, so they would probably take a slightly lower offer if you can guarantee a swift completion."

So he can take advantage of their need for a garden and another bedroom if he wishes. His first instinct is to offer four and work his way up, still the salesman. But it then strikes him this is what he is supposed to be leaving behind. "I'll offer full asking price, cash, and I can move when they can."

The agent is caught off guard for the first time, and she can't prevent the furtive smile or the cheap response. "I think that's such a wise move. Properties like this go so quickly." She'll go far, he thinks, as long as the market holds.

★

It takes only eight weeks, a miracle of speed by London standards. This is also quick enough for the sale of the Battersea flat to go through. A Ukrainian buyer paid one-point-seven, a hundred above the inflated asking price, so the agent from Executive Properties got as much as she would have without his beating down her commission. This time has a dead feel to it, part of a past he wants to get away from but can't quite leave. He sees family and starts going to exhibitions again. He needs some sort of plan for what he will now do and develops a vague ambition of cultural improvement. His initial focus is film, and he starts compiling lists from Sound and Vision. He has *The Apu Trilogy* express delivered but makes it only half way through the second installment before losing any determination. This is better than he does with *Andrei Rublev*, which he begins at ten in the evening after a drink with a former squash partner from Lazards. When he wakes up, he realises he must have seen only twenty minutes or so before dozing off, and he decides to change tack. He is far more engaged in the *Alien* series and finds the director's cut of *Aliens* to be obviously superior to the cinema release. All the back-story with Ripley losing her own daughter allows him to make much more sense of her obsessive protection of Newt. He also has plenty of time to dip into the porn tubes between Hollywood productions. By the time he moves, he has taken in collections by Hitchcock, John Ford, and David Fincher. He leaves the Tarkovsky and Bergman box sets behind in the unlikely hope that if the Ukrainian oligarch ever turns up he may get more out of them than Mat ever did.

He also gets rid of much of the furniture, most of which he starts to find increasingly irritating. His initial impulse on buying a modern apartment had been to acquire what he thought would be an appropriately up-to-date series of pieces that would suit the style. He spent absurd afternoons in Kartell and Poliform show rooms, selecting chairs with bright square cushions set in tubular steel frames. He was given detailed seminars on the nature of each piece by interior engineers who explained the relationship between the aesthetic, functional, and traditional aspects of each item. Mat considers texting Executive Properties to see if the new owner would like them, but he saw the look of instant recognition on the face of the estate agent when she walked in, and he is sure she would take the stuff herself. The used furniture dealer from London Bridge can't believe his eyes, and when he gets it all for three thousand he can't suppress a smile, knowing each armchair may fetch more than that when it goes on eBay.

By the time he moves, he is therefore without so much of the paraphernalia of wealth that he had up until just a few weeks earlier. His salary, home, furniture, and previously designated future have now gone, but there is an understanding of the contradictions that remain. Even the act of giving all this up has made him a millionaire once again. He has forfeited the externalities of his previous life but retained most of the advantages. There is a background awareness of this, but on the occasions such thoughts confront him he satisfies himself with arguments whose weakness he already suspects. If he is sincerely disgusted by the source of his wealth, then why retain so much of it? Well, what good would it do if he just gave it all away?

The most glaring challenge to the integrity of his actions is the Carrera he sits in as he pulls up to the new place. There is an enduring satisfaction in the feel of the leather seats and the instant sensation of power at the touch of the accelerator. This pleasure easily survives any thoughts about the immaturity of his attachment, but he receives an unpleasant shock when he pulls into the pebble driveway. The other car parked there is an ancient Zafira, light grey with the dents and scratches from countless years on London's bruising roads. He has chosen this area because he thought it would be a compromise between the lavish excess of where he was, and the remote exile of a deathly suburb. The idea of moving to an area that is gentrifying conjured images of well-educated couples buying a first home and sipping cappuccinos in new, independent cafés. What if he has bought a place above some hellish chavs with a posse of dirty, screaming children? He imagines endless nights of "Fuckin' shuh up!" rising through the thin Victorian floorboards. There is a sudden desire for the sound proof walls and the strict controls of the twenty-four-hour portered block he has just left. It is surely sensible to minimise contact with anyone who might conceivably disturb him, but now he is trapped in a place with a communal front door where he may have to talk to people with homemade tattoos.

He is still nervous by the time the Polish removal men have carried up the stairs the few items of furniture he brought with him. They carefully extract all the objects they had swathed in bubble wrap the day before, and by four in the afternoon he is sitting in a flat in Streatham Hill with Ocado having brought enough supplies to see him through the first week. He opens a bottle of Burgundy and goes to sit on the battered leather sofa the previous tenants offered to leave behind as part of the sale. He sinks so far into it that he spills some of the wine on his shorts, and curses as he rubs at the stain with a tissue. But before his irritation grows any further he becomes aware of some voices from outside. He opens the door onto the balcony and listens. It is clearly a man and a young girl, and there is some sort of game with an odd recurring sound that causes the girl to squeal ecstatically. Mat is reluctant to look out, but his curiosity is too strong. He moves gently forward and looks over into the garden. The girl has long, dark, wavy hair. She is dressed only in shorts and a tee shirt but is still flushed in the afternoon heat. The man is more difficult to describe at first, largely because he is on all fours and wearing a cycle helmet. The sound is the result of the girl repeatedly kicking a plastic football against the man's helmet from close range, with the victim screaming in mock pain, all to the girl's delight. Mat wishes to laugh out loud but remains quiet for fear of being detected. After five or six clean strikes the ball veers off to one side, and the girl must run off to retrieve it. The man rises and looks at her, smiling. "Enough," he says.

"No daddy. More, more!"

"No more. My turn. Come here."

"No. We can stop if I can have some chocolate."

"All right."

"For real?"

"Yes, for real."

Mat is still smiling, but the girl's head then snaps up, and she looks straight at him. He immediately pulls back, although he hears the exchange below. "Who's that man?"

"What man?"

"That man up there."

Silence now, with the father doubtless looking up at the empty balcony. After a while, "Come on. You can have chocolate, and I can have some rest." The girl then says something else, and the man responds, followed by a further silence suggesting they have now gone inside. Mat is partly intrigued and partly ill at ease that their first impression of him is that of a voyeur. Maybe the father will doubt that the girl actually saw anyone. But there is something else that initially passed him by as he sought to hide, and it is this recognition which sparks his curiosity still further. The girl's final words were spoken in perfect Spanish, and he was sure the father had responded in the same language.

Chapter Three

She is immediately recognisable. Godard was a director whose work he found initially interesting, and the short blond hair with the waifish figure is straight out of the New Wave. He will later learn that she had studied *A Bout de Souffle* as part of an undergraduate course. Just walked into the hairdresser's on impulse the next day, and has stuck with it. He sees her as he turns into the driveway with a couple of books he has picked up from a charity shop on Streatham High Road, and realises she is examining the car, just standing there as she looks it over. Both are embarrassed by his catching her like this, but she is first to recover. She smiles, and he's unsure if she's amused by him or the general situation. "Hello." She extends her hand with the arm absolutely straight, and they shake in what seems like an overly traditional introduction. "Welcome to Woodley Avenue. I'm Miriam."

"Mathew."

There is an unfortunate silence, and just before it starts to become excruciating she looks quickly at the books and then back at him. "Well, see you later." He watches her as she strides off, a bulky messenger bag slung over the right shoulder, and by the time he gets upstairs, his thoughts have moved forward in a strange direction. He assumes she must be the mother of the child he saw a few days earlier. Both parents share a similar style, with baggy clothes hanging casually from a slim frame. He places her around thirty, and the man was certainly older, closer to forty, although it was difficult to judge confidently through the cycle helmet. What leaves Mat ill at ease is the contrast with his own physique. He is not exactly fat, but the years of frantic energy in the City were all spent sitting in front of monitors, with long workdays often followed by exquisite meals. Early years included intense squash matches, but promotion brought greater demands and increasing opportunities to use money in ways that minimised effort. Holidays were spent in villas designed to promote inactivity, and where the heat made any sort of exertion deeply unappealing. Social etiquette determined that dining at an increasingly exotic range of restaurants was simply part of ordinary life. But he also became aware of his decreasing ability to compete in ways that had previously been straightforward. The free membership of the ultra-modern sports club also went to new recruits at the bank, and he began to realise that his speed and stamina were declining, with merciless defeats now handed out by players whom he would once have beaten. He disliked being humbled by staff who were junior to him, and after a couple of years slipping down the internal leagues, he claimed he had too little time and simply dropped out.

His initial impulse is to dismiss these concerns as nothing more than dealing poorly with the consequences of aging. But he finds it difficult to reconcile this with the simple facts of being free to do more or less what he wants, and of being thirty-nine rather than ninety-nine. So he strips off and looks at himself in the wood-framed, seven-foot mirror that now stands in the hall, part of a monstrous delivery of products from John Lewis the previous day. He has opted for the traditional, French style, which he was told will create the relaxing atmosphere of a provincial farmhouse. This sentiment was somewhat at odds with what he took to be the relentless swearing of the two Romanians who manoeuvred tables, a sideboard, chairs and an emperor-size bed up the narrow staircase. Their mood was transformed when he slipped each of them a twenty-pound note which they shoved into their sweat-stained overalls before disappearing off for god knows how many other similar calls.

The wooden theme was intended as a contrast to the steel of the Battersea apartment, but once in place it starts to annoy him that everything looks so similar, and his favourite piece now becomes the battered leather sofa that had been left behind. It is here where he sits for breakfast each day with the espresso from the Oracle coffee maker he brought with him, a two-thousand-pound ex-

travagance he has never regretted. He knows how much vanity
is implied by the presence of the huge mirror, but this thought
is far from his mind as he stands before it now. The thick dark
hair is the generous endowment from his mother's side, and he is
relieved there is not yet any hint of thinning or greying. But the
cheekbones and the line running from his chin down to his neck
are unmistakably covered with a sagging layer. Budding breasts sit
above an impressively consistent ring of flab, and as he looks at this
he is irritated by the memory of the couple who live downstairs.
Mat wants to have the same easy elegance they have, with his shirts
undisturbed by the bulge of his stomach, and a face restored to the
angular shape it had in his twenties.

"Only one way," he thinks. And he pulls the shorts and under-
wear back on before lying down full-length on the sofa with the
MacBook and a carton of orange juice. It takes an hour to make his
selection, and the six-week package he orders will start within a
couple of days. The first step is to download the dietary recommendations attached to the email welcoming him to Slimmer Solutions.
It is a predictable list of do's and don'ts, and the first of his set of
meals will arrive in two days. The diet will start at the same time as
the sessions with the personal trainer he will meet at Tooting Bec
Common. The claim is that he will shed around twenty pounds, after which he will need to follow the guidance on food and exercise
if he is to avoid the usual fate of simply recovering all he has lost
over the following few weeks. His aim is to lose the most weight
with the least effort in the shortest period. He is sure that the exter-
nal encouragement of someone standing over him and others making his food will make this far more achievable, and the restoration
of his self-image in such a short period seems well worth the three
thousand it will cost him. He is mildly amused that marketing consultants have obviously missed the danger of giving a firm dealing
in discipline the acronym SS.

The rest of his day is spent with the first of his new novels, and
then browsing new film releases on Amazon. By six he is bored of
both, pours himself a kir and takes it out on the balcony. The girl is
once again in the garden, and this time she is looking at him when

he comes out, doubtless having heard the balcony door. She looks down, opens her arms and tries to catch a tennis ball that drops between her hands. "Bad throw. Bad throw." He can hear the man laughing. "Bad catch. Bad catch." The girl looks up at Mat again and moves back towards the house and out of sight. Then he hears the voice of a woman speaking in Spanish. The man responds in what sounds like the accent of a native speaker, the tone negative. After that, the voice of another woman, this time impatient, hectoring. A moment later the man walks out into the middle of the garden and looks up at Mat. "Hello. Uh ... Mathew? We thought you might like to join us for a drink."

Mat is uncertain. He guesses the man has been bullied into the invitation by the women, but he can't easily refuse. "I'd love to." He goes to the kitchen to find a bottle of wine, selecting from the supporting cast of reds, and makes his way down to the communal hallway, from where he sees the man standing in the front door of the ground floor flat. He extends his hand. "Tom. Nice to meet you." Mat follows him inside, the door leading straight into the toy-covered lounge. Tom registers the look of surprise and is obviously embarrassed. "I'm sorry. I promise this isn't what it usually looks like ... Actually, yes it is. It's just we try to tidy it a little when people come over. This is the danger of spontaneity."

They both laugh, and Mat hopes that the resistance he detected in Tom's voice earlier was because he didn't want a guest to enter this carnage. Beneath the army of Lego people, assorted vehicles and the full spread of the animal kingdom there is an Ikea show room. Oak-effect tables and chairs sit on a laminate floor, and ceiling-high bookshelves run the length of one wall, each filled with books lying sideways on top of the upright ones. Around half appear to be Spanish, the remainder a combination of novels and philosophy in English. Mat suddenly feels self-conscious of the paltry collection he has sitting on the stand beside the TV, and he resolves to supplement them with a couple of hundred classics. Tom catches him looking at the shelves. "It's all for show. We've never read any of them." He then ushers Mat outside where the two women are sitting in white plastic chairs, the girl standing between them, all three smiling at him. He guesses the one he hasn't seen before is taller than Miriam, the jet-black hair indicating that this must be the girl's mother and that Miriam may therefore be single. The dark-haired woman rises. "Hello. Sofia." She then looks down at her daughter. "Alicia!" The girl approaches him, holds out a rigidly straight arm. "Hello. I'm Alicia. Very pleased to meet you." Mat kneels down, sits the bottle of wine on the ground, and takes the girl's hand. "Hello. I'm Mat, and I'm very pleased to meet you."

Tom then emerges from the house with one of the dining chairs, and he offers Mat a glass of the red they are already drinking. He almost recoils at the taste. Far too young, almost acidic. He looks up and smiles. "Delicious. So, how long have you been living here." A standard entry into polite middle-class conversation. It is Sofia who answers, barely able to conceal what is clearly a shared curiosity. "Oh, four years now. But tell me, what would bring someone with a Porsche to Streatham Hill?"

What follows is not a pre-planned effort at deception, and he doesn't even really intend to lie. It is more part of a sublimated attempt to get away from where he once was without acknowledging even to himself just how much he has benefitted from it. "I lost my job in the financial crisis and decided I wanted out of that life. I just thought it would be more interesting to live in this sort of area."

All three adults seem intrigued by this, although Alicia has already drifted off into helping Buzz Lightyear make his way around the cosmos. Miriam nods at this explanation. "It must have been very difficult to lose your job like that. You must really resent the people who were dealing in these complex securities."

"I've been able to come to terms with it. They didn't really foresee the full effect of what they were doing. It was just this sort of lucrative joyride they all jumped on without realising where it was all headed." The effort to hide any sense of irony is almost as great as the shock that anyone outside the City might speak of securities with apparent understanding. He also realises there is a danger of appearing a little too sympathetic before an audience who may well share the general preference for using pitchforks to deal with the banking community. "There was definitely a sense of absurdity about how it was all handled."

Tom looks even more curious. "You were against the bailouts? I thought everyone in the City was arguing they were necessary."

"There was no way all the banks could simply be allowed to go under, but the way the US government handled it was driven more by panic than any rational reflection." He then suffers an increased sense of fear that he may either start boring them with the dull technical nature of it all, or else simply antagonise them. "Are you really interested in this?"

Now Sofia joins the discussion for the first time. "Actually it's a source of fascination for us. Tom passed round Lanchester's book, which is better than any thriller. Did you actually have any idea of what was happening?"

"There was a sort of formal concern, but everyone was doing so well it didn't really seem much more than the usual background noise about potential problems further down the line. Then all of a sudden the talk was of the worst crisis since twenty-nine, and we all grasped how serious it was."

Now Tom breaks in again. "You seemed to suggest you were against the bailouts."

"They couldn't just let all the banks go, but what it all came down to was institutions everywhere owning the mortgages of poor Americans who couldn't repay them. The US government could have paid off the mortgages, but instead they just gave the money to the banks and they in turn foreclosed on all the borrowers and kicked them out of their homes."

Miriam smiles at him. "You sound very cynical."

He sighs. "I'm not sure it's cynicism, just a loss of faith in the prevailing economic religion. The moral premise of modern finance is that everyone comes out ahead if you unleash the free market. All of a sudden, the same people who had spent years arguing for this reached the view that governments around the world had a moral obligation to save banks that the free market wanted to kill off. Then you read an article in the morning about troops coming back from Afghanistan to find their regiment is being disbanded, and later the same day you sit down for a drink with someone who tells you about his bonus and the need for austerity … Well, you see how much wishful thinking there is behind all the so-called theory, and how it becomes so dangerous. That's why the crisis had to happen, and why it will happen again."

The three are still staring at him. Tom reaches over to fill his glass. "Please go on, Cassandra."

"People are recruited out of top universities and told they are being employed because they are smart. They are then offered the possibility of enormous earnings, and these come for correctly judging where the future lies. Except when they invest, they are always investing someone else's money, so the risk is never fully personal. And when it comes off, they attract the sort of reputation that guarantees ever more money, and you live in a world so enclosed that you only really compare your life to others in the same line."

Miriam looks at him quizzically. "So why must it happen again?"

"The most misused term in all this is 'casino banking'. The problem lies precisely in the fact that investment banking isn't enough like gambling. If I sit down at a roulette table and see that red has come up ten times in a row, I still know my chances are only fifty-fifty of it coming up the next time, and I'd be a fool to think I *know* what will happen. But if I see a company has performed well ten years in a row, then I have good reason to think it's a sound bet. It's the possibility of predicting the future that generates the real risk because it creates the illusion that you can turn it into a science. Then you start offering the biggest rewards for the greatest risk, and you must produce a crisis because people are bound to overstretch in the belief they're fully in control. It's so mesmerising to watch the money pour in, that people simply lose sight of their own limitations.

He stops and looks at them, uncomfortable at the silence. "I'm sorry, these thoughts had been swirling around in my head, and they just sort of popped out when you asked about what happened." He looks over at Tom, who is holding what is now an empty bottle of wine, and he spies the one he brought downstairs with him sitting on the ground beside Sofia. "Any chance of another drink? Try mine if you like."

"Oh, sorry. Of course." Tom leaps up to get the bottle. Mat is keen to switch the conversation to something lighter, fearing that this is too much personal confession for a first meeting. He tries for a subject he believes to be one of interest for such an audience. "So, I hear childcare is really expensive these days."

Both women are surprised by the change of direction, and even Alicia looks up. Sofia reacts first. "Actually, we don't really have to pay for it. Tom does it."

The girl now interrupts. "Can I watch *Charlie and Lola?*" A nod from her mother and she is gone. Sofia now tastes the wine and looks up at Tom. "My god, this is quite good. Where did you get it?"

"I must have picked it up at Lidl on special offer," says Tom, oblivious this was the one that Mat had brought. Mat is annoyed that he will not receive the credit for his wine, but more relieved that he will be spared any more of the earlier poison. His satisfaction diminishes as he sees Tom pouring enormous quantities for Miriam and himself, before refilling Sofia's now half-empty glass. By the time the bottle reaches him there is only a third of a glass left. "You know what, I have some wine upstairs. Why don't I pop up and get some more?"

Sofia shakes her head vigorously and raises a hand to stop him. "We wouldn't hear of it. Please, let us treat you this evening. A pause, and then, "So, are you officially retired?"

"Actually, I was thinking of trying to enter teaching." He simply has no idea where these words have come from. When he later tries to reconstruct the line of thought that must have produced them, the best account he comes up with is some combination of reading an article on the shortage of maths teachers and perhaps some subliminal recollection of Pete Spelling. Whatever its provenance, the impact is impressive. Miriam looks over at him, obviously shocked. "So what would you teach?"

He was once told by a hedge fund manager who had committed far too much on the prospect of the Yuan falling that there

are times when the hole you're in is so deep all you can do is keep
digging. "I would really like to try art history." At least the reason
for this answer is clearer to him, having read *The Story of Art* the
previous week, and being broadly confident that he could make
it through a couple of rounds before revealing he knew virtually
nothing about the subject. Tom is in the process of dipping his sour
cream Pringles into the guacamole, and looks up. "We told Alicia
that we would take her to the National Gallery to do the Katie tour.
Why don't you come with us?"

"Great idea. I think I read a really positive review of the exhibition."

"Ah, no. Sorry, that must be something else. The Katie books
are a series in which a little girl enters various classic works of art
and meets the characters in the paintings. I don't think they have
ever put all the pieces together in a single exhibition."

Miriam nods. "I was thinking of taking her tomorrow, why
don't you join us? Tom can have a day off."

"Wonderful," he thinks, realising he will now have to find out
later what the hell the books focus on and try to ensure he has
something intelligent, but not pretentious, to say about them. As
for teaching art history, how the fuck is he going to get out of
that one? The conversation moves mercifully away from any other
topics that might tempt him to either develop some fantasy future
or force him to conceal his past, and by seven Alicia is escorted to
bed by Tom with only minimal resistance. When he returns, he
brings a further bottle of the first wine, and Mat feels that enough is
enough. "I'm just going to nip upstairs for a sweater." Two minutes
later he has returned with a couple more bottles of his own. "Look! I
must have bought some wine from the same stash that Tom found."
He doesn't know what Lidl is, but has already concluded they are
unlikely to be selling red at the minimum of forty pounds a bottle
he always pays. He opens the wine himself. "So, Alicia seems lovely," he says, pouring himself a full glass to ensure he doesn't miss
out again.

Tom smiles at him. "She's a little better now, but she's only just
got through this rather difficult biting phase. She would get frus-

trated and just regress to some primal stage of human development. I once left her micro scooter in the back of the car and she bit the bumper when she couldn't get to it. The couple you bought your flat from had a girl who was a couple of months younger, and we realised that all of a sudden she wasn't being invited upstairs to play anymore. We had to sit her down and ask if there was any problem, and it turned out she took the heads of the girl's two favourite Barbies when she couldn't get their shoes on. I think the parents were worried their kid was next."

"Oh well, at least she didn't attack any people."

"Not at first, but when she realised the impact on humans was more impressive than anything she could elicit from the insentient, she moved on. I once took her to this playgroup on Trinity Road, where it was just her and a couple of boys jumping on the equipment. There was a sort of mini slide, and just as she was about to climb up the ladder this thuggish little brute pulled her back and she just stood there looking up at him as he bundled past her. I looked over at the mother, who didn't look away quite fast enough to avoid eye contact with me, and she reluctantly called over to her son, "Play nicely, Tarquin."

"Tarquin?"

"Yes. This was the Wandsworth Common end of Trinity Road."

"Alicia didn't look too upset, so I decided not to make an issue of it and went back to my book. Then there was this piercing scream, I looked up, and Tarquin was face down on the super-soft play mat with Alicia sitting astride him. She must have waited at the foot of the slide and then pounced. She'd found a nice piece of loose flesh just below his right shoulder blade and she looked as if she was trying to gnaw her way through it. Then she started jerking her head from side-to-side to tear it free. Tarquin was just lying there crying miserably, the mother and I descended on them, and I had to pull her off. She'd gone right through the kid's Ralph Lauren polo, and she kept snapping her neck towards him as I held her back. The mother made some snotty comment about the need to control my child, which just pissed me off more than before. I looked at Alicia and said something like, 'Now what have we been told about biting, darling? It's very naughty. Say sorry to Tarquin.' She looked over and said, 'Sorry, Barkin,' and I had to bite my lip." He takes a sip of wine, and looks down reflectively. "You know the worst part? I actually left her clamped on there for a few more seconds than I needed to. When I saw her on top of him, I had this terrible urge to start cheering."

Sofia is now shaking her head. "That is terrible, Tom."

"I know. I felt as ashamed as you did when you started laughing at the Barkin bit that evening."

Mat leans back in his chair. The good wine, the warm evening. Yet there is something more oddly relaxing about it, which he cannot yet put his finger on. By the time he goes upstairs, he already knows he is looking forward to seeing them again. Them? Yes, he wants to see Tom and Sofia, and even Alicia. But above all he wishes to see Miriam, and he is excited at the prospect of meeting her the next morning for a trip to the National Gallery. He then realises he can't recall the name of the children's books with the paintings they will be viewing and will therefore have no chance of reading up on them. "Fuck it," he thinks. "I've spent years pretending I knew what I was talking about."

Chapter Four

When he knocks on the door, it is Miriam who opens. "Come in, come in", and he follows her through to the lounge. The toys that were strewn across the floor the previous evening are stowed in functional, plastic boxes that stand in front of the bookshelves. Their presence badly undermines the rustic style the rest of the furniture is intended to create, and has the effect of making the room feel cramped. Alicia is sitting at the dining table, concentrating intently on the crayons and paper in front of her. Miriam calls across to her. "Alicia, say hello to Mathew."

"Hello, Mathew." Not even a glance in his direction.

Miriam is wearing the same figure-hugging jeans from the evening before, with a French fisherman style tee. The white and navy hoops remind him still further of Seberg, and he wonders if she's not overdoing it. This thought evaporates when she looks directly at him and smiles. "Can I ask you a favour? I said I would pick up some things. Instead of all three of us going up to the supermarket, would you mind staying with Alicia, and I'll be back in a couple of minutes?"

He is uncomfortable with this, suddenly seeing visions of the girl losing her cool and launching herself at him in some Hannibal-like attack. "No problem." He hopes she will retain the fanatical focus on her drawing until Miriam returns. As she leaves, he looks at his watch. Nine-thirty, so there shouldn't be any queues to delay her, and he sits opposite the girl. "So, Alicia, what do you like doing aside from drawing?"

She answers without looking up. "Daddy and mummy took me to Legoland for my birthday. It was *so* awesome. We went in Lego saucers that went round. And we went in a Lego boat that went down a hill and water splashed on us. And we had pizza."

Mat is bored with this story even before they reach the pizza but feels he ought to persist in some sort of social exchange. He tries to decipher the impenetrable mess she is working on with such devotion. "That looks very interesting. Can I ask what it is?"

"Guess. It begins with wuh," she says, still not looking up.

He suspects some of the lines may be wires. "Is it a washing-machine?"

"No. Guess again." A smile now as she feels herself moving ahead in the game.

"Is it a windmill?"

"Nooo," with the smile now broader. "Try again."

He can't think of any machines she might know that begin with the appropriate letter, so he changes strategy and goes for what he thinks a child may be interested in. "Is it a witch?"

She throws back her head and howls. "Noooooo." She now looks at him for the first time, her face illuminated by the amusement at his poor attempts. "It's a wobot." Full concentration is then restored as the mass of jagged lines and curves on the paper become ever denser, but her eyes soon rise in suspicion and the drawing ceases as she sees Mat pick up a tiny, plastic show jumper from the middle of the table. Her right hand continues to grip the colouring pencil with ferocious force, instantly ready for a return to action. But the eyes are now trained on the figure, and after a few moments a look of fury sweeps across her face. "Hey, you're not sharing!" And the left hand snakes out with astonishing speed to whip her little friend from the open palm in which Mat is holding it.

He senses he should probably do something responsible. "Now, that's not very nice. Shouldn't you say 'please'?"

"No. It's my toy. It's not yours." The figure remains hidden within the left hand as she returns to her artwork, and Mat decides he has made his point. He checks his watch to find it is now nine-thirty-four and realises his best chance of avoiding conflict may lie in doing nothing that may disturb her. This possibility recedes when, with head still bent over the paper, she addresses him for the first time without provocation or compulsion. "Do you have a friend called Charlie?"

Mat's first thought is of an equities analyst from Fieldings called Charlie Driggs, but he hasn't seen him for years, and he is sure the name hadn't come up the previous evening. "No I don't. Do you have a friend called Charlie?"

"No. Do you know someone called Charlie?"

"I used to, but I don't know him anymore."

"Is he very small?"

"Not really. He was over six feet."

"What's six feet?"

"It means he was quite tall. Why do you think I know someone called Charlie?"

"I heard mummy say you probably put lots of Charlie in your nose. How do you do that?"

For reasons he does not fully understand he feels he cannot simply state he has never put anyone in his nose, and that mummy made a mistake. He feels a sort of inarticulate desire to engage in conversation as honestly as possible. This first thought combines unfortunately with a specific recollection from a dinner party some years before. He was part of the only couple at the table without young children and recalled the proselytising of a mother who had delivered all of her three kids without an anaesthetic. Her response to Mat's curiosity about enduring unnecessary pain was a lecture on the undiluted wonder of feeling absolutely and fully alive, at which point Mat stifled a belly laugh and tried as best he could to sit politely through the endless anecdotes about shitting, screaming and sleep deprivation. He nevertheless came away with a sense of the authority these people must have on the issue of children, and a particular piece of wisdom now comes back to him. It is important not to mystify the world. Children must receive care and love but must also be brought to understand that there are aspects of what they will face that are not present in books about hungry caterpillars and colourful dragons. For Mat, these thoughts don't take the form of a careful process of reflection but come more as a jumbled supply of apparent knowledge he thinks he can draw on. He looks down at Alicia and smiles. "When mummy said Charlie, she didn't mean a person, she meant cocaine." As soon as the word is said, the mere sound of it freezes him, and there is a horrifying recognition that even if he can now somehow manoeuvre the girl off the topic without revealing too much, there is a severe risk of this exchange leaking out. This in turn imperils not only his early attraction to Miriam but also any possibility of a good relationship with his new neighbours. "So, how would you like to go outside and play football in the garden? Maybe I can put on daddy's cycling helmet and you can kick the ball against my head. Go right for the face if you want."

"What's cocaine?"

"Oh, forget I said that. Let's play football."

"What's cocaine?"

"Football, football. Let's talk about that?"

"What's cocaine?"

He fears the constant repetition of the word may help to embed it in her vocabulary. New worries now start to emerge about police involvement. "Sit down please, sir. If I understand correctly, you are a single, unemployed middle-aged man without children of your own living above a family with a young child. And I believe you spoke with this child about a class A drug. Is that correct, sir?" He can now feel himself beginning to sweat, and he wonders if the best strategy might not be to give up on trying to drive her off the path immediately, and instead to gently lure her away from it with some rather more carefully selected answers. "It's a white powder."

"What's a powder?"

"How the fuck is this supposed to work if you keep doing vocab checks?" he thinks. "A powder is lots of little bits of stuff all together in a little pile."

"Why do you put it in your nose?"

"It makes people feel really good."

"Can I have some?"

"I'm afraid not. Only big people can have it." He is relieved at having avoided the repetition of the key word himself, and hopes that Alicia may not yet have internalised it. This fleeting moment of hope is quickly succeeded by a heart-pounding nervousness as he hears the front door opening and realises that the next few moments will be critical. Miriam walks in with a couple of shopping bags that she deposits in the kitchen before sitting down at the table with them. "So, what have you two been talking about?"

Alicia looks up, first at Mat, then at Miriam. Big smile on her face. "Mathew thought this was a witch." Miriam smiles. "That's funny. What else were you talking about, darling? Remember, it's important to try and listen to exactly what people say and to answer when they ask you something." These last words produce in Mat a clear understanding that at this rate the content of what he has told her will soon come out in some sort of corrupted form, and that Alicia's innocence will ensure everyone believes her. He considers asking Miriam to step into the kitchen where he might try explaining why he was discussing cocaine with a four-year-old. Instead, inspiration strikes. He leaps to his feet, spreads his arms, and beams down at the two of them. "Who wants to go to Legoland for the day?"

Both look back at him open-mouthed, but Alicia is first to react. "I do! I do! I do!"

Miriam's state of disbelief delays her response a little longer. "I thought you wanted to go to the National?"

"Well, it'll still be there tomorrow."

Alicia now looks up at him with deep concern. "Is Legoland going away?"

"No, no," he says, desperate to avoid any further mishaps. "But look at that glorious sunshine. Much nicer to be outside. Come on, let's pack some bags and go."

Miriam is still in apparent shock. "'Pack some bags'? How long are we going for?"

"Well, I mean nappies and food parcels and dummies. All the essentials."

"She's a four-year-old from Streatham, not an abandoned baby in a Lebanese camp." She then sighs and looks down at Alicia. "All right, find Percy Penguin, take your blue sweatshirt just in case, and go to the toilet." She then looks over at Mat and smiles. "Give me a couple of minutes to put together some emergency supplies in case we find ourselves stranded in Legoland."

"Great. I'll just get the car keys." He races upstairs with a breath-taking sense of relief. That girl is about as likely to have cocaine on her mind over the next few hours as she would have been if he'd said nothing about it. If he can get through that first key period without her talking then surely the memory of it would be overwhelmed by the excitement of all those bricks. He grabs the keys and makes his way outside where he finds Miriam and Alicia already standing by the car. Alicia is now wearing a neat little back-pack with Buzz and Woody smiling out from each side. He fits the booster seat that Miriam has retrieved from Tom and Sofia's car, positioning it behind Miriam so he can keep his own seat pushed back as far as possible. Fifteen minutes after he first mentioned co-caine, they are ready to leave. The car eases back over the pebbles, and he pulls slowly away. The mid-morning departure ought to mean that there should be less traffic around, and a desire to re-veal the power of the car leads him to accelerate unnecessarily as they turn onto the first main road. An unfortunate robin is hopping across the road and is unable to react quickly enough before one of the immense wheels flattens it. Mat hopes this has gone unnoticed, but from the rear seat there comes a detailed appreciation of what has happened. "You killed that bird. It had a worm in its mouth. It was probably going to its nest. Now all its baby chicks will die."

This wasn't the effect Mat had imagined when he ushered them into the car. "You know what—those chicks are probably already big enough to fly, and I bet they're already off to start families of their own." But after a brief silence, there is now a low, persistent sobbing. Mat looks over at Miriam, assuming that she will be able to deal with the situation, and he is angry to see her searching through her handbag as the outpouring of grief in the back seat continues. But she then pulls something from the bag and turns to Alicia with it. "Would you like an organic, dried strawberry?" The girl is trans-formed. "Yes, please." She grabs the entire bag and begins work on consuming the contents as quickly as possible, all concerns about avian infant mortality now gone.

The journey takes around an hour, much of it spent on the M4, where they pass everything at what feels like lightning speed. Even after all the years of driving such cars, there is the residual pleasure on feeling his head pulled back against the seat in immediate response to touching the accelerator. Vehicles previously moving alongside disappear from peripheral vision and reappear in the mirror as if time has slowed for them. Alicia pesters him to go ever faster, but even he has enough awareness to recognise this impulse has to be controlled. He is also able to ask Miriam some of the questions that had come to him the previous evening but that he'd been unable to raise. "Can you tell me how you and Sofia came to speak such immaculate English?"

"Sofia has lived here for almost twenty years. I studied here before I went back to Spain."

"'Went back'? I thought you lived here."

"I'm here only until the end of the summer. I teach at the University of Castile."

"What did you study?"

"I did my PhD in philosophy with Tom at King's. When we worked out the Spanish connection, I got to know Sofia as well, and we all kept in touch."

"You're a philosopher?"

"Sort of. I teach it, and the point of being here is I'm trying to write a couple of papers. I was given a term off, and I get the spare room in return for looking after Alicia from time to time."

"Do you have some sort of specialisation?"

"I'm trying to write on justice."

"Trying?"

"I've been here two months, and I've slipped into the mindset of believing there is always just one more article or book I have to read before I actually start writing. Now I have only three months left and I've read so much that I have no idea where to begin."

"This may be naïve, but can't you just write a longer piece?"

"Journals don't like anything more than six thousand words. You basically have to make an incredibly narrow point and then defend it against any conceivable attack. You hope it gets into a good journal and will be read by a few dozen people around the

globe who are interested in the same tiny corner of the philosophical landscape. That is success."

Mat's curiosity is diminished by the knowledge that Miriam
will be leaving, but he is also intrigued by these people. It turns
out that all three of the adults living below him have doctorates,
the obvious anomaly being that Tom no longer works. There is
something about the clipped tone in which Miriam says this that
tells him not to ask any more questions, and by the time they pull
up to the apparently infinite car park, he resents the fact that trudg-
ing round a plastic playground will delay the possibility of finding
out more. When he retrieves his messenger bag from the back and
locks the car, he turns to find Alicia smiling up at him. She holds out
her hand, he takes it, and the three of them walk to the gates where
he pulls out his AmEx card before Miriam can get there. "Please,"
he says. "My idea. I get to pay for it."

In truth, he is dreading what will be his first visit to a theme park
and is starting to regret his decision not to explain his error back
in Streatham when he had the chance. His concerns are reinforced
when he realises how many cars have beaten them there, and the
multitudes he can see from the hilltop entrance make him feel as
if he's on the set of *The Ten Commandments*. It is only when Miriam explains that they are in the middle of the summer half-term
holiday that the full force of his earlier mistake now strikes home.
She tells him this twenty minutes into their half-hour wait for the
first ride, by which time Alicia is becoming increasingly difficult.
After they emerge from the ten-minute trip in a mini-submarine
from which they viewed a series of exotic creatures made entirely
from plastic, they decide on a strategy that will alleviate the danger
of Alicia becoming upset at spending fifty minutes of every hour
standing in a line dominated by other whiney children. She chooses
the sequence of rides she finds most appealing, and Mat queues for
the next but one, meaning Alicia and Miriam can move straight to
the front of the queue once they finish the previous ride. Mat then
moves on to reprise his role at the next attraction, an exercise made
somewhat less dull by the fact that during each wait he can read
the Franzen novel he has downloaded on his iPad. Nevertheless, by

late afternoon he has been standing vigil for over four hours, a process broken only by some miserable Bolognese poured over watery pasta. His rising irritation is made worse by Alicia's ecstasy at the prospect of each further ride, suggesting the day may never end. He texts Miriam that he will be waiting at one of the cafés, and when the girl bounces up to him he is determined that no matter how much disappointment it will cause there will be no more queuing. She smiles up at him. "Can we go on the helicopters?"

"No, I think it may be time to go now. It's getting late." He then turns to Miriam. "It would be really good to get back before the rush hour. It could cost us two hours if we get caught in it." The tone says more than the words, and she looks down at the girl and says something in Spanish. Her face crumples, and Mat fears the prospect of driving home with her blubbing away in the back. "Wait one moment."

He heads off for an ice-cream stall, surely the way to keep her quiet, but then worries she may stain the car seats. Five minutes later he is standing in front of the two of them with a version of Emmett around eight inches taller than Alicia. Her eyes widen in disbelief and she grabs it, almost tumbling over before Miriam saves her. "What do we say to Mathew?"

"Thank you, Mathew," she says, her face lit up.

The ride home is uncomfortable. He feels from Miriam's silence that he is going too fast, but he's had enough now. Not his kid, and nothing in the day that was for him to enjoy. They make it back in under an hour, the girl conversing constantly with Emmett, who sits beside her. When they open the front door, Tom comes to welcome them and thanks him, but without any offer to pay. Alicia immediately starts talking about all they have done, with Tom expressing mock surprise at each story. He then looks over at Miriam. "You got a Skype message from León, I think it was urgent."

"Oh God, I was supposed to call this morning." She's about to rush in but suddenly turns to Tom. "Can Mat come in for a drink? He's spent the whole day standing around for us."

"Of course, I've still got some wine left from last night."

Even without the prospect of stale wine, Mat is now reluctant.

"Thanks, but I've actually got a series of things I need to catch up with. It was really a great today. I hope Alicia enjoyed it." He trudges upstairs, throws the car keys into the bowl by the front door and flops down onto the sofa, his thoughts turning with irritation to the news that Miriam will be leaving. "It's not as if I actually know her enough to be disappointed," he thinks. Yet he is, and there's no getting away from it. The only reason he doesn't feel more disheartened is that he is sidetracked by a thought he's had many times before but never with such crystalline clarity. "Why the fuck does anyone have children?"

Chapter Five

He feels something close to excitement at the prospect of his new regime, relishing the idea of recovering the shape he had in his twenties. The buzzer goes just before eight, exactly as he'd been told, and the east European delivery man politely hands over the monogrammed bag. The company logo is written in letters that combine the images of various fruits and vegetables: Health & Fitness = Happiness. He opens the bag to find three boxes containing the meals for the day, and the first indication of trouble is the simple fact of the breakfast being green. This is consistent with the range of distinct flavours he is able to discern on tasting the food and the accompanying drink. In the thickish porridge he detects cucumber, carrot, and a sharpness suggesting celery. The drink is made more palatable by the sweetness of the fruits, but in the ten minutes it takes him to polish off this gunk he is already starting to lose confidence in his ability to sustain this for the six-week spell he has signed up for. The cost is no issue, but he objects on principle to paying for something that is so appalling to consume. To make matters worse, he is soon struck by the conflicting sensations of remaining ravenously hungry and dreading the contents of the lunch compartment he must imbibe at some stage between midday and one. This means he is already in a foul mood on setting off for Tooting Bec Common, where he finds the personal trainer is passing the time till his arrival by doing single-handed push-ups. He is approaching from behind her, so she is initially unaware of his presence, and at first he thinks she is grunting as she rises and falls with impressive ease. But when he gets closer he, realises she is saying, "Be the best you can!" at the start of each ascent. Mat gulps in trepidation and silently turns for home. Before he makes it more than a couple of yards, he hears the sharp South African accent behind him. "Mathew! Come back here. I'm Tish. You're late! Come on, we have a lot of work to do."

What he acquires above all from the ninety minutes that follow is a sense of the absolute relativity of time. The idea that a minute always lasts sixty seconds and that these measurements of duration are somehow universal becomes absurd. The nearest he has come to understanding that hours can be longer or shorter depending on the experience that fills them came during some of the Scandinavian cinema he'd endured after leaving Fieldings. He would glance at the elapsed time to see that the four hours he felt he had sat through had in fact been compressed into a mere forty minutes on the clock, yet that was nothing in comparison to what he is now undergoing. He is told to lie backwards over a large, inflated ball and hold the position for thirty seconds. Hours of real, lived experience later, he is still in the same pose, with Tish snarling at him. "Be strong! Be better! Be your best!" At the end of each burst of pain there is an orgy of praise and backslapping to acknowledge his first baby steps into the world of those who are the best they can be. After this first session comes to a close, Tish displays a touch of kindness that takes him by surprise. "All right, I have to wait here for an hour before my next appointment. Come on, we're doing a run to warm down. Once round the park. What's your target?"

"Survival?"

"Ha, ha! This is about real challenges. Your flabby pecs have to go. We'll aim for twenty-five minutes, and then we'll beat it next time. Lit's go."

Most of the exercises have focused on the upper body, so the initial phase of the run is manageable on legs that have been relatively undamaged during the previous hour. But after the first half-mile, they start rebelling and clearly want to stop and be carried home. The moment his pace slows, Tish drops back beside him and begins seething in his ear. "Pain is nothing. We laugh at pain. We push. We strive. We reach. Say it! Say it!"

"We push. We strive. We reach," he says, releasing each word in a pathetic sob.

"Agin."

"We push, we strive, we reach. We push, we strive, we reach."

"Good, Mathew. I want to run with the winner in you!"

By the time they return to their starting point around forty minutes later, he can think only of the few hundred yards he must travel to make it back home for a day. Once there, he will allow his body to rest, and he hopes he will be forgiven for the crimes inflicted upon it. He limps slowly up Woodley Avenue and struggles to fit the key in the lock of the front door with his trembling arm. The climb up the stairs is followed by the most satisfying descent into a sofa he has ever experienced. He decides he will wait until mid-afternoon before calling to cancel any further sessions with Tish or any other practitioner of the legalised torture and psychobabble he has just been through, telling the company he's found another job and won't have the time. There are vague thoughts of some alternative diet to the natural gunk they have sent him, but the physical exhaustion makes it impossible to formulate any serious plan.

He picks up the MacBook to do some aimless surfing and sees there are three new messages. The first is spam that has made it through the filters. The second is from his mother, which he is about to open when his eyes fall upon the third message – from Miriam. There is momentary confusion over how she has acquired his email address, but he remembers it is part of his signature on the iPhone, and she must have seen it in the texts they exchanged the previous day at Legoland. He opens the message to see a brief note. "Thought this may be of interest ..." The link takes him to a site about converting to teaching. There is a further moment of confusion before he recalls his claims about the future he was planning. He's uncomfortable that the vaguest of thoughts has now been translated into something like a firm project, but this is trumped by a further reflection. She has taken the time to do some research for him. Maybe she already knew of the organisation, and it took no more than a few moments to send the link, maybe not. He's excited at the mere fact of her having thought about him, but he also wishes to avoid making a fool of himself, and this means finding out certain key information. It takes him some time to work out how best to do this, but inspiration comes when he hears some movement from the flat below, and he realises Tom must be home.

He quickly starts downstairs and is immediately reminded of his earlier exertions when his right leg almost gives way in protest at being made to work again so soon after Tish's brutal session. He taps gently on the door and smiles with all the sincerity he can muster when Tom opens. "Hi, I'm just going to do some shopping. I wondered if you wanted anything."

Tom is obviously caught by surprise. "Uh, sure. Actually, I sort of have to do some food shopping myself."

"Good. I'll buy you a coffee afterwards."

"Just come in for a second. I need a list."

Mat enters to find the place surprisingly well-organised, and deserted aside from Tom. "No Alicia."

"She's in nursery."

"Did she enjoy herself yesterday?"

"God, she loved it. Thanks again for taking her out like that. Believe it or not, we still managed to have a huge scene before she went to bed."

"What happened?"

"She has to sleep with whichever animal is her current favourite. We assumed that Emmett would be squeezing in with her, but she kept shouting for one of the others and we couldn't work out who the hell it was. Just kept screaming, 'I want Charlie! I want Charlie!' "

"Oh dear. So, let's go."

Tom leads them to Lidl, the cheapest of the supermarkets on the high road, and while Mat loads a basket with supplies for which he has no need, Tom makes his way to the special deals. His basket has an odd combination of frozen lobster, brandy, baking potatoes, and fresh herbs. "I lost a bet, and the price was that I had to cook an exotic meal. At the checkout, he types in his PIN, but as he's about to continue the exchange with Mat the cashier tells him with perfect economy, "Card declined." He tries the PIN again with the same result. "Sorry. I'll use another one." There is some impatient shuffling in the queue behind them to which Tom seems wholly indifferent. The second card is also declined, and he now turns to Mat in obvious embarrassment. Before Tom can speak, Mat smiles and passes over the cash. "Right, let's get a coffee. I'll pay." He is happy to help out and knows that pride will dictate that the trifling sum will be reimbursed later.

As soon as they sit in the expensive little independent café Mat had spotted during a stroll a couple of days earlier, he wonders how he can manoeuvre the discussion round to Miriam without appearing desperate. "So what was the bet you lost?"

We watched *Paris at Midnight* and got into a discussion about Woody's best films. This led to a disagreement about which ones Diane Keaton was in, and I bet she wasn't in *Love and Death*.

"Sonja."

Tom recoils. "How the fuck did you know that?"

"I watched it quite recently." (Part of a later boxset.)

"Not his best."

"No, but it has his ever best line."

"Go on."

"He's lying next to a duchess he's just seduced. She looks at him in awe and says, 'You're the greatest lover I've ever had.' And Woody fires back: 'Thanks. I practise a lot on my own.'"

Tom laughs. "Would be good to be able to use that line in real life."

"I sort of came close once with this rather eccentric refinancing specialist from the Bank of Japan."

"She said you were a great lover?"

"No. She said I should practise more on my own. Didn't even spend the night."

The coffees arrive, each cup on a small, wooden platter with a porcelain saucer of warm milk and a glass of roughly-cut sugar lumps. The miniature spoons are sterling silver. Tom smiles at the presentation. "When we moved here, there was no one in Streatham who would have come into this sort of place. Now it fills up on a weekday morning."

"You know you're in trouble once the bankers think it's all right to live somewhere." He tries to find a form of words that will not be too obvious. "So, is León a friend of yours from your time in Spain?"

There is a moment of confusion, before Tom visibly undergoes a double recognition of both what Mat is talking about and why. "He's this incredibly good-looking guy we've known for years."

The obvious irony annoys Mat, who was hoping to be less transparent, but the humour suggests that he has made some sort of fortunate error. "I just assumed that was true of all your friends."

"León is a city in northern Spain. There's some stuff going on there Miriam is mixed up in, and she missed an important call yesterday."

"Stuff?"

"Part of the Spanish government's austerity measures include rolling back state support for just about anything except the banking system. The coal mines are massively dependent on state subsidies, and the government wants to cut them. If the mines close, half the people in the region will lose their jobs and half the local businesses will go under after that. They've been in dispute for a couple of months."

"How is Miriam involved?"

"Her father is a mining engineer, and the fear is if the pits close, his job is one of those that will go. She's also a local representative for one of the teachers' unions, and they've been organising collections and protests in support of the miners. The guy who took over from her keeps her up to speed."

Mat is at a loss how to react. He's unsure if he's ever met anyone active in a union before, and his perspective is one formed growing up in the eighties, when aggressive, working-class men were systematically annihilated by the greengrocer's daughter. It just strikes him that in the age of minimum wage, employment protection, and a more advanced culture, surely their time has passed. His surprise must have been obvious, because Tom detects his reservation.

"You look as if you disapprove."

"No, no. It's just ... well ... Haven't we moved beyond the point where unions are so essential. I can see why they are needed in the dispute you're talking about, but it just seems we're past the stage where employers can do as they please. Hasn't there been a shift in attitudes in the sense that even companies recognise it makes sense to look after their staff?"

"Actually, I'd say the opposite. The modern approach is that it's healthy for companies to squeeze every drop out of people on the lowest income because this is what benefits everyone. Try reading some of the articles on what it's like working for Amazon or Sports Direct. People employed on lousy conditions who get fired if they're off sick. They don't like unions because the last thing they want is a workforce with any sort of ability to fight."

The tone is oddly neutral, steeped in resignation despite the obvious note of disgust. Something has happened to this man, and Mat is keen to avoid any impression that he sympathises with the sort of Victorian industrial policy Tom is describing. "I suppose I've just not really seen this sort of thing. I'm used to working in places where they demand a lot of you, but they generally just pay you off if they don't think you fit, or they pay you well enough so that you don't mind how badly they treat you. At the first place I worked, the CEO met each member of the senior management individually every day. They were called the daily meetings but came to be known as the daily beatings. It's a lot easier to put up with someone humiliating you if he's paying you two hundred thousand a year for the privilege."

"Unfortunately, the public sector has only implemented part of that. They just demand more of you, and a lot of the senior managers pay themselves well enough, but no one else. Sometimes, it's down to austerity, but that attitude of shitting on everyone below you seems more like part of the wallpaper. At the last college I worked, someone sent round an internal email that hadn't been proofread. When she was typing 'human resources' she mistakenly put a 'w' at the start of 'resources' and the spellchecker changed it so that news came round that there was now an opening in human wreckage. The name stuck."

"That sounds rather more familiar. I was forced to sit on the interview panel for a new head of HR at my last bank, and we had a couple of these candidates who emphasised how much they enjoyed working with people and how they relished the chances to support those in difficulty and develop new ways of bringing staff closer together. Neither of them made the final shortlist because the last thing anyone wanted in an HR director was someone who gave a shit about the people they were working with. Basically, all they did was make sure redundancies were fast and clean, and that you got rid of any difficult characters as quietly as possible."

Mat sips the coffee. It is not as smooth as the one he makes at home, and the homemade cake he has ordered has too much ginger in it. He's also irritated by the Victorian style school furniture that is the latest café fashion despite offering such minimal comfort. Yet the place is almost full. A couple with a young child. A middle-aged man reading *The Guardian* from an antique-looking newspaper holder, doubtless imported from China and having been produced at roughly the same cost an original would have been a century earlier. Two women in their twenties, expensive looking casual clothes, sitting opposite each other with MacBooks open as they engage in impossibly serious discussion. None of these people can be unemployed given what they are paying for the new obsession of independents over chains. He has no idea what they do.

By the time they finish, Mat feels that his body has returned to something close to its normal strength despite the morning's physical desecration. He carries the shopping bags back to the house, and as he's leaving Tom thanks him, but then hesitates, as if unsure of whether he should say what's on his mind. "Look, I'm not sure if this is really my business, and I'm sorry if this seems out of line. It's just … Well, Miriam went through quite a bad divorce not so long ago. And …"

Mat nods. "Believe me, I know what that's like." There is a difficult silence as each is uncomfortable with the intimacy. Tom smiles at him. "I need to look up a recipe and start cooking. Thanks again."

As soon as Mat gets upstairs, he opens his emails once again and scrutinises the one Miriam had sent earlier. After considering several possible interpretations, he realises that there is so little content it is absurd to make any attempt to read much into what she has said. Now he must also confront the question of what on earth the point would be of pursuing this. She is leaving the country, and God knows what kind of state she might be in if she really has been through some shocking break-up. He has no idea of what she thinks of him and would prefer not to make himself look a complete dick by getting rejected by someone who lives downstairs. "Fuck it," he thinks to himself unconvincingly. "Too many reasons not to do this."

Five minutes later he has changed his mind again and replies. "Many thanks for this. Looks really interesting. Wouldn't mind finding out a bit more about what teaching is like. Any chance we could discuss it." The response is immediate. "Sure. When is good?" He can't just ask her out for dinner. Better to find some more subtle approach to begin with. "Over coffee tomorrow?" Again, the response is instant. "Days bad, as really must work." That has to be an indirect invitation. Has to be. Must be. "Early evening drink the day after tomorrow?" That sounds all right. Can't say cocktails as it's too obvious. Meal even more obvious, but if things go well he could propose it. Delaying for a couple of days doesn't sound too desperate. He starts smiling at the embarrassing immaturity of it all. "No," comes the reply. "Dinner."

Chapter Six

He spends hours looking through reviews on four different websites. He wants a stylish place without prices she may find obscene. His normal reaction would be to take her somewhere expensive on the clear understanding that he would be paying, and then encourage her to select the most sumptuous food and wine. This is not as crude as trying to buy someone, just a way of living. He is used to people with whom there is a shared understanding that money is present and never referred to. Wealth must be weightless, a presence so natural that no one need think of it, and drawing on it is as effortless as breathing. Mat's experience of seeing Tom's card declined in a supermarket meant encountering a world he had hitherto known only in the abstract. Not since his student days had he been in the same social circle as someone unable to pay for some basic item. Even then it was no more than a temporary passage through the romantic world of student penury in a university that would propel its graduates into any sphere they chose. Discussions of poverty, austerity, waiting lists, low pay; these have no more than theoretical force at best. Yet part of his reason for leaving Fieldings had been an understanding of the unreality of his life when set against those around him. He pays cleaners, exchanges emails with someone in customer service, tips a waiter, but he has lived in a world that is literally above theirs, sitting on a balcony, gazing down on the city as they squeeze into cheaply decorated, suburban bedrooms.

He has no wish to experience the other extreme, seeing nothing noble in poverty, feeling no desire to give up the deserved result of a well-judged risk. He has never wanted to work his way up from the bottom, largely because he has worked with those who have done it. The few he has known who came from nothing had excelled because they had sublimated the bad imitations of their accents, or the modesty of their school, or the demands of selecting the right suit, or coming to appreciate the appropriate food. Whatever value might be attached to such relentlessness, the price always struck Mat as being far too high. His first job in the City was as a trainee with a French bank. He had started with five others, one of whom, Angus Forster, was brought up in a ninth floor council flat near the docks in eastern Glasgow. Mat would sit uncomfortably as those around them would wheel out mindless stereotypes in a horribly exaggerated version of the accent, with Gus smiling gamely as even his bosses joined in. Mat lost touch with him when he moved on after a couple of years, but was stunned to be sitting opposite him a few years later at a job interview that would have made Gus his line manager had Mat taken the post. From the moment Gus offered the most cursory nod to acknowledge their shared history, to the point where Mat rose to leave without receiving even a minimal glance, it was clear what the outcome would be. Gus would never forgive him for having witnessed his hideously low status all those years ago, and would be sure only to hire precisely the sorts of people who had humiliated him back then. The only way he would be able to rationalise choosing to live in a world where he was scorned was by subjugating those who looked down on him. The saddest irony of the whole piece was that it didn't matter how high he rose because the further he got the more likely he was to be surrounded by those who made him feel most uncomfortable about where he was from.

Mat's own background meant he could blend in with a certain degree of comfort whilst never fully giving the impression of benefitting from unfair degrees of privilege. His parents were both doctors, having met and married in medical school in Bristol, where they lived until they retired. At a time when the hours and the pay of a GP were still consistent with the status of the profession, this meant they could afford the most stylish of townhouses. Three storeys of deep carpets, and enormous rooms with original, intricate Victorian cornices and ceiling roses. They were on call at the weekend from time to time but still had plenty of money to send their only son to Clifton College, the city's most prestigious private school. They picked up a farmhouse in Burgundy for nine thousand pounds and thought nothing of spending another thirty to turn it into the sort of English, romantic vision of France the French had never known. This meant that from as young as six Mat found it normal to be standing next to his parents as they studied the labels on bottles of red they could not have found back home. A holiday meant touring round a château and playing while his parents read classic literature. When he got old enough to be bored of his solitude on such breaks, he would bring a school friend with him. By the time he left home, he simply didn't realise just how deeply he had internalised the values of relaxation and a sensual appreciation of what the world had to offer.

On arriving at Cambridge, he experienced little change. This was in a time before university tuition fees, when undergraduate study could be completed without any invasive sense of it being a luxury for which one would pay over the course of an entire working life. He pursued a range of courses before settling on mathematics and spent his time doing what was required to achieve reasonable success. Yet for all the continuity, there were also certain points of departure. He arrived at university a virgin, and for the first time in his life he found himself studying in the same room as women. There was a sort of relief when he discovered that many were as ill at ease as he was. The sudden release from any parental presence created both a greatly improved chance of romance and an almost equally powerful anxiety at the prospect of being unable to attract anyone despite the promising circumstances. He looked on with disbelieving envy at the endless parade of women who trooped back and forth from the room of the leonine Marxist poet a couple of doors down. As yet, Mat was too naïve to recognise that the man's appeal was rooted in a shallowness that wasn't entirely obvious until he bumped into him again six years later, unpublished, neatly trimmed, and flourishing in the hot new world of derivatives. But as a first-year undergraduate, Mat was simply in awe of a lifestyle that hinted at a world filled with unimaginable excitement, one which appeared all the more intoxicating precisely because it remained such a mystery.

He was ultimately delighted that the first time he slept with someone was within a relationship that endured until shortly before the end of his studies. For years he had longed for some crudely quick, drunken episode so that the most primitive hurdle could be overcome and there could be basic relief from his sense of being a sexual lepor. Instead, he met Maya celebrating in a pub with some of her friends after Thatcher had announced she would not stand against Heseltine in the second round. She was a painter from the Cambridge School of Art, and one explanation Mat hit upon for why he had somehow come up with the claim twenty years later that he wanted to teach art history was that this was an unconscious desire to return to those extraordinary days. Friends would rib him for being unable even to register the existence of other women, having moved directly from a state of desperate inexperience to trance-like devotion. Despite never actually living together they contrived to spend almost every evening and night in one another's company, often simply entwined in bed.

Largely thanks to her commitment as an artist, they were able to combine their mutual obsession with a sensible allocation of time to their respective studies. But the speed and intensity of Mat's head-long fall into such a relationship obscured the problems that would later divide them. By the time they entered their third year, there were aspects of her that began to antagonise him with increasing force. She had briefly been out with one of the sculptors before meeting Mat, and it annoyed him that she never seemed ready to confront the fact that this man's continuing desire to be her friend was so obviously rooted in the fact he had never gotten over her. When Mat tried to raise this, he was met with what he felt was a deeply unfair comment about how she would not tolerate his being possessive. It also began to irk him that she seemed to prioritise the importance of her own studies over his. It was clear from the outset that he could never disturb her when she was painting and that under no circumstances could he watch her at work or discuss what she was doing with others. Yet she was impatient if he insisted on working on an assignment instead of traveling to London to see an exhibition. She would denigrate the lifeless nature of mathematics compared to the importance of art in enriching humanity. When Mat responded that real bridges were possibly more important than painted ones, she was scornful. When he cited Bertrand Russell's comment about the austere beauty of mathematics, she gave a belly laugh.

These exchanges were overwhelmed by mutual affection for two years, but Mat came to the point where he began to find her overbearing and self-righteous. He resented what he felt was the unreasonable prominence that always had to be placed on her interests but was too foolish to realise that he felt this way only because he no longer loved her with the unquestioning commitment he had felt when fully under her spell. As his frustration grew, he did the typical thing a mature man does. He fucked someone else and told Maya under the guise of wishing to be honest. He didn't deliberately select a Roedean girl in order to maximise the insult, but Maya had seen her a couple of times at parties and commented with irritation at an eighteen-year-old wearing a genuine pashmina and real pearls to a student party. Whatever the depth psychology, anyone with left-wing sympathies was likely to find this to be a particularly harsh form of infidelity, and Maya did the typical thing a mature woman does. She told him how hurt she was, asked him to leave, and made him feel like the idiot that he now realised he had been.

His initial reaction was to try and repair the damage he had done, but he quickly understood that this was no more than a desire to feel better about himself by acquiring her forgiveness. So he wrote to her, apologising and saying she clearly deserved far better. He never saw her again, and beyond his sense of shame he was mystified by his own emotions. He was aware of how complete his affection had been but now knew this only as a memory stripped of all the immersive passion he had felt at the time. He also realised how his current frustration with her had tainted all that had gone before, with positive memories now diluted by the power of his immediate doubts. Over the years, he would do online searches, but never found her, and he suspected she may have changed her name on marriage. He hoped things went well for her.

Much of this now returns to Mat because he recalls hints of the same primitive excitement he felt when he first pursued Maya, and he engages in a sort of childish fantasy about the possibilities lying before him. The fact that he barely knows her is irrelevant, and when he arrives at the point of choosing a restaurant he is desperate not to endanger a relationship that has not yet started with a woman he has known for a matter of hours. The reservations he had the previous day about whether he should even respond to her have disappeared, and the absurd immaturity of his behaviour is something he has set aside as a boring triviality.

*

He knocks on the door around eight, and it is Sofia who opens, barely able to suppress a smile. "Miriam's almost ready. Come in. Tom's out playing tennis. Have a drink."

He walks in to see normal chaos resumed. Toys and children's books are strewn across the floor. Plates with partially eaten food sit on both the dining and coffee tables. Alicia is watching a Spanish cartoon and doesn't look at him until Sofia orders it. She says hello without looking away from the TV, and her mother is apparently too weary to enforce any greater degree of courtesy. Mat sits on one of the armchairs, and this comically produces the sound of a steam engine from the book hidden beneath the cushion. The room is stifling, the south-facing windows and glass doors offering no protection from the abnormally hot English summer. When the cartoon ends, the girl asks for another, but her mother tells her impatiently that it is time for bed. Alicia looks down, aware that her mother is looking at her. "Can Mathew read me a story?"

It takes Mat a moment to realise that this means him, and he is caught between not wishing to be rude and the rather higher priority of getting to the restaurant on time. "I'd love to, but maybe we should do it another night when I have more time."

"I want Mathew to read to me." The voice is a pathetic whimper, and Sofia looks at him imploringly.

"Of course. Let's go."

She kisses her mother, and then walks over to Mat, taking his hand to lead him upstairs where she lies down on the cot bed. She hands him *Paddington at the Zoo*. "This is my favourite. Daddy showed me the movie. Read, please."

Mat works his way through it at a pace he hopes is just slow enough not to appear hasty. He then looks down at her and smiles. She sits up and kisses him on the cheek, but as he switches the light out she whispers to him, "Can you tell me a story now, please."

"I'm not sure I know any stories."

"Can you make one up, please."

He inhales deeply. "Well, once upon a time there was a beautiful princess who lived in a big castle. And she …

"Did she have superpowers?"

"Oh yes. She could fly?"

"And could she make webs?"

"Yes, she could."

"Wow. Awesome. What happened next?"

"Well, when night came the princess decided …"

"What was she called?"

"Leia. So Princess Leia decided to go out flying, but when she'd been out for a while she saw her good friend Luke was being attacked, so she quickly flew down to help him. And these two horrible men called Darth and … Darth and Larry were trying to take his magic cloak. So Leia …

"What could the magic cloak do?"

"Well, it could make Luke invisible, but he had forgotten to turn it on. So Darth and Larry were able to see him, and they wanted the cloak for themselves. And when Leia saw this, she quickly flew down, pulled the two horrible men off and spun a web that was so tight they couldn't move. Then she called the police with her magic phone …"

"What magic could the phone do?"

"It meant Leia could call anyone anywhere in the universe whenever she wanted. So the police arrived, took the two men away, Leia flew back to the castle with Luke, and they had a lovely dinner and lived happily ever after. The end."

"Can you tell me another story, please."

"I'm sorry," he whispers, "but I have to go now. Someone is waiting for me."

"OK." And she sits up, puts her arms around his neck and kisses him on the cheek before lying down again. He slowly rises and moves as quietly as he can towards the door, closing it gently behind him. When he turns, he sees Miriam standing in front of him smiling broadly. "Larry?"

"I couldn't think of the emperor's real name."

"Darth Sidious, although you could have used Palpatine to avoid the repetition of 'Darth'. At any rate, I like the post-feminist twist of the brave princess saving the helpless prince. I'm hungry, let's go."

The figure-hugging jeans and the slimline black cotton shirt make him feel terribly conscious once again of his own shape, and this in turn prompts a hideous memory of his session with Tish. But these thoughts are soon dismissed as they start walking down Bedford Hill in the warmth of the summer evening. The restaurant is only half-full, and the table is conveniently distant from any other diners, creating a welcome sense of privacy. When they sit, the waiter immediately asks them if they wish to order a drink, and Miriam looks over at Mat. "I'll let you order the wine, but on the clear understanding we split the bill." He orders a moderately expensive Chianti. As soon as the waiter leaves, she looks over at him. "Nice restaurant. Anyway, do you want to go first or do you want me to?"

"I'm not with you."

"Tom is a good father and a good husband, and he was probably a really good teacher. But under no circumstances should you tell him anything you wouldn't want others to know. He told me you were divorced, and I've no doubt he told you I was, and as I'm always curious to see if someone managed to screw up their marriage more spectacularly than I, why don't we compare disasters? Are you happy to go first?"

The honest answer to this was that he had no wish to go first or second, and that there was nothing he would rather conceal more than this particular episode. What kind of discussion was this for a first date? Maybe she was a weirdo, but if so then this would surely come out when she described her own break-up, and it was better to find out now. He also realised that if she was going to be repelled by what he had done, it was also better to have this happen earlier rather than later. "All right, but if you get up and walk out then you still have to pay for your half of the meal, and no throwing any glasses of wine."

"I promise to pay for my half, but I quite like the possibility of throwing the wine over you and then flinging a few notes onto the table. The double movement will heighten the dramatic effect."

"I can see that. Do you want the full story or just the blood-soaked final scenes?"

"Give me a few background details. What was her name, and how did you meet her?"

"Jo, and she was the younger sister of someone I worked with. There was some charity event organised by the bank, and all those involved were invited to a club afterwards that the bank had hired out. People could bring guests, and her brother introduced us and asked me if I would look after her because he was supposed to be entertaining some wealthy clients our boss wished to diplomatically avoid so he could get off his head on the free cocktails. Anyway, we got on all right, I took her out again, and we started seeing each other."

"How long before you got married?"

"Six months of going out, and then a year of being engaged so she could arrange the wedding."

"Was it some obscenely expensive location with two hundred guests?"

"A stately home in Surrey, and only the catering was expensive."

"You found a cheap castle?"

"No, we just used her parents' one for free."

"You did choose well. Were they aristocracy?"

"Not quite. The great-grandparents had done very well trading tea in India and sent a lot of the money back home. They bought

up half of Surrey before independence. A lot of the land was countryside when they bought, but as London expanded they found
they were sitting on property worth more than they could have
dreamed of. They bought a pile from a baron who lost his two sons
in the First World War and didn't really want to stay in the home
where he'd raised them. Even with all land being diluted through
the generations, Jo will inherit a fortune."

"Seems a very conventional name for someone from that background. All the sloanie types I came across at King's were Cleodie
or Arabella or Ottilie. Jo's parents were quite merciful."

"Not really."

"What do you mean? It's not short for Joanna?"

He shakes his head.

"Josephine?"

"Try again?"

"Jocelyn?"

"That's a man's name."

"Go on, then."

He gulps in uncomfortable anticipation of the likely reaction.
"Jocasta."

Miriam throws back her head and roars with laughter. "Jesus,
did you kill your father as well?"

"You'll like the names she had planned for her children even
more. She wanted a boy and girl. The boy was to be Hyperion,
and the girl Hippolyta. At any rate, one of the many reasons why
divorce was the right decision is the reduced number of occasions
when I have to hear jokes about murdering my dad or fucking my
mother."

"So what were the other reasons?"

He sighs heavily. Privately, he has worked through all the details of what happened countless times, with everything now neatly
rationalised. Friends and family were always given carefully cen-
sored accounts, and part of him is reluctant to expose his sanitised
version to any scrutiny, yet there is also the enduring appeal of confession. He wants to hear that he isn't so bad, that Jo was somehow
impossible, that any decent person might have acted the way he

did. Even as he begins, he knows he is offering an account that he himself has come to believe, but one that has certainly undergone many small and subtle revisions to make it easier for him to come to terms with it all.

"There's a particular moment that often comes back to me as the one when I was first disappointed in her. We were staying with her parents, and I got into this very difficult exchange with the father. The whole family bought into eighties' conservatism, and he made some comment about how sick he was of people always discussing difficulties in the NHS. I had been in Bristol with my parents the previous weekend, and they had been lamenting the latest reorganisation, talking about how much more time they now spent managing money instead of seeing patients. I mentioned this in a way that I thought was quite restrained, and the old man exploded. 'Typical of the whinging I hear everywhere. How can someone in your line of work complain about how the country has moved forward? People should stop carping and get out and work harder the way I have'. This was all in front of Jo's brothers and a couple of other guests. I was completely shocked but felt a kind of loyalty to my parents, so I made some comments about how doctors also worked very hard, but the old fool just carried on. In the end, I just lost patience and said he was talking nonsense, at which point everyone sat up in righteous anger at my rudeness. Jo insisted that I hadn't really meant it like that and that he had also been a little aggressive. I didn't expect her to stab him through the heart with her steak knife, but it seemed so obvious he was being outrageously over the top, and she should have stepped in to stop him. It really irritated me that he had been such a dick, but it annoyed me even more that she tried to pass this off as eccentricity."

"Did he really think of himself as someone who worked hard?"

"He did work very hard. He had a massive estate he managed himself. Dozens of employees, a private gallery from which he was always lending pictures, dinners, charity events. It went on forever. The idiocy didn't lie in the claim that he was hard-working but more in the absurdity of thinking this somehow explained why he was so rich. I used to fantasise about telling him the sorts of hours my parents' friends put in at the local hospitals and asking him if they deserved more money than him because they worked harder. Or I imagined asking him whether hard work or inheritance was the greater cause of his wealth. Instead, this little exchange was just set aside, and we went back to being polite to one another."

"Did you enjoy that sort of life?"

"We never lived it. We both wanted to be in London, and Jo took on responsibility for designing our life there. We had to buy a house in Notting Hill, and she spent endless amounts of time paying people to decorate this bedroom or change that bathroom or landscape this tiny section of the garden. Then it would all have to be done again a few months later. I was bringing in a good salary, and she had her allowance, so cost was never an obstacle to the insanity of turning your home into an eternal building site."

"She didn't work."

"Actually, she was very proud to have her own career."

"Was she also in the City?"

"Yes, but not in the conventional way."

"I can't wait."

"She was a life coach."

"What the hell is that?"

"It's about allowing the individual to release their inner wisdom so they can make decisions they already know are right but lack the confidence to accept."

"Sounds like Plato."

"Unless Plato was charging a thousand an hour to City execs to develop their soul intelligence, I doubt very much they had anything in common."

"A thousand an hour!"

"She had about fifteen clients, most of whom she saw around once a fortnight, but often she did it over the phone. When we went on holiday, she would slot half of them in on a Monday, the other half on a Tuesday, and on the Wednesday we would fly out to a Greek island for ten days."

"What did she actually do with them?"

"I stood outside the bedroom once, and listened to her when she

was on with some senior guy at J. P. Morgan. The strategy seemed
to be that you ask what someone wants to achieve, followed by
what's possible, and then which option they really want. There was
a sort of miraculous art of stringing out common sense questions
far beyond any necessary length of time and then making obvious
solutions sound like the discovery of a new element."

"I assume you never told her what you thought of all this."

"It came out towards the end in spectacular fashion, but not
before."

"So what went wrong?"

"I'm afraid I'm going to over-simplify this, but I just started
getting more and more impatient with all the shit going on in the
house and her stupid family. She insisted on seeing them really regularly even after the blow-up with her dad. But it wasn't only the
politics, they were just deeply dull. There would be endless conversations about trivial events around the estate. Some horse had got
into the wrong field, or the seventeenth-century roof on one wing
may have to be replaced, and this would excite them for an entire
evening. It reached a climax one Sunday when the father started
talking about a problem he had whenever they had a shoot."

"They were in the film industry?"

"Not shooting film, birds. He found that whenever they organised one of these events they were slaughtering so many of the
poor creatures they couldn't get rid of them all. Jo and the mother
were full of suggestions about carting them off to local butchers
or distributing them to the beaters, and in the end I just excused
myself and went upstairs. When I told Jo on the drive home that I
was basically bored by the discussion, she was offended that I wasn't
prepared to make an effort with her family. And I have this distinct
memory of thinking how unremittingly stupid they all were. It sort
of hit me like a religious conversion, and I never really felt the same
way about her again. All the qualities I had liked now seemed more
of a misunderstanding. Her arty ambitions for the house were just
a foolish obsession with appearing stylish. All her social skills now
felt like a PR exercise to promote the image of a successful London
couple. Even her looks started to appall me. When I first knew her,

I thought she had this beautifully sculpted nose that tapered perfect-ly. Now I just thought it looked pointy. I'm not saying all of this was crystal clear at the time. It was sort of dressed up as a realisation that we both wanted different things. She wanted children straight away, and I wasn't ready. She wanted to be in London permanent-ly, whereas I quite liked the idea of living abroad for a few years. And … well …"

"Can I take your hesitation to mean there may be something else that was even more important?"

"I also wanted to carry on seeing this accountant from KPMG, and she didn't want that either."

"You must have been very unhappy if you were sleeping with an accountant."

"That's more or less what Jo said, but rather more dramatically. 'How could you fuck someone who looks so common?'"

"Oh, they knew each other?"

"No. When Jo found out she looked her up on Facebook. Found some unfortunate photos of her in Ibiza in a cheap sombre-ro. I'm not sure if it would have been better or worse if she'd been more expensively dressed."

"Well, at least you told her about it."

This is followed by a silence is far more eloquent than any words would have been. "I see. So how did she find out?"

"I was watching an important cricket match on the laptop, and navigating between screens to exchange emails with the accoun-tant. I exited my Hotmail but didn't sign out. She came home later, went to open her own account, and went straight into a message I had received earlier in the day."

"Wasn't there any ambiguity? 'Just someone I met a couple of times for a drink. Likes making risqué jokes about affairs.' That sort of thing."

"I'm afraid it was far too explicit for that. I tried claiming that it had been a terrible mistake that had only happened once, but she'd been through my entire inbox by that stage. I was almost as shocked as her to find out how long it had been going on."

"Sounds impressively thorough. I'm actually starting to like her, although I can see how the endless redecoration would be a real drag. So was that it? She walked out."

"You're joking. Nothing short of nuclear Armageddon could have shifted her from that house. I knew that if it ever went to court she would be pitiless, and as the tabloids like City divorces I offered my half of the house in return for a quick divorce, and she took it."

"No attempt at reconciliation."

"..."

"Excellent. What happened?"

"We went for a couple of days without talking, and then she was waiting for me in the lounge when I got home one evening and asked me to sit down. She said she wanted to try and understand why things had gone wrong and to see if we could work things through. Up until then I had just felt lost. I was ashamed at all the lies, and I felt I had to take seriously the promises I had made when we married, but part of me was relieved at the possibility it was over. Then I heard her say these ridiculous clichés, and I couldn't help myself. I looked at her and said we should set some goals, consider the options, and work out the way forward. She threw this fucking great glass ashtray at me. I tell you, if I hadn't ducked it could have killed me, and she'd be decorating her prison cell."

Miriam looks unconvinced. "Mmm ... Probably not. The rich don't go to prison."

"Anyway, I moved into a hotel that night and found a flat to rent a couple of days later. The lawyers sorted it all out over the next few weeks, and I've never seen her since." He sighs deeply. "I'll tell you the worst part of it. I don't feel genuine guilt about betraying *her*. I know that the deception and the lies were wrong, but the sense of immorality has a curiously abstract feel to it. It seems wrong to do it as a general rule, but I don't feel bad as a result of doing it to Jo. I think of her worthless family and her superficiality, and I feel worse about being idiotic enough to have been seduced into that world in the first place."

"Is that what it was? You were seduced by that world?"

"I know how it sounds. The best analogy I can think of is that it's like watching some accomplished costume drama. If it's well done, you don't consider any issues of depth because you're so mesmerised by the aesthetic. Now I just feel embarrassed." He inhales deeply, and for a moment he is lost in a series of reflections he has been through so many times. Why be taken in at all? Why not recognise it sooner? Why not get out with more dignity and fewer lies? Then he revives and looks up at her. "So, do you think you can match that level of failure?"

"What do you mean?"

"I mean I hope you didn't come out of your divorce looking as bad as I do."

"Oh, I don't want to discuss what happened with me."

He looks at her open-mouthed. "I thought you said … we agreed …" Then he stops. "Is this an attempt at irony?"

"You obviously don't think it worked."

"Frankly, no. I think you have to wait till the topic isn't quite so serious."

"All right, I'll bear that in mind. I'm afraid I still struggle with English humour."

"So I see. Anyway, what did he do?"

Before she answers, the waiter is by their table asking if everything is all right, and Miriam asks him to bring another bottle of Chianti.

"He was Richard the writer."

Mat is immediately uncomfortable at the yawning gap between his own status as a former banker and the ex-husband's cooler profession. He pictures Ethan Hawke in the Linklater trilogy and hopes the divorce was down to the husband being too far up himself. "Has he published anything I might have come across?"

"Unlikely. He travelled along the conventional road for anyone looking to break into literature these days. MA in creative writing followed by some short stories accepted on the more prestigious websites. One of the Derrideans he knew at uni started an avant-garde publishing house, and that's where he eventually got his break.

"What's a Derridean?"

"Someone who says nothing of value in a very complex way. Trust me, you don't want to know any more."

"OK, so how did you meet?"

"At Tom and Sofia's wedding. He was in the dying stages of a relationship with one of Tom's colleagues, and we were sat at the same table. The two of them were all snippy, little remarks and cold, tight-lipped exchanges, but I thought he did the better job of faking some satisfaction at their being there together. Anyway, a couple of months later, he emailed to say Tom had given up my address and he wondered if I would like to meet up for a drink. There was a nice little line about promising not to spend the evening criticising the ex-girlfriend, and I met him at this café-bookstore in Camden."

The tone in which all this is delivered suggests a sort of wistfulness, as if she should have known better. There is also a measure of composure that reveals she has been through this account before, perhaps running over it time and again to understand why she had been drawn in. "It seemed ideal at first. He had this flat in Islington. Stripped wooden floors, beaten up leather sofa, bistro table and chairs by the window. Here he was struggling away to make it as a writer, publishing reviews to make some cash, and spending days on a single paragraph for his first novel. When I moved in, I was still working on my PhD and he wouldn't let me pay anything towards the flat."

"To be honest, I didn't know writing reviews earned enough to pay the rent on a flat in Islington."

"It doesn't. It was all bullshit. He also had this big thing about not taking his parents' cash, and objecting to the values he felt they'd adopted. Except he was living in the flat they had bought together twenty-five years before, and he wasn't paying anything towards it either. To hear him talk you'd think they made their money selling weapons to ISIS. Instead, they'd launched an IT start-up in the nineties doing web design before most people even knew what the Internet was. Then the mother came up with some clever breakthrough for how supermarkets could organise their online shopping sites, and they were made overnight. By the time I met them, I was expecting Lord and Lady Macbeth. Instead, they were just a fairly normal couple curious to see if their only child was going out with someone sane. I thought at first this was just some sort of act they were putting on, but I realised by the end that he was just a fucking, spoilt brat, and the whole struggling writer act was this awful cliché that he could finance using money he pretended to accept only because he had to."

"Do you mind if I ask why you were attracted to him?"

"Look, none of this was obvious at the time. I would come home from a day of writing in the library and there would be this amazing tagine waiting for me. Or he would go out early on a weekday morning and bring back fresh croissants. Whenever he seemed short with me, I thought it was just because this is the pressure you live under when so much is invested in trying to make it in a profession where ability is little or no guarantee of success, where no one really seems to know what it means to be talented."

"You thought he was that good."

"I never really knew. I just understood how much it meant to him, and how committed he was, and what I thought he was sacrificing to try to make it. So much of what he claimed about himself relied on this sense of integrity, when the truth is he was just another rich kid wearing ripped jeans. All of his rebellion was funded by the money he claimed to despise, and even that was a sham because his parents didn't have Rockefeller type wealth. They didn't even vote Conservative."

"I'm guessing you married him before all this became clear to you."

"After I finished my doctorate, I was offered a fellowship in London, and six months later, the friend from university offered him a contract for his book. He proposed to me over dinner the same evening. It just seemed as if everything was now complete, that we had both made it. We married two months later in the town Hall in Upper Street, just our parents there. We had a week in Biarritz, where the pretentious twerp managed to book the room Hemingway wrote about in *The Sun Also Rises*."

Mat is gripped by this but is now ready to move on to the bit where things go downhill. He looks directly at her and tries to effect the most sympathetic tone he can. "It must have been devastating when things didn't work out."

"Aside from his moodiness, I was generally quite happy until his book came out. He told me he didn't want me to read any of his work in progress because he feared the impact it may have if I was critical of what he wrote. Small fucking wonder. Set aside the wanky, postmodern style where you don't bother with narrative or structure. The whole thing was a barely penetrable monologue about a talented novelist being stifled by his philosopher girlfriend for whom logic conquers all, and who's blind to the importance of the writer's quest for beauty and the deeper truth that lies in an emotional grasp of the way the world is. Believe me, this is a merciful summary of the two hundred pages he had worked on for years."

"Your marriage ended because you don't like postmodernism?"

"To be honest, that would be reason enough. The awful style was forgivable, but he'd thrown in a lot of personal stuff I had told him. There were lines about my relationship with my mother that he had just dropped in and that she would have recognised. He wrote about … well it was fucking outrageous."

"Given what you know about me, can't you just save me the trouble of reading the book by telling me what almost slipped out there?"

She looks him directly in the eyes, all humour now gone. "When I was younger, I … I had a procedure that didn't go well. It means I can't have a family. I told him this when things started to become serious and it went in the book. The female character was driven partly by jealousy and partly by a coldness that stemmed from her being unable to have children. This explained why she used every strategy she could to prevent his success. When I confronted him, he started by saying it was purely fictional and that he didn't believe for a second that I was motivated by the same concerns as the char-

acter in the book. But when I said how angry I was that he had used
this, he got incredibly sanctimonious. He felt that literature was in
some way sacrosanct and that my response was sinister because I felt
that my personal life was so precious it could justify the suppression
of art. We spent hours arguing over this, and not once did he ever
acknowledge that I may have had some point." She starts shaking
her head as the sense of disbelief she had obviously felt at the time
returns. "The irony is that he spent so much time trying to present
himself as a rebel, yet he couldn't have been more hackneyed. He
tried living the life of the poor artist and funded it with his parents'
money. He wanted to write like Joyce, which would have been
radical a hundred years earlier. He launched discussions about de
Beauvoir and Irigaray, but he thought that every woman either
secretly or overtly craves to be a mother and becomes some bitter
shrew if she can't achieve it." She shakes her head once again, but
this time with a smile of resignation as she looks up. "You must
think I'm a fool for having taken so long to work this out."

Mat is now unsure how to respond. So much has taken him by
surprise that he fears offending her if he asks about any of the more
sensitive issues, or uncaring if he avoids them. "Did it end there
and then?"

"Not quite. I thought the right thing to do was to try and get
through it, but I also didn't think what had happened could just be
set aside, so I tried raising it in ways that were intended to bring
him to see there was some merit in the way I felt. He occasionally
seemed to express some sort of regret, but I'm afraid I decided that
the only way forward was if he came to understand what it was like
to be really betrayed like this."

"You published a book about a poor little rich kid?"

"Jesus, no. That would have been far too much work. When the
book came out, he mounted a huge campaign to try to attract publicity for it, paying for reviews, ads on book sites, that sort of thing."

"He paid for people to write good reviews of his book?"

"It wasn't quite that bad. You can pay companies to write an
honest review. If you don't like it, they keep it to themselves, and
if it's good you can pay them again to get it onto the net. He had

enough contacts to get some sympathetic comments and found a couple of companies to give him some more positive reviews. All told, he had about half a dozen pieces that came out, but he came home one day and showed me some btl comment that was pretty unpleasant."

"What's a beetle comment?"

"B-T-L. Below the line. There's a whole world out there for oddballs who spend their lives reading books and posting about them in the comments section on serious websites."

"You mean Amazon reviews."

"That's the least of it. I don't mean two-line comments, and anyway, Amazon doesn't have the status these people are after. I'm talking about what you find under reviews by professional critics, where these people think they're making their own serious contribution to an understanding of the text. You've read some of these, right?"

"Not really."

"Neither has anyone else, but imagine some saddo who fancies himself an important critic and regularly posts some extended analysis where they pick up on the subtext everyone has missed. It's just one more way in which the net has fucked up everything. All the people producing serious content are losing their jobs because they want to be paid, and the field is now open for these losers who think they're stars because the ideas they used to hold privately and were unseen by anyone are now public, and the fact they're still unseen by anyone matters less because they can tell themselves they have an audience. The key thing is to make it clear it is either the best or the worst book that has ever been written, and it's usually the worst."

"And one of these characters posted something under a review of Richard's book?"

"Something about a victory of form over content. Anyway, he comes home and wants me to sympathise with him even though his publisher has told him never to read this stuff. I was still furious with what he'd written, but after I got over the shock of his expecting me to worry about this, I thought this might be a way forward."

She looks at him in anticipation of his support. "You see what I mean?"

Mat is bemused. "Not really."

"Well, I thought that if he was really taking these comments seriously, then I might be able to get him to think again about what he'd done."

"You started posting comments under the reviews?"

"He wouldn't take my objections seriously as his wife, but as he was much more interested in what a reader might say, it just seemed at first like a more effective way of trying to communicate with him."

"What did you write?"

"I started off by suggesting more or less exactly what I'd said to him personally and hoped that if he felt there was a bit of a consensus, then he might come to see things differently."

"If he was so thin-skinned about all this, then wasn't it obvious he might react badly to you criticising him publicly?"

"Oh I didn't use my own name. I had to invent an online ID and then posted anonymously. I did it in the morning at work and then waited to see if he would say anything that evening. But instead of raising it in conversation, he replied to my post with one of his own. He just repeated the same nonsense as before but added some really nasty personal remarks about how I was doubtless attacking him out of envy and concealing it beneath some pseudo-feminist rhetoric. Well, I wasn't having that. If he was stupid enough to start replying to online critics, and he was offering up such idiotic views, then it felt like he deserved everything he got. So I started inventing more IDs and posting on all the sites where he'd been reviewed. I mean I varied what I was saying. A man here complaining about how boring it was. A woman there unhappy it was so self-indulgent. Another Londoner pointing out he had lost touch with modern gender relations in the city. A New Yorker saying that he had seen a similar phase that several writers there went through twenty years earlier. And every time I posted, he always replied, until I was having to limit myself to an hour a day. After a few weeks he was starting to lose a lot of weight, and he asked me to sit down and talk with him. He said he had something serious he wanted to discuss about the book, and when I settled into the sofa, he looked at me and said, 'I think I may have made a major error in writing the whole text in the first person singular. I'm just not sure this speaks to contemporary readers.' I'm honestly not proud of this, but I was so sickened by him that after I told him I didn't think that was such an issue and he smiled a little and went to bed, I stayed up for another four hours and blitzed all six sites. I made it look as if all the comments were from North America so that it would seem as if people were all posting during the day there. I really hadn't started out with any thought of doing this to him, but I was so angry to begin with, and every time he refused the chance to apologise or just to see that he may have done something wrong it just infuriated me even more."

Mat sighs, caught between disbelief and admiration at such a well-organised assault. "What happened?"

"When I came home the next day, he was gone. Went home to live with his mum and dad. The mother called me a few days later and asked to meet up. Said he had decided to give up on his writing career and was entering the family firm. He'd be drafting content for the sites they were developing for blue chip companies. She wondered if I had any idea why he had suffered such a dramatic loss of confidence. He wrote himself a few days later. Some predictable shit about how he felt we had rushed into marriage and how we had both been naïve about living in some intellectual fairytale. Told me to take my time in finding somewhere else to live."

"So you divorced."

"After only two years of marriage." She stops and looks down. Then she smiles at him. "There are two things I keep coming back to. The first is that I'm convinced if he'd fucked someone else it would have hurt less than using that material in the book. No matter how much you despise infidelity, it's possible to understand it. But there's a degree of calculation in what he did that frightened me. I wasn't just angry, I really couldn't fathom how he could do it." She stops and looks down again. She appears completely lost in some attempt at understanding how he could have hurt her like this, doubtless pondering a matter she has contemplated a thousand times before.

Mat is unsure whether or not he should say anything, but silence seems worse. "You still seem very upset about it, even all these years later."

"I said there are two things that come back to me. The second is a sense of revulsion with myself. I should have just continued to stand my ground after I read the book and demanded an apology, just never let it drop until he did the right thing. The truth is that I knew what I was doing and I knew that I was simply taking revenge in the most effective way possible. When his mother called me, I was terrified she was going to tell me he had been diagnosed with depression instead of having just run home to mummy and daddy. And all the stuff I wrote is permanently recorded, visible to anyone who decides they want to take a look at it."

"I thought you said no one ever looks below the line."

"They don't, but you still live with the constant possibility someone might. I hate him, but mostly because of what he provoked me into doing and because there's this permanent record of it."

"I take it you're not in touch."

"Actually, he emailed me a couple of years ago. 'Still think about you. Sorry things finished so badly between us. Married again now.' And the delicious little touch at the end. 'Expecting our first child in a few months. Hope you have also moved on to better times. Blah, blah. Lots of love.'

"Jesus Christ."

"Not bad, is it? It's the only good line he ever wrote. Just enough ambiguity to defend the noble thought he hoped I was as happy as he was, but he knew I would understand the true meaning. He would never forgive me for being with him when he failed, and I couldn't be allowed to escape without at least a hint of the suffering he went through." She smiles at Mat again. "Good job he never worked out what really happened. Anyway, his message really just made me pity the weak, little fuck even more. If he needed to write that, it's difficult to believe he'll be happy doing the school run in

Surrey. He'll end up shagging someone twenty years younger than he is, talking about his novel as they drive back to her place in his Z4."

Mat sighs deeply. "I have to say I feel boringly normal."

"It's not a bad place to be sometimes. I said it would have been easier to deal with his betrayal if he had simply slept with someone else. I also wouldn't feel as bad as I do now if I had simply messed around with someone instead of posting all those comments. There's something worse about finding someone's distinctly personal weak spot and exploiting it like that."

"He was a complete dick."

"I know, but it makes it worse that I did it because I deliberately wanted to be like him. If I'd just walked out then, I would feel a lot better than I do now."

Mat shakes his head. "I don't know. It may be a stretch, but I saw people who had bought and sold complete shit. They got bailed out by the government and still managed to pontificate about the virtues of the free market. There are plenty I wouldn't mind seeing personally bankrupted in some elaborate scam. In a rigged game, all you can hope for is that people get their comeuppance in whatever way possible."

She ponders this. "Maybe you're right. I'd probably be more pissed off right now if he was appearing on BBC Four and had people describing his unreadable shit as ground-breaking."

They order a Spanish liqueur Mat has never heard of, and when the bill comes, she allows him to pick it up on the strict understanding that she will pay the next time. He is relieved she will see him again despite all she now knows, and everything she told him has simply strengthened the erotic charge he has felt since first seeing her. By the time they leave, it is just after eleven but still warm. They walk the fifteen minutes back to Woodley Avenue, and when they get there nothing is said. There is the briefest of looks and the simplest of smiles.

Chapter Seven

When he wakes in the morning, she is gone. There is an awful moment during which he doubts whether she had really come back with him, and when he is reassured that she had he wonders if he has said or done something that has caused her to leave. This fear is still with him when he shuffles into the kitchen to make some coffee, the previous night's drinking now weighing down each thought and movement. He is desperately searching through the memories he can piece together when he sees the handwritten note on the table. *Must work till mid-afternoon. Why not meet me at the Tate Britain around four to see the Turner exhibition. Text me if you fancy it. M*

In the midst of the sleep-addled haze in which he is now reading, even the note looks like a work of art. There is the distinctive continental writing style, all curls and flourishes, so much more extravagant than the Anglo-Saxon one to which he is accustomed. The mere fact of the words being hand-written instead of transmitted in the generic font of a text makes it seem more powerful. He considers waiting for a respectable period of time before responding but quickly sets aside such thoughts. *See you at 4.*

He spends the day ensuring he will be ready to meet her, downloading articles on Turner and analysing the comments by the curators. He doesn't wish to show off, merely to avoid looking like a fool. He also does searches on the miners' dispute in Spain. The loss of the subsidies will essentially mean the end of an industry in a region that is already ravaged by industrial decline. The government has a majority that includes virtually no representatives from that area, and it is simply ignoring the complaints of politicians who are equally tainted. All of them are seen as far too intimate with the developers and bankers who built an illusion of prosperity on shady deals for unwanted homes. So now a community that experienced no more than a ripple of investment during the good years must pay for the bust. He is struck not simply by the apparent injustice but by the uncomfortable parallel with his own life. He reads these articles on a sleek, twelve-hundred-pound MacBook, with millions in an offshore account that is part of the same process. Such ideas emerge and are then quickly suppressed, as he has already confronted the moral issues surrounding his past. He has left that world behind precisely because of the damage it did and has no reason to feel any residual guilt about events wholly outside his control. This is what he tells himself each time these uneasy doubts surface, always accompanied by a nagging sense of mystery as to why they return.

When he finishes with the miners, he also begins looking up Spanish language courses. He knows how ludicrously premature this is but has already fantasised about meeting her family and being able to converse fluently over good Rioja. He finds options that vary from a couple of evenings a week up to one-to-one sessions for six hours a day. He is attracted by the prospect of the quickest possible route to competence but is still literally feeling the pain of his recent attempt at high-speed weight loss and decides that even if he does take a course it won't be another attempted short cut.

The thought of language courses is still uppermost in his mind when he climbs the steps of the Tate. It is years since he has been there, and he has always retained the impression that the transformation of a prison into a gallery is the perfect symbol of civilisation progressing. He finds it typical that it requires someone from outside the country to nudge him into visiting a free institution he would otherwise continue to pass without ever stopping to go in. She is sitting on the marble bench to the left of the entrance and scowls at him when he enters. "What's wrong? I'm early."

"Some fucker in the States has already put forward the thesis I was working on. I found two of his articles this morning. The bastard isn't even thirty yet, and he's staked out the position I've been thinking about for years."

"I'm very sorry. Does this mean all the work you've done has been wasted?"

"Probably not. I'll just have to start by summarising what he said, then state he was almost right before setting out some claims that are barely distinguishable from his. That way the fifty or so people on the planet who may read our work will see us as engaged in some sort of important debate."

"So you'll be at the start of some new movement. Sounds impressive."

"No, the two of us will be fighting it out for the position of who gets to the be more important footnote in someone else's movement." The anger then melts away and she smiles at him. She wraps a hand around the back of his neck, pulls him gently down towards her, and kisses him softly on the lips, then on the cheek. She holds him for a moment longer, her face touching his, and then releases him, looking up and smiling at him as she does so. "Come on. I've bought the tickets. Let's see the exhibition."

It takes them an hour to amble round, the luxury of going midweek meaning they can take in the vast canvases without the distraction of too many others. They go to the upstairs café when they finish, and Mat picks up some coffee for them. Miriam is studying the guide when he sits down but instantly looks up. "I promised Tom and Sofia I would get back for seven-thirty so they can go out. Do you mind if we go after this?"

"Of course not." He then hesitates, unsure if he is entitled to ask this so soon. "Now that you've exploited my body so heartlessly, am I allowed to know what's going on there?"

"With Tom and Sofia? You think one night is enough for that sort of information?"

"You're probably right. Sorry for asking. It's just I pick up these hints, and I was curious, but I see it's not really my business."

She takes another sip of the coffee and sighs. "Obviously, it can never come out that you know this."

"Obviously."

"Up until a year ago, Tom had a job at what had been a good college. They then got into financial difficulty, and they brought in some senior managers who set about gutting the staff in order to make ends meet. Tom was one of the union leaders and they got into a really vicious dispute. Strikes, war of words in the local press, negotiators shouting at each other across the table. It went on for months, and even though it was a strong union, in the end they got butchered. Management wouldn't compromise. Instead they sacked the entire staff and told them to accept new contracts or they were out. The offer was they had to work longer hours for less money, and lots of nasty little clauses which meant that unless your results improved you got fired. So he's got classes to teach, managers putting out press notices blaming the union for trying to bankrupt the college, his own members demanding to know why the leadership hasn't managed to protect them, and a three-year-old at home. I'm not sure if something specific triggered the final descent, but Sofia comes home one night and goes in to see Alicia, who asks her why daddy was crying. The two of them talk things through, and they decide it would be best if he gets out. They do some pretty rushed calculations and reckon that her salary is enough, so he gives up work, and everything seems fine at first because they have a couple of thousand in their account and they save all this money on childcare. I don't really know all the details, but they basically just squeeze by."

This is a world Mat has only read about. "Sounds like a nightmare."

She shrugs. "It's not as bad as you think. When Sofia speaks about it, she sounds much happier now than she was when Tom was on a full salary working at the college. She reckons his mood lifted more or less the day after he left. Most of the pressure just disappeared, and he was transformed."

"You say most of it?"

"I never really know how much I can ask him about it. My impression is that he was outmatched and he lost. I'm convinced he feels some sort of guilt, as if he personally was responsible for what happened. Given how immense the defeat, then it's not the sort of thing you want to feel you could have avoided."

"What makes you think he's feeling better since he left work?"

"Look, he's poor, and he's homicidally bitter, but that is a much better state than dreading the thought of getting up each day because you have to go to a place you hate and face the kind of managers who treat you as an irritating obstacle in the path of their genius. Just watch him when he's with Alicia. He's like a little kid himself. If he gets another job, they'll be fine."

She glances down at her watch, and he nods. "OK. Let's get a taxi."

"No. We'll take the bus from outside."

"I'll pay."

"No. I don't want to take a taxi. Let's get the bus."

As he's keen to avoid a first argument, he agrees without understanding why they must pass the line of empty cabs and wait to find themselves sardined into what is now a rush-hour bus. They make it back just before seven, and there is a moment of uncertainty when they reach the hallway. Miriam sighs. "Well, I suppose you had better go upstairs, get some of your expensive wine and come back down a little later so you can practise your babysitting."

"Exactly the sort of second date I've always dreamed of."

★

He waits until he hears Tom and Sofia leave, feeling somewhat uncomfortable at the thought of seeing them. Having been warned that Miriam is rather vulnerable, he leapt into bed with her a couple of days later and is now so committed to repeating the act he is even prepared to babysit their cannibalistic child. He taps quietly on the door, rightly anticipating that Alicia has been tucked in by the parents before they go out. Miriam opens, and he sees two glasses set out on the coffee table beside a bottle of red. Mat inwardly decides that he will take this bottle back upstairs with him later to make it look as if its poisonous contents have been gratefully consumed. Miriam is in the process of navigating through the contents of a memory stick inserted into the side of the TV. "I can't believe how they get all this stuff."

Mat looks at the list of films, recognising only around half and fearing he may be forced to watch some worthy, subtitled epic. "I'm afraid I don't know all of them. Can I assume they're arthouse classics beyond a philistine like me?"

"No, they're not into that stuff anymore. Too tired after looking after the little monster for anything demanding, so they go for semi-intelligent Hollywood stuff."

Mat looks again. "I still don't know them."

"That's because most of them haven't come out yet. Tom has got a list of sites with advance copies of stuff. He gets some of them even before they're released in the cinema."

Mat inhales, ill at ease with this. "Are you referring to illegal download sites? If so, aren't such operations killing the film industry, and it's wrong to be supporting them?"

She turns to him, clearly unmoved by his argument. "The film industry is composed of hugely profitable corporations making hundreds of millions. They're not dying, they're just belting out ever more profitable formulaic shit and buying up any of the original talent they think might make them even more money." She turns back to the screen, the cursor lands on a forthcoming Tarantino film, and her eyes light up. "Fuckin' hell. Do you fancy this one?"

Mat is unhappy at being so swiftly dismissed but is also tempted by the thought of seeing a film that has already generated such enormous advance publicity. He nevertheless feels he ought to make one more attempt. "Does your study of ethics not lead you to think that breaking the law is something one should not do?"

She looks at him again. "Are you serious about this?"

"Yes I am," he says with growing confidence that he has exposed an important contradiction.

"OK. Firstly, it is never wrong in itself to break any law. One must ask if the law is just, and as justice is a higher value than legality it is always morally acceptable to break any law that is unjust. Copyright law is morally complicated because it protects a variety of individuals and organisations, some of whom fully merit such protection. Small production companies, struggling screenwriters, independent producers. It also protects vile corporations who pay millions to those who are obscenely wealthy whilst refusing more peripheral staff the right to unionise, and fire those who demand fair pay. Taking from such organisations is just because it is a form of redistribution that is fairer than the one that would take place under laws introduced by politicians funded by these organisations. It is therefore morally acceptable to illegally download any film from a corporation."

He looks at her in shock. "Really?"

"No, but I've already had my fill of justice for today, so can we just watch this. I've got a feeling they may be back home sooner rather than later."

"I thought people with kids never get to go out."

"They don't, which is why they never have anything to say to one another. Anyway, they were kind of sniping at each other when they went out the door. Tom was pissed off that Sofia was taking so long to get ready, and … well you know what it's like." A mischievous smile then spreads across her face. "Although I'm sure Jocasta never posed any such problems. 'Won't be a moment. Just tucking my son in. Oh wait! No, I'm not. He's the one who's taking me out for dinner.'" She then giggles at her own joke.

"Ha, fucking ha. I never should have told you."

He opens the wine and pours them each a glass as Miriam hits play. He had hoped they could simply spend the evening talking, but he is drawn into the film with increasing enthusiasm for a director whose work he hadn't reached during his cultural phase. When it ends, Miriam switches off the set and continues to look at the screen with the same degree of concentration she had invested in the film. After a while she turns to him. "What did you think?"

"The guy's a genius. It's funny, it's stylish, and it's powerful."

She looks back at the darkened screen and slowly begins shaking her head. "No. You can't mix comedy with an analysis of slavery. Some subjects have to be treated seriously because of the subject matter. It's self-indulgent to make parts of the film look like a costume drama and to throw in one-liners. It should have been straight drama without any concern for style or humour."

"He's original."

She throws back her head and rolls her eyes. "The modern obsession with all artists is the search for originality. The mindset seems to be that because some great artists made breakthroughs, all great art must strive to be different. Why not use a traditional form in an intelligent way to deal with an important issue?"

"You told me earlier today that you had wasted weeks of research because someone had already said what you were hoping to."

"It's not the same. I have a contract that tells me I must do something new in order to sustain my career. If I was writing a novel or making a film about slavery or the Holocaust, I wouldn't dare to make light of it. You say he's a genius, and you're right, but his talent is purely technical. Everything he does is eye-catching, but he'll never be a great filmmaker because he's more interested in spraying blood everywhere than exploring the moral content of his subject matter."

"Jesus, can't you just lighten up a little when you watch this sort of thing. Surely part of what he's trying to do is just to entertain."

"It's the fucking curse of philosophy. You can't stop yourself from analysing what's in front of you." She looks at her watch. "Well, maybe I was wrong. They've been out for more than the one moody drink I predicted."

"Are you really as cynical about parenthood as you pretend to be?"

"I'm not cynical, I just think that it's treated as a condition every rational human ought to aspire to. I love Alicia, and I enjoy looking after her, but I don't want children of my own and resent the way I'm looked at because of that. At best, I'm pitied because everyone thinks it's sad that my life is so empty. When I say I'm perfectly happy with the way things are, I'm seen as unnatural."

"Surely that's a view you might find in a Catholic country like Spain, but if you lived in London it's not the same." He is aware how obvious the implication must appear, but he's already at the stage where he doesn't care. Miriam is nevertheless oblivious to the glaring subtext and just carries on.

"Look, if I was a lesbian mother shacked up with my girlfriend and our two lovely IVF twins, I would be seen as more normal than someone who doesn't want children. If Tom and Sofia were killed walking back from the bar tonight and I had to adopt Alicia, people would think it was a tragedy with the unforeseen benefit of giving me this wonderful chance to be a real woman. Even though I didn't want it, those around me would think to themselves that once I have spent a little time with my unexpected little bundle of happiness, I'll see what all the fuss is about." She sips some more of the wine and then fixes him. "Tom once had a couple more drinks than he should have, and he told me that when Alicia was two, he was carrying her back from the park one weekday morning and the roads were deserted. He was walking over the railway bridge and had this momentary fantasy of throwing her onto the tracks and saying she had jumped."

"I thought you said he adored her."

"He does, and that's my point. Even a good father like Tom, with a relatively human child, spends half his time putting away Barbie's clothes and the rest of it, worrying how he should react when Alicia turns thirteen and brings back her twenty-five-year-old boyfriend with the jumbo pack of condoms sticking out of his rear pocket. Why am I a freak because I don't want that?"

He is considering how to respond to this when they hear the front door quietly opening. Tom and Sofia enter with smiles so forced that Mat instantly wishes to leave. They go through the conventional motions of offering him a drink but the tension between the two of them is so tangible that it reminds him of the prevailing mood in the days after his wife found out about the accountant. He offers a transparent excuse about being tired and makes his way upstairs, hoping that Miriam will be able to follow him. Five minutes later, he hears the ping of a text. *Really bad atmosphere downstairs. Any chance of a glass of wine?*

Brought Tom's wine up with me. All yours. LOL btw that's an example of appropriate irony.

Within a few minutes they are in bed, just in time to hear from two floors below a beautifully distinct "Oh fuck off!" from Sofia. This and everything that follows is delivered in a seething whisper that carries with remarkable clarity through windows left open in the warm night air. "No, you fuck off! We get to go out for once, and I have to wait for half an hour because you want to try on your whole fucking wardrobe for a trip to a Streatham bar."

"Oh get over yourself. Yes, for once we get to go out, and I want to put on something I like. How is that so fucking bad?"

"It's about being considerate."

"No it isn't. It's about you having to set down some unnecessary law that results in execution if it's not obeyed."

"How fucking dare you? Half my life is governed by rules you set down, which are all about your fucking control freakery and nothing to do with how things need to be done."

"Oh here we fucking go again. I get blamed whenever I try to organise anything around the house. If I try to say which day we should do the washing, it's me being a control freak. Well, fine. You fucking do everything yourself from now on, and let's not bother going out again in case you actually have to sit down for eight seconds before we leave."

"Oh no, please! How could I live without squeezing in those two-minute conversations about buying new sheets between you checking your mobile or drifting off into dreamland?"

"Oh, fuck you!"

"Well that's a fucking mature way to resolve an argument."

Two floors above, Mat experiences immense relief when they stop, but through the silence he still feels their hostility, and he is stunned by the viciousness of the exchange. He is also aware that if he has heard everything from below, then any sound or movement he makes may travel back in the opposite direction and that Miriam must be conscious of the same possibility. But his discomfort is tempered by her presence beside him, and he turns slowly and breathes the words into her ear. "I don't suppose there's any chance of full-on sex tonight?"

"Not with a screamer like you," she replies in a barely audible voice. "Anyway, how can you want to roll around after hearing that?"

"They're probably having an epic, silent, make-up fuck as we speak."

"They're married with a kid. They don't have sex anymore."

He kisses her gently on the neck and rolls over on his back, gazing silently up at the ceiling, with any chance of sleep utterly remote. He can hear from Miriam's breathing pattern that she is also hopelessly awake, and he knows why. She has also recognised the boundless spite in a relationship splitting apart.

Chapter Eight

When he wakes, there is another note waiting for him. *Why not pop down to see Tom. Try to make sure he doesn't end up a divorced loser like us. X.*

Mat ponders this. It's all very well for Miriam to talk about major intervention, but he barely knows them. Is he supposed to go down and talk about how awful it is to be living in a hotel after you've separated from your wife? It's bad enough divorcing when you're rich, but God knows how these two could afford it. Or maybe the advice should be more practical. "Look, if you try sleeping with someone else, then make sure you leave no trail that might be discovered." Come to think of it, that's not really very funny when a child is involved. In the end, he decides to revert to a traditional masculine approach to personal conflict resolution, which is to feign ignorance and say absolutely nothing about it.

It is ten by the time he knocks on the door with the miserably transparent lie that he is going for a walk and wondered if Tom and Alicia would like to come with him. He is surprised when Sofia opens the door, clearly preparing to go out with the girl. "Oh, thanks, but it's actually sports day at Alicia's nursery." Then hesitation. "Why don't you come with us?"

Mat is initially unenthusiastic at the prospect of watching toddlers competing to see who can put their trousers on the right way round in under six hours, but he also experiences a sick fascination at the idea of children so young being inducted into the realm of competitive sports. A fantasy flashes before his mind of a gladiatorial contest in which the little beasts must struggle to inflict a fatal bite on the opponent. He pictures Alicia victoriously removing the fallen victim's flesh from her teeth and holding it aloft as parents and other combatants rapturously chant her name. "I'd love to."

A few moments later, Alicia is racing ahead of them on the inevitable micro scooter. When she is clearly out of earshot, Sofia turns to Mat rather self-consciously. "I'm sorry about last night."

"What do you mean?"

"We heard you snoring while we were simmering away downstairs not having an epic make-up fuck."

Mat is thrown off guard. How could they possibly have heard this? Then Sofia smiles at him. "Miriam came down this morning to pick up some fresh clothes, and when we apologised to her she told us your rather amusing line."

A first glimmer of doubt. Miriam shouldn't have said this, and Mat is acutely embarrassed, unsure how to react. Sofia seems to detect his discomfort. "Don't worry. Once you come to know Miriam better, you'll understand she has this rather unfortunate combination of indiscretion and an odd inability to know which jokes are appropriate. She's nice enough that everyone forgives her for it."

Mat smiles at her, and they walk a few more paces in silence before Sofia looks at him again. "It's not as bad as it sounds. I mean I know how awful it must appear, but it's not what you think."

"Look, I really ... you don't have to ..."

"I know, I just don't want anyone to get the wrong idea. You devote so much effort and concern to your child that very little else seems important any more. The danger is that you forget how to get along with others, but we actually really enjoy the life we have."

Before he can stop himself, the word is out. "Why?"

She laughs at him. "Have you really never felt the urge to have children?"

"Look, I'm sorry. I didn't mean it like that. I'm sure there are very good reasons I'm overlooking. Well ... it's just you say how much effort it requires and then how much you enjoy it."

"It's difficult to explain without falling into cliché. There's a sort of wonder at watching a human develop and realising you are somehow responsible for it, part of the whole process. The only time I've ever had any sort of insight into religious conviction is the moment I heard Alicia cry after she came out. There's also something extraordinary about being held by a child, an odd combination of being loved and needed. Beyond that you start to get into territory reminiscent of the clips people send into TV shows with children throwing a breakfast bowl on the floor because the milk was poured from the wrong angle. They're just very funny." Just as she gives the impression of being about to continue, she stops abruptly. "I hope this doesn't sound too preachy, I hate sitting with some of the other mums who either bore you to death with endless anecdotes or deliver a sermon on the moral superiority of those who procreate. I don't come across like that, do I?"

She doesn't, and he is grateful for the analytical approach to a life whose appeal still seems mysterious to him. "No, but I'm surprised by how uncritically people seem to recommend it. You compare it to religion, and when I was married I found people would speak to me as if I had completed my preparation for the major part of my life, which would only be fulfilled once I had become a father."

"You'll be relieved to know the attraction of not being a parent actually becomes clearer from the other side of the fence. When we were in Spain last year, I went over to see one of my cousins on a Sunday morning. I got there about eleven, and she and her boyfriend had clearly crawled out of bed only a few minutes earlier. Stylish apartment on the eighth floor of a modern block, smooth jazz playing in the background, Sunday papers spread across the furniture, fresh coffee percolating."

"How come they had the Sunday papers if they'd only just got up?"

"They bought the first edition at the main station on their way back from the theatre the previous night."

"Nice. You know I'm starting to feel better about my life."

She looks at him oddly, and he sees that for all her understanding of why he leads the life he does, she would never choose to go back to it. Before this thought crystallises, they have arrived at a corner of the park where around twenty other children are gathered in an excited mass, with five nursery teachers watching and listening to each child with such exaggerated interest one might think every semi-coherent sentence was revealing next week's winning lottery number. Mat finds it difficult to discern the different ages, finding

everyone falling between one and five to be more or less indistin-
guishable. Yet the staff somehow manage to sift the younger from
the older, and organise the initial races, which involve a ten-me-
tre sprint in which the two-year-olds are released from the hands
of a teacher and must advance as quickly as possible towards their
mothers. Two of the five competitors make it the full distance, resisting the temptation to lie down and play with their shoes before
half way. All of them receive a gold medal, including the one who
refused to leave the teacher's hands despite his mother's best efforts
at tempting him away.

Alicia's first contest has her in a team of four. They must compete against one other group, dribbling a football five metres and
firing it into a mini goal before picking it up, and carrying it back
to the next team member. Alicia goes first, tapping the ball with
extraordinary care for the few steps before blasting it into the tiny
goal, retrieving it, and racing back to the start line. Mat finds himself
willing her team to do well, and when he turns to smile at Sofia he
sees her face taut, head bobbing back and forth, teeth clenched. Alicia has put her team well ahead, and the next two players maintain
the advantage. The final child is the diminutive Philomena in her
full Prada sports outfit. She tops the ball with her first kick, moving
it only a few inches. Still, they are so far ahead that Mat remains
relaxed. She then nudges the ball broadly in the right direction,
and closes in on goal. From around two feet away, she then strikes
the ball with all her little might, making good contact with the left
side of it and sending it well wide of the goal. Mat turns to walk for
the ball but sees Sofia thunder past him at full speed, retrieve it and
race back to give it to Philomena. The other team's final player is
now approaching the goal, and Sofia hands the ball over just as the
opposition score, with the two girls now side by side. Philomena
then places the ball on the ground and begins scuffing it roughly
in the direction of her teammates, all of whom are now shouting at
her to pick it up. Too late she realises she is supposed to be carrying
the ball, but by the time she has lifted it, her rival has run into the
delighted arms of her friends, all of whom high-five her to celebrate
their impossible victory.

Sofia stands there expressionless but then leans over to Mat and whispers in his ear, "As soon as I saw that fucking useless midget was on our team, I knew we were in trouble." Her mood visibly worsens when the mother's loud, plummy voice carries to them. "Mummy's so proud of you, Philly. You were so fast. Mummy's little footballer." Mat smiles but finds Sofia gazing at him with barely concealed rage at the betrayal of her daughter. After some more variations of these micro-distance contests, there is a sumptuous picnic of low-calorie sandwiches and sugar-free drinks, and after a couple of hours the children begin hugging one another as they part.

Mat must disentangle Alicia's scooter from its twenty near-identical sisters, and when he returns his eyes widen as he sees her playing with Philomena. The mother soon walks up to Sofia. "My, isn't Alicia a wonderful athlete. Such strong legs."

"Thank you so much. But Philly tries so hard as well."

"So useful to be a bit lanky sometimes."

"Yes, but what commitment from one so stunted."

"Well, she has grown quite a lot over the last year!"

"Oh I can see that. She must be almost two feet high now."

Mat then cuts in. "Look, how about a muffin at Caffè Néro?" The mothers then agree that they must organise a playdate soon, and they part with an impressive display of artificial affection. They walk for a few metres before Sofia turns to him. "Nice idea to have a muffin, but let's go to a café that doesn't evade tax." She leads them to a Polish place on Streatham High Road and texts Tom when they get there. "He has a job interview. Just want to find out what happened." This task is made easier when Tom walks in ten minutes later, dressed in a suit and tie despite the blazing hot sun. Sofia smiles at him and then kisses him gently on the cheek, the previous night's hostility having apparently dissipated. "Well?"

"You are now officially married to someone in employment."

"Whoah! Well done."

"Don't get too excited. Two hundred pounds a day, but a zero hours contract. I teach two days a week for the summer term, and if it works out then maybe a one-year contract from the autumn."

"What's the place like?"

"Two huge Victorian mansions knocked together just off Sloane Square. Classes of six students taking intensive courses, paying forty thousand a year for the prospect of getting into a Russell group uni."

Mat is shocked at the price. "That's more than I would have thought."

"Only if you're thinking in terms of old Europe. All their students are Chinese and Russian. I assume someone's pitching the chance of being the next Harry Potter, and all these people are biting."

Sofia is smiling. "Well done, really. Does this mean you're paying for the coffee?"

"I haven't started work yet. Mat can pay." He then turns to him. "So, did Sofia poison the drinks of the other children so Alicia would win?"

The girl looks up from her muffin. "Did you mummy?"

"No, darling. Daddy's just making a very old joke he has made so many times before. Why don't you go and play with the toys in the children's area?" The girl's eyes move swiftly to the mats in one corner of the room, with toys strewn across them. She then forces the remaining third of her muffin into her mouth and runs off with her cheeks bulging.

Mat looks back at Tom, and the pleasure is so clear. "How long since you gave up your last job?"

"'Gave up'?" That's a delicate way of putting it, and he and Sofia both laugh. "I had to walk out before I got fired. I'm sure Miriam has given you some of the details."

"She mentioned in passing that things got very difficult."

"I was one of the union representatives at this large college, part of which involved issuing press notices. At one stage, I gave an interview to a local journalist about what it was like working as a teacher in a college that had seen almost two years of continuous strikes. We thought it would be good PR, but management claimed that as I was going beyond just setting out the union's official position, this was a personal interview, which no member of staff had the right to do without the written permission of the principal. So I ended up trying to lead a strike and fight a gross misconduct charge at the same time. In the end, I just had enough and walked out."

Mat is initially silent and then shakes his head in disbelief. "Would they definitely have sacked you?"

"Absolutely. The national union put up this very good full-time official to represent me, and she told me as soon as we came out of the first interrogation from the new head of HR that they had already taken the decision. All the HR person did was ask a series of prepared questions and then write down the answers as if she was a note-taker instead of someone supposed to be considering the facts. 'Do you think you have behaved in a way that is trustworthy? Do you think you have acted in the best interests of the college? What would you say to the suggestion that the reason you did not contact me to seek permission to speak with a journalist is because you knew I would not have granted it?'"

"It sounds like Orwell."

"Actually, it was perversely interesting at times. I once went through a phase of reading a lot of east European dissident writers, and it was like being transported into the middle of a play to hear the same questions put to me that they had fielded." He stops, apparently caught in reflection about events that must have been far worse at the time than his relaxed tone indicates. Sofia places a hand on his, and she holds it. "I'll tell you the precise moment at which it struck me that we couldn't possibly win. At one stage, I had to meet with the principal and some of the senior managers he hired. I went in with this head-banging business lecturer who never really had much time for delicate negotiation, and at one point this guy asks the principal if he really has any interest in the proper running of the college. The reaction was like something out of a comic. His eyes actually bulged out with shock, and he shouts back, 'I take *great* exception to the suggestion I'm not interested.' And it suddenly dawned on me that this man actually believed in what he was doing. All the destruction of people's jobs, all the money spent on hiring expensive venues for set piece speeches, the fortune wasted on hiring unnecessary managers while he got rid of teachers. He believed in all of it. We thought he was just this inadequate little man who liked to make himself feel bigger by shouting at his staff in front of an audience of obedient managers, but acknowledging that would have required a certain degree of self-awareness on his part. The story he obviously told himself was that he was this visionary, and those who disagreed were threatening a college only he could save."

Mat smiles. He had seen the same sort of personal fantasy in the City. Even after it was clear just how badly things had gone wrong, and after being kept alive by governments they had derided for years, he saw senior executives without any real doubt over the wonder of financial services. It was just this blip in the otherwise immaculate progress of the most impressive of free markets. Even the experience of catastrophic failure followed by salvation from what was supposed to be the greatest obstacle to success did not shake anyone's faith, and he remains convinced this myth of infallibility will eventually bring them down. These institutions are so immune from doubt that they're incapable of diagnosing their own shortcomings, and because no government can afford to anger them, all they can do is move profitably towards their own destruction.

Alicia appears at their side, and Sofia quickly moves to pay before Mat has the chance. They all then make their way back to Woodley Avenue. The girl is full of stories about the various contests from earlier in the day, and Tom responds with exaggerated enthusiasm to each one. By the time they are a few hundred yards from the house, he picks her up, and she wraps her arms around his neck. Her head lies flat on his shoulder, and she is still telling him about the races she won and the medals the teachers draped around her. Her father walks with an almost childish smile as he holds her, and for the first time Mat has a flicker of understanding.

Chapter Nine

Nothing is said. There is no pre-planned discussion during which one of them raises the issue and they talk it through. Instead, there is just a seamless transition from the point where Miriam first sleeps upstairs, through the stage where she has been sleeping there for a number of consecutive nights, until they arrive at the unspoken understanding that she is now living there. Living there? Is that what it's called when they both know she plans to leave? Shouldn't there be another name for it, like temporary cohabitation, or extended stay? He entertains vague fantasies about what it would be like to live in Spain, but hopes she will consider staying in London. At any rate, the issue is largely sublimated as warm days turn into weeks. There is the odd reference to her teaching responsibilities, or friends from home who have emailed her, but these are lost in a sort of semi-routine that evolves without ever being articulated. She rises early and endures the horror of the rush-hour commute up the Northern Line each day. This is treated as a punishment that must be endured in light of her need for the works stored in the British Library and because she feels she is sharpest early in the day. She works until four, always leaving in time to beat the commuters on the way back down to southwest London.

His days are shaped entirely around the anticipation of her. After the debacle of his initial attempts at weight loss, he tries for a slower but more plausible route. He signs up at a local gym and starts working out every day from ten till eleven. He cuts down on carbs and sugar, and joins Tom and Sofia's tennis club, which also includes three crumbling squash courts. He plays twice a week, with the bonus of this being an old club struggling to attract stronger players who have grown up playing in front of Perspex walls at the rear of perfectly dehumidified courts. This means he is able to compete once again at a respectable level, with his success increasing as he becomes lighter and quicker. He also starts burning through the contemporary literature recommended by Sofia. He takes out subscriptions to *The New Yorker* and the *The London Review of Books*, but also starts checking daily a number of websites she recommends that review a broader range of novels than those picked up by the major journals.

These activities occupy his time, but they are secondary to Miriam's return each day. This moment is often celebrated by rolling around for an hour or so, experiencing that very particular satisfaction of sex during the day rather than its ritual performance before sleep. He starts cooking, and they settle into evenings where they sit out on the small balcony with a meal he has made and a wine he has selected to go with it. This pattern is broken for the two days a week when Tom now works, with Miriam charged with looking after Alicia until he or Sofia gets home. Miriam's proximity makes the thought of childcare a burden worth bearing, and he comes downstairs with her each Tuesday and Wednesday, days when Alicia is not in nursery. This makes it possible to do day trips in the car, although he understands that these must be economical in order to avoid the danger of the girl's parents also being expected to splash out on theme parks and play centres they can scarcely afford. He is surprised just how much of London is either free or so cheap he wonders why they bother with the administrative pain of charging at all. Aside from parks and playgrounds, they find city farms where she can sit on a pony that is led twice round a tiny field. They do make it to the National Gallery where she draws *Whistlejacket* with a degree of precision that astonishes him. He is surprised how concerned he becomes that she should be happy on each day out, but always prefers those trips to cafés with a play area in which Alicia amuses herself with other children while Mat can talk with Miriam in circumstances approaching normality despite the presence of children.

He is happier than he can remember, and it is therefore a moment of shattering disappointment when he wakes up on one of the days when Miriam usually works, and finds her sitting in the lounge, eyes staring straight ahead, face like death. "I may have to go back early." The words are issued in a lifeless, robotic tone.

"What are you talking about? What's happened?"

She inhales deeply. "I told you before about what was happening back home, about the miners. I was sent an email last night that I didn't see till this morning. I just came off Skype with my dad. Talks have broken down again between the union and the government. The minister won't shift. Won't even delay any of the changes. The union is going to ballot for an all-out indefinite strike. They want to bring everyone out and keep them out until there is some sort of improved offer." She hesitates, holding his stare as she speaks. "I'm sorry, but I have to go. I can't stay here reading in libraries, and … Well, I can't."

"Reading in libraries and what?"

"I can't feast here in London while this is going on. Almost everyone I know depends on those mines in some way. I feel I have to go back and do something."

Part of his reaction is a genuine confusion over what on earth someone in her position might achieve. Why must this end because of a dispute in which she could have so little effect? "What exactly can you do?"

"Everyone will support them. Even those who don't like the miners know that they need them, and as everyone hates the government it should be possible to organise some sort of opposition to this. I have to be there to help out."

He looks down. He knows she is trying to be diplomatic, but even he is aware of the decadence of their life over the previous two months. He was also aware that there was always the probability of her returning to Spain, but he had fantasised about her finding some sort of position in London. It wouldn't matter how little it paid because he could easily fund their life here, and she herself had spoken about the difference between working in a city with just a couple of other academic philosophers and being in London with limitless opportunities for meeting others in the same field. But what did this mean about him? Had he been deluded about how much she seemed to be enjoying this life? Was he just a means of helping her to pad out the time before going back to a more serious life and a relationship with some writer whose life she approved of more than his?

She looks at him and clearly seems to have anticipated these thoughts. "I'm sorry, I know how all this must appear. Everything has been a bit of a shock to me too, and I haven't really had the time to think things through, but here's my best attempt after reflecting on matters for the last hour. I … I have to go back, and I'm not sure a separation would work out."

It takes him a moment to process this, but once he grasps the meaning and sees her nervous half-smile, he sits down opposite her. "This is one hell of a way to ask me to leave my country." She remains silent, simply looking at him.

"What do you imagine I would do there?"

She inhales deeply. "Why did you leave the City?"

"I just didn't feel comfortable there anymore. I didn't want to be a part of what they were doing."

"Are you going to feel patronised if I start quoting moral philosophy at you?"

"Probably, but I suppose I'd better hear it anyway."

"Do you know the myth of Gyges?"

"Didn't Kristin Scott Thomas do a turn on this in *The English Patient*?"

"The myth has it that he discovered a ring which gave him the power of invisibility. He used it to steal, to rape, and ultimately to murder his way to becoming the king of Lydia."

"I was a currency trader not a serial killer."

"Hear me out. When Plato uses the myth he's trying to point out what he thinks is a fundamental mistake about morality. He thinks that people wrongly assume that if you are able to act purely in your own self-interest and get away with it, then you'll be happy. He suggests that living what you believe to be a moral life is the only way happiness is possible and that anyone who is selfish will never be satisfied because they will always want more."

"I'm sure there's a straightforward answer to this, but how exactly do I fit into this?"

"I'm saying help us, help me."

"It's not exactly something I'm terribly experienced in."

"You must have been involved in some campaigns when you were a student"

"..."

"Nothing, not ever? Jesus, don't you think it's time you started?"

"What exactly could *I* do?"

"What anyone else does. You just make as much noise as you can to try to and make the fuckers so uncomfortable they think again. You march, you write letters, you turn up to meetings, you raise money. You're a native English speaker, which means you can try to reach people that others can't. Set up a website, a Facebook page, a Twitter account, write to British journalists. You can make sure anyone who's interested and speaks English can find out about what's going on and help in whatever way they can."

They are both silent, with Mat unsure what to think of this. It is one thing to have left behind a life with which he was ill at ease, but without ever having been a member of a union he is now asked to run an international campaign. It's also true that he *does* feel patronised. He doesn't perceive himself as being so awful that he deserves this sort of lecture. Yet these concerns seem trivial beside the possibility of being with her, and for all his reservations about the crusading attitudes, there is something in this he admires, something he wants to emulate. He smiles at her, and when he speaks it sounds more like a capitulation than the sort of commitment she was seeking. "All right," he says. "All right."

*

It is only a week before she goes back. From Mat's perspective, the only upside of such a rapid departure is that she gives up the daily trips to the library and sits down to carve one pristine piece of writing from the mountain of books and articles she has read. The original plan had been two articles, but she doesn't have the time. The downside is that she puts in ten hours a day to produce a first draft before she goes back, terrified she will discover she needs further access to a work that will be unavailable in Spain. She works in the bedroom, and Mat finds it bizarre to uncover the way in which she writes. He is intrigued by the fact that he hears the keys struck so infrequently, having expected a constant tapping. She tells him on the second evening that having planned out exactly what she will say and how she will structure the article, she never writes more than one sentence at a time before pausing to review it. She removes any unnecessary words, simplifying each claim until it is boiled down to a pure essence, an argument composed of elements that make it utterly transparent because all ambiguity or excess has been stripped out. By the fifth day she has a first draft, which she will set aside for a week and then reread at home, satisfied she won't need any further material in London. She will send it to her former supervisor at King's and a selection of others writing in the same field with whom she has always kept in touch. If she is lucky, the finished article will emerge in a leading journal in a year's time, and she will have added an atom of original thought to the growing mountain of material appearing in every academic field.

The morning after she completes it, he comes down and sees a printout sitting on the dining room table. She comes down a few minutes later and sees him looking at it. "Am I allowed to ask what it's about?"

"Do you really want to know?"

"Actually, I do."

She smiles. "Some of the ancient Greeks believed there was a relationship between justice, beauty and love, and I try to defend that view. If you really want a boiled-down version, then the just person is also beautiful, and genuine love is the appreciation of that moral beauty regardless of what the person looks like."

"So you'll still love me even when I lose my amazing looks?"

"Get rid of the vanity and we'll see."

*

On the day she must leave, he drives her to Stansted. She has a suitcase that costs more to check in than the ticket for the low-cost flight, and as they sit in the café she asks him something that smacks of an artificial attempt at being casual. "How are you going to travel over?"

"Drive to Portsmouth, ferry to Bilbao, and drive down from there."

She draws a deep breath. "You can't come in that car."

He is initially surprised, but quickly realises the tension in supporting striking miners as he races around in a Porsche. "It's my favourite toy."

"Mat!"

"Don't worry. I understand the kind of sacrifice one must make to unite the workers of the world."

"You once told me about my problems with irony."

"All right, I'll try to be more careful." Then a pause while he tries to think of something to fit the moment. Somehow, the knowledge that they have planned for him join her in a little more than a month doesn't diminish the sense he has as they walk towards the gates that he will never see her again. Maybe she'll think better of the idea, or meet someone else before he flies out. "I wish I could come with you now."

She raises a hand to his face, pulls him gently towards her, and kisses him softly. Then she releases him, turns, and she's gone. He stares through the departure gate for a few moments in case she comes back, but soon realises this is futile, and he is already trying to sort through in his own mind all he must do in the five weeks before he travels out. He has signed up for a language course at the Cervantes Institute. Four hours a day for four weeks. He considered the individual sessions for six hours a day, but Tom put him off with stories of what it had been like when he did one-to-one lessons in Valencia. There are very few people you would ever choose to spend six waking hours with every day, and it is not worth taking the risk that you will get the wrong one.

He must also deal with the flat. He decides against renting it out, partly because he doesn't need the money, but mostly because he wishes to avoid the danger of dealing with difficult tenants. Instead, he will give Tom and Sofia the keys so they can lease it through Airbnb, asking only that they pay the bills and cover any breakages.

There is also the vague thought that having the flat quickly available will make it easier to come back if things don't work out. He travels back to Bristol the following weekend to stay with his parents and to tell them what he is about to do. When it emerges why he is going, he is surprised by the reaction. There is the predictable concern about how often they will see him, and whether it isn't a little quick, but they are intrigued by Miriam. They met her over dinner when Mat invited them up to London for a weekend and took them all to the National Theatre to see a Stoppard revival, but they were unaware of her political commitments. His father pokes fun at him over the fact that he had been working at one of the banks whose continued existence requires the closure of Europe's mines, but his mother is curiously relieved. It is she, after all, who had emailed him the article that had unleashed the thoughts that had led him here. "I'm sorry you're going so far away to do this, but I'm pleased you're out of that world. I never really liked your previous job very much." This is the closest she has ever come to voicing the old-fashioned values to which both his parents subscribe. They have always had a distrust of any form of radicalism, and the infatuation with free markets has made them uncomfortable because they have only seen danger in the determination to remould every organisation in the imagined form of a competitive business. His father had once likened it to a modern form of Jacobinism. These views make them oddly sympathetic to preventing the destruction of industries they feel are so central to the ability of any community to sustain itself. He sets up a Skype account for them and explains they will see more of him while he's in Spain than they ever did in London.

The language lessons mean he is constantly busy during the weeks between Miriam's departure and his own. Aside from the work he is given in class, he reinforces what he has learned each day by working through relevant sections in other course books he has bought, and it becomes a running joke with Sofia and Tom when he asks them for explanations of irregular verbs or for clarification on a particular grammatical rule. The fact that he will not be driving also makes it easier to decide what he will take, as he is now restricted to a couple of suitcases, although the coffee maker will be sent on ahead. He spends many of the evenings downstairs and agrees to look after Alicia on a couple of occasions each week so that Tom and Sofia can go out. She giggles at his Spanish but also delights in it when he begs her to speak with him. He even comes to look forward to the time he now spends with her, sitting next to her on the sofa as they watch the latest Pixar film Tom has downloaded.

Two days before his departure Mat finishes the language course, and he is set. No job to leave or to worry about. No flat to sell or rent out. No questions over how long he can afford to be away for. He picks up an international SIM card from one of the shops in Streatham High Road, and as he comes through the front door into the communal hallway he sees some of the junk mail that now constitutes his only source of incoming post. He picks up the letters for the downstairs flat and is on the verge of pushing them under the door when he stops and looks at one of them. He reflects for a moment and decides to take it up with him, knowing he can always claim it was a mistake if he's wrong. He sits down on the beautifully deep sofa and opens it. He laughs at first, but then the thought comes to him that maybe he has been conned, that the figure is too small to be correct. He picks up his MacBook and logs in, spending only a few moments on what would have taken the other two twenty years to achieve. Two days later he is gone. Three days after that, Tom and Sofia receive confirmation their mortgage has been repaid in full. The source of the final payment is untraceable.

PART TWO

———

LEÓN

Chapter Ten

She takes a large gulp of the dry white, her second glass. She checks again, but still there is no indication how late the flight will be. Having organised a petition in support of air traffic controllers, she is now irritated that it should be this day of all days that there is so much disruption. She tells herself she is having the second glass because of the delay, but she knows it's a lie and on recognising this she is amused at the memory of a talk she once attended about the impossibility of self-deception. You may deceive others, and you may hold false beliefs yourself, but the act of deception requires the knowledge that the belief one is trying to bring others to accept is false. That knowledge makes deceiving oneself impossible because if you know the belief is false then you cannot believe it to be true. So why is she attempting the impossibility of deceiving herself? Because she's not sure about this. Even though *she* suggested he move with her, and despite all that has happened over the summer, still she's not sure. Her doubts are not rooted in reservations about Mat but about herself. It had been a year since she slept with anyone, two since she had been involved in what one might consider a relationship, a disastrous four-month romp with a more junior colleague from another department. She thought at first that he possessed the talent she had mistakenly attributed to her husband. He was a published poet with a local cult following due to his use of the regional language. He showed an open contempt for academic hierarchy, refusing to submit research proposals or even to inform his head of department of where and when he was publishing. It was his good fortune that some of those in positions of seniority recognised the considerable commercial appeal of this image and happily watched as he published articles in radical, online journals where he attacked the innate conservatism of academia. The result was a surge in applications from local discontents and American cultural studies majors interested in the crossover between art, politics, and regional identity. The more he insulted those above him, the more money he brought into a faculty wilting under austerity. Miriam would attend readings with him at independent bookshops and anarchist collectives, and the more he raged, the more he enhanced his reputation as part of a challenge to a system that had bankrupted the country.

What irritates her in hindsight is not the immature hypocrisy, but the time it took her to recognise it for what it was. She was initially in thrall to the impassioned commitment to his poetry, his politics, his sex, his everything. Yes, *his* everything, and it was the sex that first bothered her, the facile claim that opposition to authority included resisting all norms, including sexual ones. This meant an absence of any restrictions on which sorts of act they should engage in, as well as a conveniently well-hidden absence of any restrictions on whom he performed them with. What made the truth so difficult to discern was that he was so utterly oblivious to the fact that nothing could be more traditional than the artist fucking everyone he could, any way he could. When she put this to him after finding out about two of the undergraduates he was also sleeping with, he was sincerely outraged at the accusation of conformity to the rules of old-fashioned masculinity and accused her in turn of clinging to traditions she ought to be resisting. When she laughed at him, he stormed out but predictably returned a couple of days later. By this stage, her early excitement had faded into dislike of just how far he was into himself. The clear sight of just how badly he needed some reassuring maternal figure he could also fuck led her to be probably a little harsher than she intended. The obvious parallel with Richard riled her, and she ruled out the possibility of ever dating another artist, regardless of his politics or his talent. She felt vindicated in her judgement of him when he accepted a professorship a year later, and she knew he would be conservative when older.

This experience did little damage in itself, the sort of silly misjudgement many have made. But it added to a growing loss of confidence that ultimately led her to Mat. She sees the unfairness of the labels under which she falls, but finds she just cannot ignore them. At thirty-eight, she is childless, the very term suggesting that she is lacking something. Why not 'child-free', or 'still able to go out spontaneously', or 'capable of having conversations unrelated to infant faecal production'? She is also divorced, another term bearing the imprint of failure, an open advertisement of having committed herself absolutely to someone and then fallen miserably short of the standard she publicly claimed she would meet. The only consolation here is that those who have never married receive either pity for never having found someone, or contempt for being too immature or cowardly to try it out. In the twisted world of social convention she has lost out in a higher game than the one played by those who have never wed. Another irresistible source of concern is the approach of her fortieth year, a stage of biological betrayal in which she is aware of slowing physically, with the body resisting ever more forcefully the social shape it's expected to maintain. She perceives without a trace of doubt both the artificiality and the injustice of these categories, yet still they bear down on her. She does not want others to think less of her because she doesn't want children. She feels no guilt at her divorce and does not want others to look at her with pity. She resents a world that denies her the possibility of being beautiful for arbitrary reasons no one could defend.

These personal doubts are made worse by what she sees around her. A country humiliated by those who run it, funnelling money between one another's banks and construction companies until the façade crumbles away and everyone must pay for this farce except those who are responsible. So she had leapt at the possibility of an Erasmus grant to carry out some research back in London. She still associated it with marriage, with divorce, with failure, but also with those years at King's when she was happiest. But the issues from home pursue her, and one morning she opens an email from the colleague who has taken over her union role that tells her about a fresh round of funding cuts at the faculty. She is safe, but there will be more job losses than had previously been planned. And she walks out of Tom and Sofia's flat slamming the door, and she sees that stupid car sitting in the driveway, and she still has the house keys in

her hand, and she walks back and looks at it, and she puts the key
against the door and gets ready to dig it in as deep as she can and
pull it the whole length of the car, and suddenly he's standing there
looking at her. And now she's a thirty-eight-year-old philosophy
lecturer who's been caught trying to key a car, and when the absurdity of this strikes her she has to stop herself from giggling as she
offers the most formal introduction she can to conceal what she was
about to do. She is amused by this all day.

It is Sofia who insists that evening that they invite him down.
Tom initially resists out of nothing more than sheer laziness at the
prospect of having to make some sort of social effort, yet he takes
the usual path of following the line set down by Sofia, and they
bring him in. She is still embarrassed at having almost been caught
out that morning, but as the evening wears on she is also aware of
his glancing over at her, and she's intrigued by his backstory. A
banker, but someone who's rejected that life. Is the desire to be a
teacher real, or is she right that he has concocted this on the spur of
the moment? What first sparks a deeper interest is when she finds
herself genuinely shocked that he would take them to Legoland.
Despite the cultural horror of proposing this as an alternative to the
National Gallery, there was also a beauty in the act of taking Alicia
back to where she most wanted to go. When she emails him the details of some teacher-training course she has come across, it is in the
knowledge that she wishes to meet with him, and when Tom tells
her he is divorced she hopes to find someone who will understand
what she has been through. On listening to his catastrophe, she recognises her own stupidity in being drawn into a relationship that
should never have occurred. She also sees in his bitterness the same
distortion of her own memory, that special way in which a vicious
separation corrupts the recollection of everything good that went
before. Then he listens to what she has to say, and it's the reaction
of someone damaged in the same way, lost in the same helpless
confusion of being unable to find any way forward because of such
foolish mistakes in the past. She decides in the restaurant that she
wants to sleep with him, and if he turns out to be another disaster

then so be it. She could scarcely do any worse than when she had carefully thought things through.

Except it isn't a disaster. He is interested in what she is doing, and he reads some of the articles she's published. He never tries to pressure her into setting aside her research to spend more time with him. He doesn't spend hours talking about himself, and there is the satisfying experience of coming home each day in the knowledge he will prepare an exquisite meal which they will consume with some of his excellent wine as they sit on the balcony. After the set-backs, which had become so engrained in her life at home, it feels as if she has somehow been allowed a chance at an easier shot. She doesn't feel as if she has done anything wrong to achieve it, and there is that constant background reassurance that if things were to work out between them then his money would smooth over any obstacle they might encounter. She finds herself considering a move back to London, perhaps applying for a fellowship or funding for post-doctoral work.

She glides through the weeks in an ever more hopeful frame of mind until she skypes her father and all the contradictions suddenly confront her. She must choose between the lighter life of recent weeks, or going back to fight what will probably be a futile struggle in which she will achieve nothing. Why bother? Why not let go and seize an opportunity she may never have again instead of going back to resist a kleptocracy that is almost certainly invulnerable. These thoughts run through her mind while he sleeps upstairs, and in the end it is a casual reflection from one of her tutors at King's that returns to her. The study of ethics cannot be treated in the same way as other branches of philosophy. Logic, metaphysics, mind; they can all be addressed dispassionately, approached in the detached fashion in which one might solve a mathematical equation. But to consider the issue of how one should live is to ask about which values everyone should accept, and any answer to such a question reveals how you yourself must live. Once she reaches this point, she feels she must either go back or give up any sense of integrity in what she has taught for a decade now. She would have to set out her own position on morality in the knowledge that she refuses to live in accordance with what she claims to believe. And so she decides she must go back. Better to fight and lose than recline in sumptuous ease as she teaches material that would now involve an act of hypocrisy every time she stands up to deliver it.

What about him? He has to come with her, and he has to do it for the right reasons. He can't come over simply to be with her, but also because he sees the importance of what she is doing. So she gives him the lecture on Plato and takes the risk of his finding her condescending. Better he knows now what she thinks and decides if he is still interested. And he agrees. So why does she still have any doubts? Because it can't be this simple. Always she has chosen badly, and it has to be the same again for reasons she has not yet fathomed.

She drains the glass and looks up again. Baggage in hall. She walks over to the gates and edges towards the front in the hope she will be the first person he sees when he comes out. The automatic doors open and close relentlessly, and she wonders if he has missed the flight, perhaps changed his mind. But suddenly he is there in front of her, holding her, kissing her, and everything is better.

Chapter Eleven

She knows how small he will find the flat in comparison to what he left behind. No stylish furniture or exposed wooden beams. He sets down the two suitcases and first looks at the wall of books with the flat screen TV neatly slotted in amongst them, and the DVD player at head height a couple of shelves higher. He scans the rest of the room with the large Goya prints and the one original painting above the classic fireplace. Then he looks her in the eyes and smiles. "Perfecto!"

They spend the first four hours in bed, rising only for her to make an omelette for a late lunch while he fishes out the coffee maker from its box. It is swathed in towels and sweaters, and he heaves an immense sigh of relief on finding it wholly undamaged. He has also smuggled in the three best bottles of wine he has, and they will consume the first that evening. "We'll save the second for the day on which the dispute is settled in our favour," he tells her.

"And the third?"

"I haven't come up with an occasion for that one, but please don't break it open when you've got a couple of your girlfriends over for a cheap night in."

She has prepared a meal for their first evening, hoping to repay some of what he offered her when they were in London, but before they sit down he says there is something he needs to discuss with her. "You said you wanted me to get involved in what's happening. I wasn't sure how far I should go before getting here, but I tried following things as best I could online, and I had a couple of ideas."

She is taken by surprise, not having imagined that he would throw himself into the miners' dispute from the start. "What ideas?"

"You mentioned that there could be ways of generating some sort of international angle, and I made contact with some people

125

who I thought might be interested. I tracked down some of those in Wales and in Yorkshire who were involved in the last big miners' strikes in Britain, and they are keen to do whatever they can. They mentioned fundraising, messages of support, lobbying MEPs, that sort of thing."

"You know you're getting the hang of this already. You're really supposed to spend years marching and taking abuse in the streets by trying to get someone to sign petitions before you take over the international side of the campaign, but maybe you can be fast-tracked into a strategic role."

"In all honesty, I'd probably be most comfortable trying to invest any funds the union has in high yield bonds, or hiding their cash offshore."

"Right, I'll mention that to my counterpart in the miners' union."

"I want to meet with whoever is coordinating the dispute. I need to know exactly which figures they are using in their own publicity material and what the demands are. I think it's important that whatever prospectus I put out is completely consistent with the message being issued in Spain."

"Jesus, you really haven't done this before, have you? The 'prospectus' says, 'Don't shut the mines because everyone will be fucked,' and there are two or three real figures to remember about the size of subsidies and the number of miners. Everything else is hyperbole about how much damage it will do, which will probably turn out to be an understatement because you can't quantify what it does to a city or a region when you drain its income."

"That's fine. I've spent years talking shit about how good the product is I'm selling, I just need whatever figures the union is putting out." She smiles at him, so serious. She will introduce him to one of the union representatives over the next couple of days, and she is amused by the fact that she will have to be there as his interpreter.

After they finish eating, she takes him for a walk through the city centre, meandering down the wide boulevards that radiate out from the central plazas. She tells him that she thought he might wish to spend some time outside the city, and she has been offered the use of a place in the mountains in a couple of weeks' time. It is simple, but utterly remote. Then he stops and looks up at the immense palace before them. "Hmm ... Looks neo-Gothic, but it's also reminiscent of some of Gaudí's work."

She looks at him suspiciously. "Have you been reading your Gombrich again?"

"*The Rough Guide.* Casa Botines; commissioned in 1891, finished in 1893. I want to see round it."

"Good luck. Like everything else in the country it's now owned by a bank."

They sit in one of the bars and order a local drink she recommends. She is nervous that he will quickly tire of a city only a fraction the size of London, but he is still apparently mesmerised by the vibrancy of the clean squares on a warm evening with everyone in tee shirts even as it approaches midnight. She knows that if they were in any British city centre at the same time, there would be an endless stream of drunken groups emerging from bars with a superficial joy that barely masks the threat of violence. She hopes he is ready for something quieter, safer. In a couple of days, he is due to start at one of the local language schools at which she enrolled him at his request. Three months of intense lessons by the end of which he hopes to be reasonably articulate, and she is already impressed at the basic grasp he demonstrates when ordering and paying for the drinks. Maybe things will work out. Maybe.

Chapter Twleve

"Felipe."

"Mathew."

They shake hands with extreme formality. She had always been unsure of Wittgenstein's claim that you can actually see an emotion, that apparently private experience which occurs within a mind and may or may not be clearly expressed by the body. But when this official from the UGF, Spain's largest mining union, sees Mat pull out his MacBook and start typing notes, the shock is as plain as every other feature of his face. He may be in his forties but looks older. His prematurely greying hair is combed back, but strands of it continually escape to fall forward over a face lined with the history of defending those who have spent decades under assault. He wears an unbranded polo shirt with genuinely faded jeans, which meet over a bulging stomach, and she wonders if Mat will feel self-conscious at sitting down with someone whose work has been so dramatically opposed to his own.

Mat explains that he wishes to set up an English language site that will promote the dispute to a wider audience but needs to know exactly what the message and the strategy are so that he can fall in line. "What is the total value of current government subsidies?"

Miriam translates the questions in a tone rather less business-like than the one in which Mat issues them.

"Three hundred million euros a year."

"What is the planned reduction?"

"Just over sixty per cent. They want to cut it to just over one hundred and ten million, but we assume their plan is ultimately to get rid of it altogether."

"What is the economic argument against these cuts?"

"We have opted for an approach that combines a moral and

economic argument. We feel this is best suited to tapping into the general discontent with the government. The basic claim is that it's deeply unfair that miners should pay the price for mistakes made by politicians and speculators who have destroyed the economy. The argument is also that the cost of five thousand miners losing their jobs may exceed any savings. There will be welfare payments for all those who are out of work, and as there is already twenty per cent unemployment, it's unlikely they'll find jobs. You also have to look at what it means taking all of that income out of what is already a poor region. They will also have to import coal they are now getting from within the country. Even if you don't care about the social impact, it will probably be an economic disaster."

Mat types quickly, then stops and nods. "All right, what's your bottom line?"

Miriam looks baffled. "What do you mean?"

"What figure would they accept in order to settle?"

She is unsure whether or not she should press him further, but decides it is not for her to decide whether or not this is a question worth putting, and she translates.

"All existing subsidies should remain as part of a wider policy of trying to invest in the economy instead of squeezing it."

Mat's head goes back as he considers this. "All right, what I could do is promote your dual strategy. We can target groups who are likely to help out already. I would suggest miners' organisations in countries where they have strong domestic unions, the US, Australia, Britain. The aim will be to raise money to fund the dispute here, but also raise general awareness. There also needs to be an attempt to attract wider support from those who would not necessarily side with a trade union. I would simply follow your line about the foolishness of austerity, and how this policy will make it more difficult for Spain to repay its international debts. That may generate some further funding, but the better outcome would be if it starts to discredit the policy of austerity and if it makes the government look incompetent."

Miriam translates this to the astonished official.

"Look, if you can rally the world behind us, that would be wonderful, but I should warn you that our focus will be overwhelmingly on fighting a local dispute aimed at getting the government to climb down."

"I'm only talking about a general approach consistent with your aims. If you're happy with this, I can have a website up and running within a couple of days. It'll be basic, but it will ensure anyone who's interested will get the story we want them to hear."

He smiles back. "Sounds like you may be able to win this on your own. We'll make sure to get you a miner's helmet with your name inscribed on it."

"It's what I've always dreamed of."

He passes them a flyer about some of the events planned over the next few weeks and then rises to leave. He kisses Miriam on both cheeks and reaches out to shake Mat's hand. "Just so you know, when you're in the position of trying to take on what feels like the entire world it means a lot to have people come out of nowhere to support us. Thank you."

After he leaves, Miriam looks at Mat in disbelief. "Are you serious about all of this?"

"Why not? Everyone hates every government at the moment, and everyone is pissed off about ordinary people being shafted to pay for the banks. The story of an entire community being devastated could easily attract a lot of support." Then he smiles. "It's the perfect tale of redemption. I get to destroy the global financial system and then become a hero for saving those who had to pay for what I did."

"You know all those conversations we had about irony?"

"OK, I get it." His attention then shifts to the flyer on the table. "Well, when do I get to go to my first demonstration?"

"It's not as exciting as Legoland."

"Easy for you to say. I was the one who spent the whole day queuing."

"There's a march to one of the pits on Saturday. The aim is to stage a sit-down outside the factory gates in order to stop any coal leaving. There are some workers who are still going in, and the company that transports the coal isn't unionised. The idea is to disrupt the operation for at least a few hours and perhaps generate some wider publicity." Then she smiles broadly at him. "Not a bad way to start. If you're lucky you might even get arrested."

★

He makes sure the website is up before the demonstration. It lacks any creative flair but contains the basic information that might draw in anyone who's interested. What it's about, why the miners are right, photos of noble workers, how to donate. It includes links to the union's site, and it is at least a start for anyone who speaks English. He sends the link to Felipe, and when he and Miriam get off the bus in the village from where the march will begin, Mat is welcomed by members of the local leadership who have already seen the site. They speak to him in Spanish and he responds falteringly, but Miriam is impressed once again by how much he obviously understands already.

They begin walking at around ten, with the colliery only around fifteen minutes away. There are around forty of them, mostly miners, but also some students and members of other unions such as Miriam's. Mat is disappointed by the low turnout, but she explains that they must limit how many mass demonstrations they organise in order to avoid declining numbers. Any such trend would be used to suggest support ebbing away, so the strategy is many smaller events with the occasional mass rally. She is still explaining this when they round a bend to see the gates, and they advance to the point where they are standing only a few metres from the hundred riot police who separate them from the entrance. The fear is extraordinarily easy to analyse despite its intensity. There is the initial shock at seeing the well-organised lines of men, and there is the brute fact of being hugely outnumbered. The thick black body armour, the helmets with darkened visors, the shields. Miriam has the absurd concern that they must all be very hot under the searing morning sun, but this is offset by the implicit menace of the long truncheons. The presence of a couple of TV cameras and perhaps half a dozen journalists and photographers offers moderate reassurance. Even if some of the police may be salivating at the prospect of piling into such a small group, they will recognise the danger of images being recorded and instantly uploaded.

Felipe is standing at the front, and Miriam overhears him say to the man next to him that this is new, a shift in strategy to prevent the union from carrying out the more disruptive measures they had used over the previous few weeks. As the two groups face one another, a truck emerges from one of the loading bays inside the fence, a pile of coal clearly visible in the back. The gates are opened and the officer in charge lifts a loudspeaker and asks in a faultlessly polite manner for the demonstrators to exercise their right to protest by the side of the road. No movement. Now a second request, only this time with the additional information that the police will use force if necessary in order to clear the road. Felipe turns to his people. "My friends. You must be tired after the walk from town. Please sit down for a rest." They all sit, and the cameras and photographers approach in search of the best angle. Once again the officer issues the request to clear the road, and the demonstrators sit in silence, the threat of what may be about to come being enough to remove any incentive to shout back. So he issues some commands to his men, and they approach. They have apparently planned how they will do this, because three men move forward to grab Felipe, who is at the front. The first two each seize an arm as the third grabs his legs. He makes no effort to walk, nor does he kick or lash out in resistance. When they have travelled the few metres to the side of the road they lower him and place him on the ground. He stands and looks back over at his friends, but does not move back to the road. The same process is then repeated in turn for each of those seated, and everything advances with a sort of mutual coordination, whereby the protesters offer only passive resistance as they are removed. When they reach a woman who is a representative of a civil service union, one of the police grabs an arm but also catches a handful of hair. She shouts at him, and then tries to knee him when he swears at her. Another policeman then comes out of the line, raises his stick and brings it down into her stomach with all his force. She folds in two as they drop her, and those at the side of the road rush forward to help her. The officer bellows at the man who struck her, and a sergeant grabs him by the shoulder and hustles him back through the lines of police. The woman then rises, shocked but not as seriously injured as her reaction to the blow suggested. She flips the finger to the police as she seethes at them, a full thirty seconds of shouting during which she runs through the entire range of Spanish verbal abuse. When she stops, the officer calls to his men and the process of removal begins again.

Within half an hour the road has been cleared, and the truck rolls out. Felipe then motions them to follow him back in the direction of the village. Miriam is unsure if this signals defeat, or merely a common sense understanding that their battle will not be won or lost today. But when they arrive at the bend in the road from where they first saw the gates, the group separates. The woman who took the blow to the stomach carries on back towards the village, accompanied by most of the others. The rest are led up a small path into some woods, and after ten minutes they are at a point which looks down on the colliery from above. There are three men sitting there with a huge duffel bag, and Felipe approaches them and appears to give a rapid account of what had happened. One of the men pulls from the bag a piece of metal piping around a metre long, and places it on his left shoulder, facing roughly in the direction of the colliery gates. A second man pulls out some binoculars. A third loads the biggest firework they have ever seen into the back of the pipe, and lights it. It takes around ten seconds for the fuse to burn, at which point the rocket streaks out of the pipe and fizzes in the general direction of the police. If falls woefully short, but the explosion is a spectacular arrangement of colour that lights up the arid dust around the road. Binoculars then utters a few words about elevation, and the next missile is loaded. This one lands closer to the gates, but still a full thirty metres from the riot police, who remain where they are, apparently anticipating the protestors may return. They seem to be milling around, unsure whether to be concerned by the potential danger or reassured by the wildly inaccurate aim. This dilemma is resolved when the third attempt hits the gate full on and the police scatter in all directions to avoid the cascading sparks.

There is a spontaneous cheer from all those on the hill, and Miriam turns to Mat in elation. But when his smile suddenly evaporates, she turns back and sees the police racing towards them. Then they are running. They cannot return to the path because they will be cut off, so they crash through undergrowth and bushes, racing into the depth of the woods from where they hope to be invisible. It will take the police time to climb the hill or else work their way round so they can come up the path, and each of those now fleeing is aware they must make good ground while they have this advantage. So they run until they see that some are so exhausted they can run no further and Felipe says they should stop. He is breathing hardest of all, down on one knee, looking back in the direction from where they came. They wait with no word spoken as each watches and listens for any sign of pursuit. If they hear any voice or see any sign of the dark visors, they know they will have to run again, this time followed more closely by younger, fitter predators who will no longer be under the lens of a TV camera. Still they wait, and the longer they stay there the more reassured they feel that the police were content to drive them off and were probably reluctant to follow them into the woods.

After maybe fifteen minutes, Felipe rises and walks over to binoculars. The two whisper for a few moments before motioning for everyone to approach. Felipe smiles at them. "I'm really too old for this." The others laugh, grateful for the final release of tension and reassured that they are probably safe. "My friend here is going to lead us to the edge of the woods, but it's probably not such a good idea to go back to the place we got off the bus, as they could be waiting. There's a small station about half-an-hour's walk from here, and we'll go there. When we get close we'll split up so it just looks as if we're walkers who've been enjoying the beautiful Castilian countryside over the weekend."

So they trudge on until the trees thin out and they can see a village no more than a mile away. Felipe walks out first with one of the other men, and will text from the station if it is safe. No text will mean they must find another route home, but would also imply the police may be monitoring all of the local transport links and they face the prospect of walking the fifteen miles back to León. So once again they sit and wait, each wondering how long it will take before they must conclude that Felipe has been taken. After twenty minutes, they hear the double bleep on binoculars' phone, and they separate into smaller groups, setting off at five-minute intervals. Mat and Miriam are second from last, and they hold hands as they reach the narrow road leading up to the station, just a couple of lovers out walking for the day. There is a moment of panic when they see a police car parked in the station, but Miriam whispers to him that they are local so there is little chance of being recognised.

They must wait almost an hour for a train on a rural line carrying commuters during the week but barely used outside rush hours. Others from the protest are spread along the platform, but none of the disparate groups communicate with one another. They consider looking for a café, but there is a residual fear of running to the police and it feels safer where they are, baking in the afternoon sun. They finally get back at seven in the evening, and Mat throws himself into one of the armchairs as Miriam grabs some food and wine from the kitchen. When she sits herself, she looks at him and is unsure what to make of his demeanour. He has been silent for most of the trip back, and she was reluctant to speak about what had happened for fear of being overheard.

"Are you ok?"

"Not really." His tone is snotty.

"Look, I'm sorry. I really didn't know that anything like this was coming. I think they must have realised the police were under orders to start cracking down, but Felipe must have decided that he couldn't tell us what was planned in case it got out."

Mat looks over at her and smiles. "That's not what I meant. I just keep playing this image over and over in my mind of that woman being hit in the stomach with the truncheon. I've ... I've never seen anything like that before. There was something horribly distinctive about the sound of it. Not the clean paff of a screen sound effect. It was quieter and duller, made me feel as if something was crumpling beneath it. Then, when we were running all I could think was that if they caught us they would do the same to us."

She inhales deeply. "Look, we were all scared. I had no idea that so many of them would be there to stop us. They must have been expecting thousands of us to turn up or something."

"You want to know something bizarre? When we were running through the woods, I was scared, but I also had this incredibly powerful feeling of exhilaration. I mean a really primal sense of just loving the experience of the fear and the escape, something about the extreme nature of it."

"I tell you what. We'll ask Felipe if you can let off the fireworks next time."

"That's another thing. How the hell did they come up with that?"

"I've got this terrible urge to say it's not rocket science, but however primitive, I would have to admit that's exactly what they used."

He smiles again and opens his arms to invite her over to him. They kiss, and he looks her in the eye. "I'm afraid I'm too mentally frayed to have sex, but I would like to drink a bottle of my wine."

As she goes back to the kitchen to get the wine, he opens the MacBook and hooks up the latest iPhone he bought a couple of days before leaving London, hoping to acquire this one last toy before beginning the more austere life he knew he would lead with Miriam. On returning with the wine, she looks at the screen and her eyes widen in disbelief. "Where the fuck did you get this?"

"I shot it from the hillside. Not bad, is it?"

"You had a camcorder with you? I didn't see it."

"Darling, in order to defeat evil corporations, you need to understand just what they're capable of," and he points to the phone. He has clips of each of the three rockets being fired, and a spectacular shot of the third one both flying through the air and then striking the gates before exploding. In the first clip it is possible to see the face of one of the men with the metal pipe, but the others contain only shots from the rear in which no one is identifiable. He uploads both onto YouTube, creates a link on the website, and also sends the link to Felipe. Once this is done, Miriam asks if she can try something. She goes on to the site of one of the left-wing national newspapers and they receive their second visual shock. The whole of the front page is a picture of the woman being dragged away by the hair, capturing her just as the truncheon falls and her face is contorted with pain. The headline reads, "The Battle of León." The first image is followed by text describing hundreds of police dragging and kicking protestors who were sitting on the ground. There are further images of people being carried off, but none with the force of that first one. She scrolls down to the foot of the page and creates an ID so she can join the discussion. Hundreds have already commented, expressing disgust at the police and the government. She inserts a link to the YouTube clips, and then goes into half-a-dozen further news websites, all of whom are now carrying images of the protestors being dragged away, usually starting with the same woman. She includes the link in the comments section following each article, knowing that with such a major piece the journalists moderating the comments will follow the link. It takes only until ten o'clock before they get what they want. Three of the major channels lead with footage of police dragging protesters way, followed by the rockets being fired. There is then footage taken by the TV crews of the police trying to climb the hill to catch those firing the rockets from above. They are struggling up the steep slope, with one slipping and falling a few metres back down the hill. The oddly contrasting impression is of one of brutality combined with comic ineptitude. A government minister condemns the viciousness of the protesters but refuses to comment on whether the police had overreacted. A woman speaking on behalf of the miners is given the final word, stating that a peaceful sit-down protest had been met with violence.

Within a day, the international press has started to pick it up, with the same images dominating. The only exception is a brief item on the Fox website that reverses the order, showing the rockets being fired before some shots in which the first miners are moved from the road in more restrained fashion. The article emphasises why Latino immigration needs to be treated so seriously by voters in the forthcoming US presidential election. Mat looks at Miriam in confusion, and she is first to work it out. "They think this happened in León in Mexico rather than Spain."

He sits back and wonders at what has happened over just a few hours. "You don't think that maybe it was a mistake to upload the footage of the rockets. Makes us look violent?"

"Fuck that. People want to fight. They're sick of the government just doing as they please, and as no one got hurt we look like we're standing up for ourselves but not injuring anyone."

"We might have."

"But we didn't. Anyway, you saw all that shit they were wearing. You'd need a lot more than a few fireworks to get through it." Then she looks back at the TV screen. "This is a big deal. International coverage, all of it sympathetic to our side. Ministers must be nervous at how it all looks. If there's going to be some sort of compromise, this must move us closer towards it."

Chapter Thirteen

She smiles on seeing his excitement at driving a real jeep. His face lit up like a child's when she told him the place was so isolated they probably shouldn't try to get there in a conventional car. The one they hire is small, with two nominal seats in the back, but obviously made with just one or two people in mind. Nevertheless, when the engine ignites with a low growl he smiles at her and she can't help smiling back. "If you're good you can have an ice cream later as well."

"No need. This is much better than Legoland."

They drive for around three hours before they reach a village and she has to fish out some directions that are so intricately detailed that he wonders how far they must go. They leave the main road about a mile outside the village and turn on to a dirt track that declines in quality the further they go. After fifteen minutes they are travelling over little more than rough, open country, with the history of car tracks rutted into the ground being the only indication it is ever used by vehicles. The final few hundred yards involves turning onto a track protruding from the side of a small hill, which is barely wider than the car. When they reach the bottom there is a surprisingly straight, level approach to a tiny building sitting among several lines of perfectly symmetrical olive trees. When they pull up to the building he jumps out.

"Is this a finca?"

She laughs. "A finca is a country house. This is a casita, more like a shack."

They grab the supplies they have brought for the weekend, essentially some simple food, some bedding, and a change of clothes. The impressive wood-panelled front door opens into a small room with a couple of armchairs, a two-ring electric stove, and a tiny fridge. At the back of this room there is a further door that leads into a small bedroom, and at the back of that there is a tiny bathroom with a shower. Miriam has to open a metal cabinet at the rear of the bathroom which houses a portable generator and some jerry cans filled with fuel. She pours in enough petrol to power it for the weekend.

Outside, she finds him reclining in one of the folding chairs he has set up, already opening the first bottle of wine. There is the powerful smell of the rosemary that grows wild all around them, and she sits in a chair opposite him and accepts the glass he extends towards her. "Quiet enough for you?"

"It's perfect. Absolute escape from civilisation, but with electricity thrown in. Whose place is it?"

"It belongs to a friend called Ana, one of the painters from the faculty of fine art. It used to be an olive farm, and she inherited it from her grandparents. She spent a couple of thousand euros to make it habitable, and now she comes up here to work on major pieces so that nothing can distract her."

"What a place to have."

"Actually she hates it. She feels she has to come here to ensure she is unreachable for long enough to focus on what she's doing, but she'd be happier in a world that reverted to no internet or telephones. It's only the British who are in love with the idea of living in the Spanish countryside. We're much more into urban comfort and don't really get the attraction of the peasant lifestyle."

"It'll be interesting to see if you change back. Before you came out of the house, I was just sitting here, and I can't remember the last time I ever experienced complete silence. No background hum from cars or central heating or the music in another room. I'd love to have a retreat like this."

"It's not quite the paradise you think. The reason she has the thickened front door and the metal box is because one of the natives broke and stole her first generator. She didn't' want to buy another straight away in case it went the same way, so she had to spend four days here eating cold food and shitting under the olive trees.

The way she tells it I think you'd give up your rural fantasy pretty quickly."

"Sounds like you could be right."

She goes back in and starts cooking while he reads. Night is already descending by the time she brings out the pasta with chorizo, and the temperature drops so low they must put on sweaters and hats. They go to bed early, tired at the end of a Friday during which she taught in the morning, followed by the long car journey and making the house liveable. The bed is an ancient one, probably a cast-off from one of the neighbours, but beautifully soft. When Miriam wakes on Saturday morning there is a feeling of deep satisfaction at being only with him, and with a weekend ahead in which they will walk and drink and speak with no other person. He is still asleep, and she moves closer to him, wrapping her arms around his torso. She sees a stunning mosaic tile on the wall, which the artist herself may have painted. The sensation of beauty begins when she first notices it, and ends at precisely the moment when it begins slowly uncoiling and moving down the wall. She is aware of a sudden and immense acceleration in her heart rate, and after a moment's shock she tightens her grip on Mat to wake him. She moves her head next to his ear to whisper so quietly she hopes the snake won't hear and launch a frightened attack, but he speaks before she does. "I know. I saw it."

They both lie there in terrified stasis, neither clear what the right move would be. The hope is perhaps that the snake will conveniently slither out of the bedroom in full view, and then make its way out of the front door and into some distant world. They wait for perhaps two minutes before the flicking tongue appears over the edge of the duvet, followed by the head, at which point both of them leap up and jump off the foot of the bed. They grab for the most effective weapons they can find, Mat's shoe being rather more potentially useful than the pillow Miriam is holding. The combination of sound and motion startles the snake, which drops down from the side of the bed and moves quickly under a wardrobe in one corner of the room, while the two humans fearfully cower in another.

Mat is first to speak. "Do you know what it is?"

"A snake."

"I mean what kind of snake. Is it poisonous?"

"No idea."

"Jesus Christ! Shouldn't you know this sort of thing? It's your country."

"Yeah, I bet you know all the British butterflies."

"Butterflies! To be honest, if there was some killer version of the red admiral I think I would probably have learned how to recognise it."

"OK, never mind all the David Attenborough shit, just get ready to pounce if it comes out." She then reflects for a moment. "Look, I think that smaller ones tend to be poisonous and the bigger ones squeeze you to death."

"Well what does that make this one?"

She ponders this, nodding as she contemplates her answer. "Indeterminate."

"What the fuck does that mean?"

"It could be a small, harmless one or a giant motherfucker of a killer. How old do you think it looked?"

"How old! Who am I, fucking Tarzan? We need a plan, just think of something."

"Look, it's probably more scared than we are, so maybe we just walk confidently past the wardrobe, and it will stay there until we leave."

Now Mat reflects. "I don't know, what if it strikes as we're walking past? If one of us gets poisoned, then it might be difficult to get to a hospital in time. I think we need to wait for it to come out and then kill it."

"That means we need a better weapon. There's a spade by the front door. Look, you stay here while I go for it and just be ready to jump on it if it goes for me."

She works her way slowly around the wall in such a way that she remains as far as possible from the wardrobe at all times. When she gets close to the door she leaps through the passage. A moment later she returns clutching the spade above her head, ready to bring it down if she sees the beast emerge. Once again, she circles around the room maintaining maximum distance between herself and the wardrobe. When she is just a few feet from Mat, he reaches out for the spade, but then freezes as he sees her eyes fix on a point over his right shoulder. She also remains stock still, speaking slowly and quietly. "Don't move a muscle. Listen to me very carefully. If it strikes, then we'll have about a minute for me to suck the poison out of you. I did it with the last guy I brought up here, and he only finished up with a nasty rash around the bite marks." She then watches the succession of emotions move across his face. The fear is followed by relief at the thought she can save him, but then a brief twang of jealousy is supplanted by the anger that she has knowingly brought him into this deadly wilderness. Her face then melts from the mock seriousness into laughter, and once he realises what's going on he leaps forward and turns to see the empty wall behind him. "You fucking mad cow! I could have died from heart failure."

"That's exactly what the other guys said. Where's your sense of humour?"

He grabs the spade, laughing nervously as he now turns to ready himself for battle. She stands beside him, watching for any movement. After a few minutes the snake's head appears and Mat rushes at it, crashing the spade against the floor as the head is retracted in good time to avoid the blow. So they begin waiting again. After a few more minutes they begin to realise that the snake may simply curl up and lie there for hours, and Miriam is first to propose a strategy. "Look, I'll bang on the far side of the wardrobe and try to drive it towards you. Then you whack it and we get out of here."

"Yes, Godfather."

So she takes the shoe Mat was previously holding and once again makes her way around the room. When she is within reach, she begins banging on the huge piece of furniture and after a few seconds the snake quickly slithers out in Mat's direction. He brings down the shovel with a short jab intended to deliver maximum accuracy, but sacrificing power. He catches the snake in the middle and it begins writhing with astonishing speed, now encircling the blade as if trying to crush it. Mat begins pounding it repeatedly against the hard floor until the head is severed from the body that has dropped from the makeshift weapon. What now shocks them is the staggering quantity of blood that spurts *Shining*-like from the tiny body. He steps back, still plainly terrified but now breathing with some relief. But the respite lasts only the brief moment it takes to register the body is still spasming, a motion propelling it back in the direction of the head. Miriam wails over at him, "It's trying to re-attach itself."

"Re-attach itself! Where did it learn that?"

"Just do something."

Emboldened only slightly by the deeply buried thought that what he is seeing cannot actually be some spectacular attempt at self-healing, he reaches forward and uses the tip of the spade to move the head away. He catches it with such a fortuitous flick that it flies across the room, striking Miriam in the ankle, at which point she screams in shock and leaps in the air, splaying her feet to ensure that each leg is as far from the deadly fangs as possible when she lands. By the time she has come down and reared backwards against the wall Mat has once again lifted the spade in readiness to bring it crashing down once more on the headless body. After a few more seconds of waiting to confirm that neither half of the severed creature feels like another round, he drops the spade on the floor and sinks to his knees.

The state of sheer disbelief begins to subside, and they start the process of extricating themselves. Miriam takes the spade and picks up the head, which she carries about a hundred yards from the house, Mat walking by her side in order to avoid being left on his own. She buries it in a shallow grave before they return for the body, which they are relieved to find exactly where they left it, still in its decapitated state. They then carry it off and bury it on the opposite side of the farm in order to maximise the difficulty either part would have in digging itself out and locating its other half during the few seconds they plan to spend on packing and making good their escape. They work together to scrub the blood off the floor, then shut up the house. Before driving off, they beat the side of the jeep with a broom just in case any of the snake's friends are hiding there, perhaps hoping to strike both of them so they die slowly together, and lie undiscovered for years.

By the time they have made it back to the main road, they have started to recover near-normal heart rates, and it is Miriam who first finds the power of speech has returned. "I tell you something, this has given me a lot more respect for Ana's commitment to her art. In all honesty, I never really liked her painting, but once you realise what she has to go through, I think I can see it in a new light." She hesitates. "If you meet her, you won't tell her I had doubts about her work, will you?"

"If I ever meet her, I can honestly say that her art is the last thing I'll be thinking about."

He starts smiling, and this slowly develops into a snigger, and finally an uncontrollable belly laugh, eventually forcing out the words, "It's trying to re-attach itself," before he contorts once again in tears of laughter. She is also caught by a combination of immense relief from the earlier tension and a sudden sense of their absurdity. She turns to him, now almost as incapacitated as he is, "Where did it learn that?" And the two of them begin laughing even harder.

After a further twenty minutes' drive, they enter a small town and he pulls over to check for hotel recommendations on the tour guide app he has installed on his phone. When they enter the white-tiled, four-storey converted town house, it is Mat who insists on speaking with the woman on the front desk. "Can we have your most expensive room, please?" he says in surprisingly accurate Spanish.

"This will be the bridal suite," she replies in English. "It is free, but you will be unable to check in before midday."

"Did anyone stay there last night?"

"No, but …"

"We'll stay only one night, but I'll pay for two if we can go up there now." The tone is sharp, direct, barely polite. This is a negotiation, not a request.

"The woman smiles back at him. Of course, sir. Do you have any bags?"

"We'll carry them up ourselves."

"As you are paying for last night, you may still have breakfast if you wish. You have another forty-five minutes." He checks his watch to see it is only eight fifteen. It must have been little more than six when they commenced battle with the snake.

"Can we have it in our room?"

"No."

He nods. "We'd very much like breakfast, and we'll be down in twenty minutes. Thank you."

Miriam is uncomfortable with the tone and the style of this exchange, perhaps an insight into how he must have conducted business in the past. But she's also curious about what she sees. The demand for the most expensive product was not issued in a way intended to be ostentatious, more like a determination to extract from the world around him what he could with the money he has. It is not a demonstration of wealth for public consumption, just the rational use of the fruits that flow to the winners in a free market. Given what they've been through, she decides to let it pass.

The room occupies the entire top floor of the building. It is ludicrously overblown, but this gives it an amusing charm. The enormous four-poster bed with linen voiles stands in the middle of the room, as if the wedding night was to be spent in the round, with both families watching on to ensure that everything proceeds as it should. There is a mock renaissance sofa and armchairs under a broad, chintzy chandelier. The bathroom is a temple of white marble and imitation gold fittings, with a circular, sunken bath big enough for a small orca. They shower and change before going downstairs, now feeling that they have returned to the safety of a world with conventional access to electricity and hot water.

The breakfast is simple but they can eat as much as they like, and each is exhausted by the earlier experience. Miriam is studying one of the local flyers she has picked up from the front desk when Mat interrupts her. "Fucking hell. Look at this!" He is watching the muted TV above her head, and she turns to see Felipe speaking to a group of journalists. His appearance is unmistakably defensive, and Mat rises to turn up the sound. Questions are fired aggressively, and Miriam's face quickly descends into something close to despair.

After the interview, the presenters go to another journalist for further analysis, and when the piece finishes a few moments later, Mat turns off the sound. Miriam looks at him. "Do you mind if we go back up to the room. I just want to make a couple of calls." Then hesitation, and she puts her hand on top of his. "I know we said that we wouldn't have any talk of the dispute over the weekend, but … I'm afraid this could be really bad."

"I didn't understand what happened."

"A passenger train was derailed last night. A tree had been placed across the track and the driver didn't see it in time to stop. At first it was being reported as a random act of vandalism. Then someone pointed out that it was the line used for transporting coal from Castile to the refineries in the Asturias. The union had to deny any involvement, but now three miners have been arrested and charged. Felipe is still denying everything, but you saw how he looked."

"What are they charged with?"

"I don't know how to say it in English. Basically, acting in a way that could put someone's life at risk. Most of the injuries were minor, but a five-year-old is in hospital with a broken collar bone." She shakes her head. "So now the headlines will be about miners harming children."

She calls a colleague from the faculty to get an account of what happened. There is no official confirmation from anyone, but the story that seems most plausible is that the three men placed the tree across the line in order to halt the coal train that regularly travels on that line. They were using an outdated train schedule and thought the train they were after would reach the point they had chosen at around six in the evening, when the tree would be visible well before the sluggish engine reached it. Instead, the train they were after had passed through two hours earlier, and the next one to come along was a high-speed passenger service that arrived just as night was falling. The driver pulled the emergency brake but couldn't stop in time, and on impact the ninety people on board were thrown around like dolls.

When she hangs up, her head falls, and he quickly moves to comfort her. "It could have been worse."

"Yes, we could have actually killed the child and perhaps a few adults for good measure."

He sighs but says nothing because they both know she is right. The footage of miners on a hillside firing homemade rockets at Darth Vader's extended family had initially attracted support. But even this was short-lived as images went out of police lying in hospital beds showing off heavily bandaged limbs that had been burned after the firework struck the gate and the sparks rained down on them, the uniforms not as effective as they appeared. Having looked so menacing in their modern armour, here were vulnerable-looking young men who had merely been trying to do their job of allowing the gates of a colliery to remain open. This narrative was repeated each time the union tried a demonstration, with the government relentlessly accusing protestors of starting the violence. The reality was that no one could say with certainty whether a brick was thrown at a line of police before a riot officer clubbed someone to the ground. The upshot was the union was unable to establish the level of support it needed in order to force the government to change direction. As long as there was a consistent story of painful but necessary austerity being threatened by violent extremists, the miners could not exert the popular pressure they needed. So when Miriam's head dropped, it was not merely in horror at how close they had come to killing someone but in recognition of the fact that all their efforts were leading merely to predictable and futile defeat.

Mat kisses her on the head, still holding her. "Listen, there's something I've been thinking about for the last few days. And … well I think there could be a different way of doing this."

Chapter Fourteen

It takes an infuriating two weeks to set up the meeting. The only serious candidates are in Madrid, and Miriam must be with him in case he needs someone to translate. This means they have to wait until she finishes a Friday morning lecture before rushing for a train that will get them to the capital in time for an afternoon meeting with the firm Mat has identified, Black and Willens. They started in New York but have opened offices in every city where there are enough people to pay what they ask. When Mat walks into their offices, it is exactly what he anticipated. The building is centrally located, just of Plaza Mayor. It is a classical piece of architecture that has been gutted in order to allow for an ultra-modern combination of veined marble floors, glass walls, and staff in stylish suits. The overall impression is that of the futuristic, humming efficiency of an organisation to which you will pay a fortune for an exquisitely effective service.

For Miriam it means entry into a world wholly unfamiliar to her. She is accustomed to small offices, shelves overflowing with books and folders, colleagues struggling to maintain mastery of their field and overrun by increasing numbers of students with ever more confident demands. When she studied at King's, her approach was a sort of awestruck deference to her tutors, seeing them as a repository of wisdom she found so distant it appeared the prospect of entering the world of academia entailed some sort of mystical elevation. It was only in her latter years there, when she spent time as a teaching fellow, that she became aware of a redefinition of the academic role as that of a commercial service provider. Now she is entering the epicentre of a world she is expected to emulate but for which she has little more than contempt. She despises the obscene expense on an aesthetic so obviously designed to provide reassurance as the firm extracts the money that is the sole purpose of its existence. This contrasts with her romantic sense of doing something valuable in itself, and she feels that simulating the corporate mentality involves the corruption of a more noble ideal. Yet here she is in a luminescent foyer, and it feels like an entry into hell. She stops short of asking herself why she's here because the answer is so blatantly clear. They are desperate, and however appalling she may find it to be sitting in the discomfort of the minimalist sofa with its metal tubes and firm leather cushions, she will see what this firm can do.

They wait in silence. Mat is dressed semi-formally in an expensive designer jacket and black trousers, dress shirt but no tie. She finds herself wondering whether he too is trying to convey an image of easy wealth to those who will instantly recognise it. After ten minutes, a pencil-thin woman in a navy business suit emerges from a lift, shakes their hands, and asks them in English to follow her. They are led to a meeting room where two lawyers sit at one end of an oak table. They rise to offer formally polite greetings before sitting again. The younger one has annotated copies before him of the email exchange with Mat. There are further documents, hidden beneath these messages, and Mat hopes that there may be some possibility there.

It is the younger lawyer who begins, once again speaking in English on the automatic assumption that any non-Spanish client would wish this, and addressing Mat. "As we understand it you wish to consider the possibility of a legal challenge to the government's policy of cutting subsidies for the mining operations in the north of the country. The aim of such a strategy would be, at the very least, to delay any proposed reductions, and hopefully to prevent them altogether. Is this correct?"

"Yes. It was not in their manifesto at the last election, and given the enormous social damage it is likely to cause, we hoped it may be illegal in some way."

"There is no obvious way in which the government could be said to be acting unlawfully. The constitution stipulates that if the government is properly formed, it has authority over economic strategy. The fact that the policy was not in the manifesto raises no legal issue, as governments have a doctor's mandate, which is to say they are legally entitled to introduce what they see as necessary measures in the face of unforeseen circumstances. They will argue that the wider economic crisis requires them to act in the way they have and that what they have done is therefore lawful."

"What about the use of excessive force in suppressing some of the demonstrations?"

"Unless there is evidence that ministers have interfered to instruct the police to engage in unnecessary violence, this would, at best, be a case that could be brought against the police. Even then, it may be practically impossible to establish violent intent from the outset, and it is difficult to see how this would require a change in the policy of removing subsidies from coal production."

"The government has refused even to consider a slower pace of reform. Could this not be seen as evidence of some sort of failure to act in the best interest of all citizens?"

"Once again, they would simply claim that they have the authority to decide what is in the best interest of the Spanish people."

Mat sighs and looks at Miriam. "I'm sorry. I thought there may be some sort of opportunity. I …" But he trails off when the younger lawyer looks to the man who is obviously his superior. "We said there is no obvious means of challenging the legality of what the government is doing. We do, however, have an unobvious one. Ms Gonzalez will suggest one possibility you may wish to consider."

They turn to the woman in the navy suit who had escorted them from the foyer, realising for the first time she is also a lawyer. She inhales deeply. "I must emphasise that we cannot offer any indication of how likely any challenge would be because there is no precedent, but we believe that there is scope for a legal challenge under human rights legislation. Whilst the government has authority over how it disposes of public funds, it is also required under both the constitution and the European Convention on Human Rights to treat all individuals and groups with equal respect. They must ensure no one is either the victim of unfair discrimination or the beneficiary of favouritism."

Miriam scoffs. "That would mean everything they've ever done would be illegal." The smile disappears when she sees none of the lawyers are laughing, but it is Mat who breaks in. "How are you going to demonstrate the miners have been treated unfairly? I thought you said the government would simply claim this is what's best overall for the country."

"It could be deemed unlawful if other groups are being treated more favourably. We think that a case could be made that the mining industry has been treated unfairly in comparison to other groups who are also recipients of government support."

It is Miriam who is first to grasp what they are getting at. "The banks."

"The New Bank of Spain has received over twenty billion euros in state aid, with many questions over how this can be justified."

Mat is confused. "I haven't heard of it."

"This is their latest name. Five regional banks were merged in order to try to make them more efficient through breaking their close links with local business and political leaders. The first incarnation faced corruption allegations so it was decided to rename it, and NBS is their new title."

"I still don't understand how exactly you would establish they had benefitted unfairly instead of this simply being an economic policy the government had to implement."

"If we can show that the government was essentially handing out state money to personal friends in financial services, then this could be deemed unconstitutional. Our calculation is that there are so many key figures who may be implicated that they will wish to avoid a situation where many of them may have to testify under oath. If we were advising them, we would urge them to settle. In practice, this may mean you at least get something better than the current policy, perhaps some protection for current subsidies for a little longer."

Mat and Miriam look at one another. It seems oddly perverse that the standard practice of politicians showering money on their friends may be illegal. Miriam looks back at Gonzalez. "How much would it cost to bring a case like this?"

"Human rights law is a highly specialised field. Such a case would need to be taken on by one of the firm's senior partners. The person we would recommend has a fee of around fifteen hundred euros an hour. He would almost certainly use a more junior lawyer to support him, which would add a further three hundred euros an hour to the cost."

Miriam's eyes bulge. "How many hours would this take?"

"It is difficult to state this precisely, but if you wish to proceed we could provide you with an estimate for preparing the initial case and submitting papers to the constitutional court."

"Rough idea."

"Between ten and twelve thousand euros."

Mat seems utterly unmoved by these numbers, and she realises what an innocent she is in a world where such money is so natural. He is simply curious about where it could lead. "So we basically pay ten thousand to scare them into settling. What if it goes to court?"

"We consider this unlikely due to the sensitive nature of the case, but if it did then you will need to consider the relatively high cost of any potential trial. We would recommend a team of several lawyers, and there are other services we would suggest in this sort of case."

"Other services?"

"Much would turn on establishing the personal and subjective nature of the decisions taken by ministers who are under an obligation to act impartially. We would need to show that their personal conduct was improper, and there are private investigators we employ who would be helpful in demonstrating this. Given the high profile of the case, there is also a public relations firm that would help to ensure the version of events the press receive is one that reflects our understanding of the facts. Once again, I must emphasise we find it unlikely that the government would wish this to go to court, but one reason they may be ready to do so is the high cost which they will suspect is enough to deter a trade union."

Mat nods slowly before looking over at Miriam. "Do you want to ask anything else?"

"No." Then glancing across the table at the lawyers, "Thank you for your time."

When they return to the foyer Miriam is about to speak, but before she can do so Mat is approached by a beaming little man who ushers him into an office just behind the reception desk. When he comes out, Miriam is confused. "Another lawyer?"

"Nope. The lawyers never smile, but the people who take your money are always in a good mood."

"You had to pay for this? I thought it was just some sort of consultation."

He laughs as they walk out of the building and into a street that is now crowded with those leaving work for the weekend. "These people sleep, eat, and drink. They charge for everything else, but I would say that was eight hundred euros well spent."

"What the fuck are you talking about? The union cannot afford to use its funds to pay these bloodsuckers. I know you may find it amusing to deal with people like this, but we do not have the money to pay for this sort of thing."

"Firstly, I don't find it amusing dealing with 'people like this'. You may be astonished to know that bankers hate lawyers. We always used to feel that we were the ones who were doing the real business, and we resented the fact that they were this sort of necessary evil. Just a bunch of parasites really." Her jaw drops, but before she can speak he breaks in. "I know, I know. Who could be more parasitic than an investment banker, but there's your answer."

"So if you dislike them so much, then why did you go to them?"

"It's the same sort of logic as you heard from cold-war politicians when they spoke about nuclear weapons. You don't ever want to use them, but if you do then you want to be fucking sure yours are better than theirs."

They reach a small café in a quiet side street and walk in. She is still clearly uncomfortable with what has just transpired. "They speak English even with me. It's as if they think that in mastering it they have entered some realm higher than the one inhabited by Spanish speakers."

"They probably assumed correctly that my Spanish wasn't up

to it. Anyway, if you're an international law firm, then English *is* the language of a higher realm. That's what their American and British clients speak, as does everyone else in high-stakes business, so a firm like that would only hire people who speak the language like a native."

She shakes her head. "Listen to me, we cannot afford this, and the way forward does not involve getting into bed with people like this."

He is in the process of raising his coffee to drink but stops abruptly. "What the fuck do you think is going on here? You think that marching and letting off fireworks is going to make any difference to the sort of people who are taking the decisions. Listen, a few years after I went into the City, I got a posting to New York. I used to hang around with a group of other British guys who were also working on Wall Street. One of them was this annoying little twerp who worked for a bank advising the Mexican government on privatisation. There was some sort of uprising in a part of the country where all of a sudden they couldn't afford medicine anymore, and they had forty kids in a class because they'd cut a load of teaching jobs. He had a couple too many one night, and he told me he had formally advised the senior civil servant he dealt with at the finance ministry that the government needed to eliminate the leaders and supporters of the local opposition to ensure the smooth introduction of the next round of reforms. This guy wasn't some dribbling psycho who wanted to jerk off to footage of the army gunning down marchers. He genuinely believed that what he was doing was the Mexican people needed, and there was no evidence that would convince him otherwise. I used to follow his progress, and after New York he got posted to Asia. He was one of the geniuses who introduced CDOs into the Hong Kong markets. So, having helped destroy civilisation on two continents, he returns to England, nobly gives up banking, and enters politics. Now he's a government minister looking to use all his wisdom to help the UK into a future determined by whatever the free market thinks best, and the worst of it is he's probably better than the wankers running Spain because he doesn't take bribes."

"Don't treat me like some fucking child, and don't lecture me on Spanish politics. I'm saying that if there's going to be a legal challenge, then there are lawyers who will work for us on principle and who genuinely believe in what we're trying to achieve."

"I'm sure you're right, but if you go into battle in a just war then what do you want to be holding, a quaint little musket made by a skilled craftsman, or a fucking great Gatling gun made by some evil US corporation? There is no principled law firm that can offer the threat posed by the people you just sat down with. They'll work for anyone, but whoever they work for will have better representation than the other side. That's what you pay for, and if we're lucky, their name on the petition to the court will be enough to scare the government into some sort of climbdown."

She shakes her head again. "All of this is beside the point anyway. Even if the union wanted to go down this route, they couldn't pay the kind of money these people are asking."

"I know that." He sips the last of the coffee, then puts the cup down. "But I can."

Chapter Fifteen

It takes three weeks to file the petition, a process that proves considerably more straightforward than the arrangements Mat feels he must make in order to finance the case. He has to make sure he has instant access to his money in a way that will not attract suspicion, and he wants to maintain complete control over what he still thinks of as his own cash. He knows he will probably only need to pay a few thousand euros, but he wants to be ready in case they do go to court. Such a situation would inevitably invite questions about where the money is coming from to finance the case, and as the union isn't going to be paying, there will have to be some sort of story that will avoid any unwelcome publicity. A case being funded by a mysterious benefactor, with cash flowing from a tax haven might be a PR disaster, and he becomes obsessed with preventing anyone finding out the money is coming from the British Virgin Islands. The chances of an international law firm letting this out are remote, but he feels he must consider the danger of having to make transfers to other organisations. In the worst case, there may be the need to hire office space, book venues for events, perhaps even employ staff. He imagines scare stories about Spain's enemies using sinister means to stop the government from saving the country. His initial thought is to create a charity, but this would be highly regulated, with the need for a constitution, trustees, and detailed financial constraints. He also dislikes the idea of just setting up an account with a Spanish bank, as their reputation for dishonesty and inefficiency is so pronounced, and what if he went with a bank that found itself implicated in the attacks made by his lawyers? If they leaked his name, the rousing image of shady banks being challenged by ordinary people would be lost.

He's unhappy with any of the solutions he comes up with but eventually settles on one which he considers to be less bad than the others. He establishes a shell company in Wyoming, a location that appeals to him for two reasons. The first is that its history of coal mining makes it a plausible candidate for some story about how sympathetic groups offered to start a support network and how everything has grown from there. The rather more crucial attraction is that it's also a tax haven offering all the secrecy he needs to ensure no one will find out the truth about where the money is coming from. So he can transfer funds from the Chapelle account into the American one, and if anyone asks he can claim that some former miners from the region approached their Spanish cousins with an offer of support, and that money is now flowing in from all parts of the world from those keen to help honest, hard-working miners to protect their jobs and communities from greedy corrupt politicians. The American account will be so impregnably walled-in from any prying eyes that even those who don't believe the story will be unable to expose what's really going on.

There has to be some sort of official-looking organisation within Spain where some people will need to be at least partially aware of what is going on in order to deal with any hostile press inquiries. The discussion he has with Felipe is rather more business-like than the exchange with Miriam. As far as he's concerned, if a private individual wishes to fund a legal challenge, then this is a personal matter, and as the union has no formal connection with the case, the choice of law firm is none of their business. At the more practical level, the aim is to give the impression of a committed grassroots movement working closely with the union but also independent from it. This will be achieved through the appointment of three local union members to front Justice for Castile. They will be the public face of the organisation bringing the case, which will in reality be handled by the lawyers in Madrid, paid directly by Mat. There is a strict understanding that none of the three will have any formal, legal status, meaning that if things go wrong there is no possibility they will face any serious consequences. Felipe is initially unhappy at the thought of his members performing such an artificial role, but the opportunity seems so attractive that he sets aside these concerns. The hope is that all eyes will be on the case, and the full truth will be so well protected that it will never come out.

He explains this to Miriam as they sit at the dining table in her apartment in León, an open bottle of wine in front of them. Although he has decided to be as honest as he dares, he leaves out the details of the Chapelle account in order to conceal from her that he has money offshore. His unease at this deception is weaker than his fear of how she might react if she knew the truth. When he finishes speaking, she drinks and then looks him directly in the eyes. "Why?"

"Why what?"

"Why are you doing all this? I know I asked you to help, but it just seems so far beyond what I meant."

"I half-wondered myself when I was setting up the Wyoming account. There's an image that keeps coming back to me from the demonstration we went on. I keep replaying the moment when the policeman brought his truncheon down on the woman who was being dragged away. Rather oddly, it's the sound that still haunts me. Muffled, dull. Not the sort of impressive crack you would think is necessary to harm a body. It left me with a sense of the terrible fragility of a person, and here was this monstrous, armed man clubbing her like that." He hesitates.

"There's something else?"

"I told you my parents were both doctors. They never said as much at the time, but I knew they didn't like the fact I went to work in the City. I think they imagined that I would leave Cambridge and go into some more traditional role. Academic, teacher, civil servant. The sort of career that used to have the old-fashioned combination of public service and status and income when they were students themselves. I don't think they ever really sympathised with the purity of financial services, working only to make money with no further outcome. I suspect they've always been disappointed that I seemed to be buying into a world they never trusted."

"Is that what you were? An old-fashioned Tory?"

He laughs. "What if the answer to that was yes? Would you dump me?"

"Were you?" Her tone is neutral, and she is curious rather than trying to root out some dark secret.

"Actually, I wasn't. Perhaps at school, but when I was at university Major was in power. Black Wednesday, arms to Iraq, cash for questions. It all seemed such a sordid mess, and Blair comes along with something that looked much more attractive even when you scraped away all the veneer."

"You bought into all that New Labour stuff?"

"Look, he starts pumping all this money into schools and hospitals. My father went from watching patients with cancer die on a waiting list, to calling a specialist and having the person seen within a week. And yes, I did think it made sense. I even felt I was some part of it. My first major job at Fieldings was on a currency desk. I would make deals worth up to a hundred million pounds a day. The profits were booked in London, so the bank paid British corporation tax, and it was possible to feel that I was getting rich but also contributing to something important." He takes a sip of his wine and looks over at her. "You think all of that is just nonsense."

"I didn't say that. I suppose I just have conflicting intuitions on the matter. I respect someone who teaches more than someone who generates the profit to pay their salary."

"Well, it's not such a conflict any more. Whatever moral justification there may have been disappeared in the crisis, and now the flow of money is all in the other direction. The schools and the hospitals are being sacrificed to pay for the banks."

"In fairness, the banks did spit you out in order to reduce the cost of austerity just a little bit."

He realises this harks back to a lie he told on the first evening they met, when he thought he might attract more sympathy by implying he had been made redundant. But having deceived her about the location of his money earlier, he now wants to be more honest, to make sure she knows who he is. "Actually, I didn't lose my job. I resigned."

"I thought you said …"

"I did. I lied. For some reason I thought you might think less of me if I sounded like someone who had come out ahead in all the mayhem."

She smiles at him. "Is that what happened? You made your fortune while all around you were losing theirs?"

"Actually, everyone with a fortune kept it. It was everyone without a fortune who lost what they had."

She is unsure what to say, desperate not to appear patronising. Part of what he says suggests that what he is doing is driven by some attenuated form of guilt, as if making himself a part of this fight will somehow redeem a crime he has committed in an earlier life. But she is also unclear to what extent this is merely her own prejudice, a presumption of the moral corruption of anyone working within such an unqualified form of capitalism. She is still reflecting when his phone rings. As soon as he answers he puts down the glass of wine and his face switches instantly into business mode. He mostly listens, asking the odd, rapid-fire question. At the end he smiles, and then puts the phone on the table before picking up the wine again and looking over at Miriam.

"That was Gonzalez. The office of the prime minister issued a press notice an hour ago saying the government had been threatened with legal action by a group calling itself Justice for Castile. They make clear that they will not be swayed by threats in their pursuit of restoring Spain's economic stability."

"Fuck me, you mean they want to go to court?"

"I doubt if they want to, but they can't really back down now. There must be hundreds of groups who could bring the same kind of suit against them."

"But the lawyers said ..."

"They're lawyers not politicians. All that meant was that the case may be so embarrassing it would make more sense to settle if they could. It turns out the government thinks it can't, so they'll just have to go through with it."

She now picks up her glass and gulps down some wine. Then she remembers something apparently trivial and looks over at him.

"Why did you smile at the end of that call with Gonzalez?"

"They want me to pay three hundred thousand euros up front to cover their initial costs."

"They're asking you to pay in advance? Is that normal?"

"Only if they're worried about not getting paid at the end of it." He looks at her reassuringly. "Don't worry, it's exactly the sort of ruthlessness you want in a lawyer. Imagine what these sorts of people will do to someone on a witness stand."

Miriam doesn't know how much money he has. She has watched the ease with which he pays for everything, seen the way he picks up a bill and pays without checking. She assumes his wealth runs into millions but does not feel she can ask. Nor does she feel comfortable with it, but she doesn't wish to give him up, and she sees him doing everything he can to help her, answering a plea she made in London in the best way he can. Yet there is something else now. Those final words betrayed a nervousness she hasn't seen before, and she suddenly realises that however much he has, it is not enough to pay such sums in the same casual way he has always dealt with money before in her presence. He found these lawyers because he thought they would provide the best possible chance of winning. Yet they will also bleed every penny out of him if they can, and he knows this.

Chapter Sixteen

The press just love it. The date of the hearing is set for four weeks after the initial suit is filed, leaving plenty of time to anticipate the sight of ministers answering questions under oath live on television. A population which has just seen four years of redundancies, pay cuts, evictions and humiliation will now get to tune in and watch the public interrogation of those they see as their chief tormentors. The news channels wheel out constitutional experts to predict the likely result. There is analysis of the judges who will hear the case and relentless debates between rival politicians about the propriety of allowing a grass-roots organisation to challenge the policies of a democratically elected government. These discussions are made more compelling by the presence of new parties who are pushing aside the two political giants who have dominated since Franco.

The forthcoming trial itself is enough to make the populace salivate, but this prospect becomes all the more intriguing due to a steady drip of stories about NBS. Loans for construction companies to build on nature reserves. The repossession of luxury villas used as holiday homes by senior executives who pay nothing. Photos of one of the bank's directors at a polo match with a CEO, one of whose companies has had its NBS debts generously restructured. Each story is broken by a different paper, and Mat knows that the PR firm recommended by Black and Willens is feeding them to journalists who are hungry for all they can get. It also means that by the time of the trial the papers' editorial line should already be leaning in their favour. For its part, the government is reduced to repeating *ad nauseam* the claim that it is elected to govern, and that is what it is doing. Ministers simply decline to comment on the scandals swarming around NBS, claiming that any illegality must be handled by the police, and poor management must be addressed by the bank's directors.

Justice for Castile now starts to attract press interest of its own, but the miners who front it are generally treated with restraint. The image of three ordinary people defending their community against the power of central government is one the journalists like because it is so easy to sell. The men are armed with fact sheets supplied by the union, and Mat provides them with advice on a line to take that has come from the PR firm. This image is made easier to sustain by the support they genuinely receive from those in the area. A local printer who has had to lay off a third of his workforce gives them free office space. They start taking on volunteers who organise fundraising events, helping with the illusion that the case is one funded by a multitude of citizens who wish to defend their community. For the time being, no one asks how much money they have raised and how much they are paying their lawyers.

The union also shifts the emphasis of its campaign in order to help the case. They avoid any hint of violence or criminality and focus instead on the apparent contradiction between the government's inability to find the few hundred million to keep the mines open, whilst pouring endless billions into institutions run by their friends. The placards at each demonstration now refer to the funding of NBS, and each interview involves putting the same question about why so much is available for those who have destroyed the economy but so little for their victims. For its part, the government offers the lifeless repetition of the need for painful cuts and for banks to be preserved, and the overall effect is one created by the simplicity of the numbers: billions for the rich, penury for everyone else. The hope is that this terribly simple thought will also penetrate the minds of the judges, and that the apparent unfairness must influence their interpretation of the law.

The union's change of tack also includes the idea of using more unexpected and eye-catching forms of protest. At nine in the morning on a cool Monday in October, Miriam walks into a local branch of the NBS. She is ill at ease despite the harmless nature of what she anticipates. Just in front of her there are two women dressed in absurdly high heels and long, fake fur coats with the collars turned up. Each wears an extravagant, wide-brimmed hat and immense dark glasses covering half the face. The bank is in the modern, open-plan style, without any defensive barriers. She has been standing for only a few moments when the man who is next in line is ushered forward to speak with a member of staff. Miriam pulls her camera out and moves to the side of the queue while the man walks to the centre of the bank instead of approaching a teller. He pulls off a long coat to reveal a black shirt and trousers, each with a purple trim. He raises his right hand, looks into the distance and begins what at first sounds like miserable wailing about some tragedy that has befallen him. Staff and customers look across in embarrassed disbelief, straining at first to decipher the lyrics about the corruption of NBS, and realising only after the first few seconds they are being treated to a Flamenco performance. After the first verse, the two women in the fur coats move behind him and drop their coats to uncover intricately woven red dresses with black ruffles that begin just below the knee and radiate out until they stop an inch above the floor. Each woman stamps with the right and issues a high-pitched scream before falling into step with the man as he holds one crooked arm above his head and wraps the other around his waist, rotating and stamping as he moves through the verses of the song. The staff look on with disbelief, but Miriam is able to film someone she takes to be a manager, quickly lifting the phone. The security guard is initially unsettled but soon grasps the unthreatening nature of the event and has enough common sense to know that wading into the troupe will create the image disaster that would doubtless cost him his hourly-paid job. It takes only three minutes before singer and dancers freeze, and even some staff applaud.

The four of them walk slowly out, not wishing to look as if they are running away as they are captured on the phones of others who are now filming them. Miriam leaves them in a café on the main square before taking a bus to the outskirts of the city where Justice for Castile has its office. It is now permanently staffed by two people Mat decided they would need, one for publicity and the other for coordinating and organising events. He bought them a couple of high spec laptops, a copier, and got the fastest broadband available. Miriam hands over the memory card from the camera, but Clara, the media graduate who is running publicity, turns her laptop to face Miriam so she can see a shaky recording of the event she has only just left. "Looks like someone beat you to it. This went up on Facebook five minutes after you left the bank, and it's been on YouTube for the last half hour. Three hundred views already, and it'll be ten thousand by the end of the day."

She slots the memory card in and smiles when she sees the footage. "I need about an hour to edit it and overlay some subs. I'll get it out by early afternoon and if the journos like it we should make the evening news and tomorrow's papers." Miriam thanks her and must now rush back to the faculty to deliver a lecture at midday. As she does so, she reflects on the extraordinary efficiency with which they now fight. Mat's money pays for staff who bring an effortless speed to controlling the message of the dispute. Clara is twenty-four, but manipulates film and skypes journalists with the ease of a child playing with a toy. There is an odd inversion of the normal relationship between age and experience in that Clara has grown up in a world where the tapping of a keyboard is the most natural form of interacting with the surrounding world. When Miriam asked her about the media theory she had read, the conversation quickly stumbled to an uncomfortable close, and it became clear that this was a woman steeped in the skills of instant response and for whom the prolonged study of key texts was antiquated. Yet Miriam's initial reaction of disappointment soon gave way to a sense that Clara was better adapted to what they were trying to achieve. The immersion in contemporary social media gave her an understanding of what sort of image would make the impact they needed. It was she who had read a piece on the relationship between politics and traditional Spanish culture, leading them to the flamenco flash mob which performed in the bank.

Two of the leading TV channels include the footage she has edited as an amusing finale to their main news, and next day, three of the dailies carry pictures on their front page. No one uses the

interview Clara has given, perhaps considering the event too frivolous to merit serious comment, yet it all contributes to the same
compelling message. On one side there is a corrupt government
interested solely in the protection of its rich allies. On the other,
there are ordinary people whose communities can be saved if the
politicians can be forced to act more fairly. At one level, Miriam
despises the way the economic and social complexity of the dispute
is reduced to one-line slogans and arresting pictures, but then she
turns to the polling numbers, which have moved hugely in their
favour, or detects the unwitting sympathy in a newsreader's voice.
They are running a campaign that contains all the shallowness of a
billboard advert, but they are winning. No judgement has yet been
made, no witness called, no questions asked in court, but there are
twelve judges who simply cannot be unmoved by what they see
around them.

It is also Clara who comes up with the most stunning image of
their campaign. In order to attract support during the court hearings, Felipe decides to organise a two-hundred-mile march from
León to Madrid, the strikers' arrival coinciding with the start of
the case. Around three hundred will be involved, and it will take
around ten days before they complete the final stretch in front of
the constitutional court on the day before proceedings are due to
commence. Clara's simple thought is to arrive at night. This will
minimise the loss of sympathy caused by any disruption, and allow
more supporters to turn out after work. But there is a far more
powerful appeal that Clara has envisaged. It is after ten when the
marchers start down the main thoroughfare leading to the court,
each wearing the distinctive miner's helmet with the lamp shining,
the worker fighting to maintain light. It is this picture that will be
splashed across European papers the following day. When Miriam
and Mat make their way towards Calle de Doménico Scarlatti they
fear that only a few dozen will be present to cheer them along the
route. Instead, there are tens of thousands, many having travelled
from outside the city to line roads from where they cheer those
who seem overwhelmed at a level of support they had not expected. It takes hours to edge through streets crowded with people of

all ages who shake the hands of men and women who can scarcely hold back their tears.

It is almost one in the morning before the group reaches the court. The standard set piece for speeches is made impossible by the court's unfortunate architecture. Instead of the natural stage created by neo-classical arches at the top of a series of steps, they have had to plan for the reality of a bulging, seventies barrel protected by impenetrable wrought-iron fencing. Police lines stand in front of the gates to prevent any attempt at entering the grounds, but this was never the plan. A flatbed truck pulls up around twenty metres in front of the police, and the first speaker makes her way up the folding stairs and is handed a mic attached to a portable speaker. She is one of the many women miners who have been involved in the dispute from the beginning, and her speech is about the simple desire to work and support a family. She is received with an impossible hush by the thousands now crammed into the park facing the court, but when she thanks all those who have turned out, her voice breaking, she is met with rapturous cheers, the whole event captured by cameras that frame a worker speaking against the background of the black-clad riot police.

After the first speech, a miners' choir from Turon squeezes onto the truck to sing the anthem for disputes in the coal industry for almost a century. Felipe delivers the standard line that has been at the heart of their campaign. Corrupt politicians. Corrupt bankers. Corrupt property developers. Miners to pay a price for the corruption of others in a policy combining injustice with economic suicide. Then the crowd lights up when Iglesias rises, telling them the court has the opportunity to declare that what is unjust is also illegal, and to signal a new beginning for a country sickened by what its leaders have done to it.

It is after two by the time the rally finishes, the final flourish being the announcement that the miners who have marched to the city will occupy the park opposite the court for the duration of the case. Events will be organised, guest speakers brought in, films shown at an improvised cinema, debates conducted. And so they disperse, thousands of them melting back into the city, carried by a euphoric sense of invulnerability. All those who have marched and listened have had nothing but the reaffirmation of what they hope for, and for now the endless, unopposed support for their views gives the illusion that the whole world is with them. And watching this stand the lines of police. Silent, hidden behind darkened visors, the long brutal sticks gripped tightly. They have been given the clearest orders not to react to anything less than the most extreme provocation, and not without orders. So for now they do no more than passively concede this aesthetic triumph.

Chapter Seventeen

Gonzalez stands, and Miriam studies her with oddly conflicting feelings. The business suit with the high heels strike her as a crude compromise between a time when no woman would ever have been able to address such a court, and one where all women should perceive the absurdity of footwear that warps the spine. Yet here she is, probably thirty, with immaculately prepared straight hair, expensively subtle make-up and a carefully crafted tone. The gendered parameters within which she must speak are far narrower than those constraining the government-appointed man against whom she must struggle to dominate the witnesses. Any lapses or loss of control he suffers may be written off as forgivable errors, but if she is too sharp she will be seen as masculine, too quiet, and she's out of her depth. Miriam realises that for the law firm to have chosen her in such a high-profile case they must be sure she can tread this line, although she suspects they have also calculated the sexual appeal a young woman will hold for a panel of judges made up of middle-aged men.

The opening address begins as a repetition of the arguments that have been aired on countless channels over recent weeks. Gonzalez simply asserts a number of legal obligations with which all Spanish governments must comply. They must promote justice and equality. They must do all they can to promote dignity and a good quality of life for all Spaniards regardless of their background. They must promote economic progress. She then pauses and looks down. There is a moment when everyone wonders if she has slipped up already, but then she looks up and delivers the lines for which the delay was intended to guarantee absolute focus. "Justice for Castile is not fighting merely for the dignity of a few thousand miners who wish to protect a way of life in one part of our country. This

is a story of how every decent Spaniard has been betrayed by a
government of greed, of incompetence, of secret deals made by
ministers and their friends, deals from which the selfish few set aside
any principles of decency or justice in order to enrich themselves
at the expense of the many. In a moment you will hear from the
government's defence team how ministers have taken painful decisions in order to save the country. We will show the full extent of
the dishonesty involved in this claim. We shall show how ministers
who have pretended that they were trying to save Spain have in fact
betrayed us. You will hear evidence of how a small group of men
who helped create the economic crisis in the first place, have prof-
ited from the solutions they foisted on everyone else. What they
have done is not simply immoral, but a breach of the fundamental
rights embodied in a constitution drafted in order to free us from
the corruption of fascism. All we ask is for the court to recognise
that the government has failed utterly in the most basic require-
ment of acting in the interests of all Spaniards. In doing so, it has
breached not only the rights of the miners of Castile, but of every
decent Spanish citizen."

When she sits, Mat casts a sideways glance at Miriam. Most of
what they have heard are the speculation and general accusations of
the TV debates, but she has also made an unequivocal promise to
reveal evidence of corruption. There is something about the simple
fact of this occurring in court that creates the sense of an event
beyond mere discussion. Those in power who are the subject of so
much scorn also appear generally untouchable, but now they must
face a form of examination that has obviously greater magnitude.
If they lie, they could face prosecution on criminal charges. They
cannot simply deflect questions with a rhetorical flourish. Instead,
they must depend on a lawyer to protect them from the worst of the
attacks, and it is this man who now rises. Martinez is as flawlessly
presented as Gonzalez. Older, perhaps in his fifties, he has a slim
elegance. The dark suit hangs perfectly, and the hair is neatly styled.
He speaks with an easy confidence bordering on arrogance, and
there is something desperately attractive about both the man and

the manner in which he addresses the judges. Miriam is reminded of Clooney.

"What a great speech. Ordinary, decent people being cut down by greedy, corrupt politicians. It's a powerful story, isn't' it? My God, even I want to cry, and hug the miners who have walked here, and hand over hundreds of millions of euros so they can all go home and carry on working and living as they did before. In fact, I want to do the same for all the workers who've lost their jobs, and all the teachers who have had their pay cut, and all the people who have lost their homes. Except I can't, and the reason I can't is because I don't have the money to give to them, and that is what this is really about. No one wants austerity. No government minister enjoys the thought of people losing their jobs, but this is the tragic reality governments must sometimes confront. Ms Gonzalez will tell you that there is an alternative story to the one which has unfolded in Spain, and she is right, but her story is a fairy-tale. The current government inherited an economic disaster, and it has taken decisions that have hurt many because there was no choice. It cannot turn back time and have its predecessors do things differently, and so it does the best it can. It inflicts pain for the same reason a surgeon does, and that is because the alternative is worse. It is too easy to blame those who take unpopular decisions, and we shall show that far from breaching any part of our constitution, ministers have done all they can to protect every Spaniard from past excesses. All I ask is that you consider the facts you will hear and not be seduced into thinking that the tragedy of those who have lost out is so awful it must be illegal."

Once again Miriam looks over at Mat, and she realises that his Spanish has now developed to the point that he can follow most of what he is hearing. "What did you think?"

"It's all going to turn on the evidence Gonzalez is talking about. If she's really got something about how some of the deals have been done, then the judges will have to rule that their economic policy is illegal." He stops, then smiles at her. "I know this is completely inappropriate, but I haven't felt this much on edge since England played Germany in the world cup semi-final."

She nods. "As Spain win everything these days, it's not as exciting for me."

The first witnesses have been called by the miners' side. They have found a couple of academic experts who set out how the mine closures will affect the region, looking not only at primary unemployment, but the wider impact on related businesses and other companies likely to close when the money disappears from the region. Martinez objects on the grounds that economic hardship does not in itself indicate a breach of human rights or any other clauses in the constitution. But Gonzalez counters successfully that government policy would be unlawful if it can be established that a group of citizens has suffered hardship as a result of ministers' malfeasance, and all she is doing is demonstrating that there has been significant loss already which is set to worsen. This part is the easy victory for the miners as the court hears a stream of evidence about how harshly their community is being damaged. For all the talk of not being moved by those who are losing out, it is difficult to avoid the impression that each of the twelve judges will be more receptive to any suggestion of a minister up to no good. Martinez is reduced to asking some ineffective questions about the measures the government has put in place to help people find jobs, but this is derided by the labour economist who points to the contradiction in helping newly unemployed people to find jobs in a region where twenty per cent are out of work.

By the time they break for the day there is an impression of the miners' side having won a convincing but trivial victory. In legal terms, all they have done so far is demonstrate in impressive detail what everyone already knew, which is that austerity is painful. The emotional force of the witnesses they have heard will count for nothing unless ministers have been not simply callous but also corrupt. It is for this reason that the start of the second day is the one around which the whole case would appear to revolve. The first witness will be Juan Ramos, minister of finance, who has agreed to appear after being called by the government lawyer. At the moment he takes the stand, it is estimated that so many Spaniards stop work to watch that national productivity declines by around forty per cent.

Ramos has a low, droning, nasal voice that many commentators have suggested will prevent his ever leading the Popular Party. The high level of bass allows it to carry with surprising force, meaning that it fills any room in which he speaks. The overall effect is therefore an unfortunate combination of his being achingly dull but highly intrusive. The voice itself is enough to put off many who watch him, but he also has the rather odd quirk of lips that curl down slightly at the corners of the mouth, giving him an air of permanent misery. Even when he smiles, he only ever achieves the appearance of neutrality. Whilst this may prevent his ever acceding to the party leadership, it nevertheless marks him out as an ideal candidate to look after the country's finances, as the image of being without emotion or flair gives the feel of someone who would manage money without any undue risk.

He sits and lifts his head high as Martinez begins to question him. He begins by stating how happy he is to have the opportunity to speak to the court, and he recognises how important it is that the government not only make laws, but also be seen to fully comply with them. Martinez then structures his questions in such a way that Ramos can talk through how he reached the difficult decisions he has made, allowing him to express the sadness he feels at the suffering endured by so many Spaniards. The message of necessary pain is the lifeless reiteration of every campaign ad for years, and Martinez doubtless keeps the questioning simple because everyone has heard every answer before, and the man is already boring enough.

When Gonzalez rises, she picks up the notes she has been periodically writing and glances briefly at them before looking up at Ramos and smiling. "Mr Ramos, thank you for agreeing to attend these hearings. You said you were happy to speak to the court, but why, then, did you not agree to *our* request to appear?"

"I am here. What more do you want?"

"Do you deny that you agreed to appear only because you were advised that the court would issue a summons forcing you to come here if you refused?" Martinez is on his feet instantly, but Senderos, the presiding judge, is speaking even before the objection is raised. "Ms Gonzalez, please spare us idle speculation."

"I apologise, I wished only to clarify Mr Ramos' motivation." She then turns back to face him. "You earlier claimed that the state cannot afford to continue paying three hundred million euros to support the mines of Castile, but you have found twenty billion euros to support NBS. Is this correct?"

"I have already explained that we must have a banking system. No one regrets the possible problems for the mining sector more than I, but we are in a position whereby we must somehow accomplish the task of sorting out the terrible mess we inherited from the previous government."

"And you claim your decision to distribute state money in this way is based entirely on your economic judgement?"

"Exactly."

"You can state without any shadow of doubt that you were not moved by any personal loyalties or business interests?" There is a perceptible increase in tension among those watching. The persistence of the same line of questioning suggests Ramos is being set up, but the man himself seems equally confident in his responses. "I can. All the measures I have taken have had the sole aim of defending the interests of Spain, and no other concerns have ever distracted me."

"You are a member of the Laguna Club, is that correct?"

Martinez breaks in. "Is the constitutional court really concerned about where Spanish citizens eat their dinner?" But Gonzalez once again replies before Senderos can admonish her. "We wish to show that, despite his claims, there are a great many personal reasons for why the minister of finance may have favoured directing the state's money towards NBS rather than Castile, and I wish only to demonstrate that this is the case."

Senderos looks back impassively. "Very well, but please come to the point quickly."

She turns again to Ramos. "Are you a member of the Laguna Club?"

"Yes I am. Should I also name the tennis and bridge clubs of which I am a member?"

"You have a table reserved in your name from nine till eleven every Monday night, is that also correct?"

"Yes. Perhaps you would like the court to know that I play doubles every Wednesday from seven till nine."

"And Alberto Calderon, the president of NBS, is also a member of that club, is he not?" For the first time absolute silence descends, as everyone present senses that Gonzalez is now beginning to reel him in, yet still her tone remains direct, formal, neutral. Ramos stiffens visibly, and gulps."

"I believe so."

"'You 'believe so'? Is it not the case that Mr Calderon frequently dines with you on Monday evenings, and that this arrangement started long before you appointed him to head NBS?"

"I have been a business leader for many years, during which time I have made many contacts with other figures who are also prominent in the business world. There is nothing unusual about people in the same professional circles meeting socially."

"And you personally appointed Mr Calderon to his post?"

"I did."

"So you appointed a personal friend to the highest-paid banking position in Spain?"

"I did not say he was a friend."

"You dine together regularly for many years. He lends you his holiday home on Menorca, you attended his most recent wedding. Surely it is a fair description of events to say that you appointed your friend to be Spain's highest-paid banker and decided the state should give twenty billion euros to help out the bank." Martinez is on his feet before the final word is out. "This is outrageous speculation. The minister has already explained that he has made many contacts in the field of business over many successful years. Of course it was possible he would know the best candidates to head a major bank."

Senderos nods supportively this time. "Ms Gonzalez, you are skating on thin ice. It is a considerable leap between demonstrating that two people know one another and establishing the impropriety of an appointment. I am also losing patience when it comes to seeing how this bears any relation to constitutional matters."

"I apologise for taking so long to come to the point. I wish to establish the ongoing relationship between the minister and the head of NBS to show that the decision to prioritise this bank over the mines of Castile to such an extent constitutes a failure of the government to treat all citizens equally."

She now turns to Ramos again, who seems grateful for the brief pause. He breathes deeply and lifts his head once more to face Gonzalez. "You stated that you have many years of experience in business. You are still a major shareholder in several companies, is that right?"

"Yes I am, and all of my interests have been declared on the parliamentary record."

"Is one of the companies you part-own called Solar Future?"

"It is. We make some of the most efficient solar panels in Spain."

"How did the company fare in the years immediately after the financial crisis first hit?"

"Like all companies related to the housing market Solar Future went through a difficult period."

"How did you avoid the bankruptcy that hit so many other such firms?"

There then follows a moment of silence in which no word is uttered, but where Ramos' face betrays the unmistakable imprint of a man who sees for the first time the cliff over which his train is about to plunge. And the three hundred or so people in the courtroom and over five million watching Spaniards grasp instantly what that look means.

"We … uh … we refinanced."

"You borrowed."

"We refinanced."

"Who did you borrow from?"

"Well, we looked at a range of banks, both Spanish and foreign, and … well …"

"Was the primary lender The Business Bank of Madrid, a bank that has since been merged?"

"I believe so."

"And who was president of this bank at the time."

Ramos looks over at Martinez, who remains utterly impassive. Whatever his thoughts, he clearly sees no chance of intervening and will do nothing to reveal the concern that must be raging inside. His opening address the previous day contained the subtext that the trial was frivolous and little more than an attempt to bully the government into policy changes to avoid entering this chamber. Now he is defending a case that will shift direction if there is evidence of corruption, and he is watching the collapse of his own witness in the face of just the sort of claims he hoped would never materialise. Ramos then steadies himself and delivers his answer with all the composure he can. "Alberto Calderon."

"And the bank into which The Business Bank of Madrid was merged is now called NBS?"

"I believe so."

"And they retain the debt that was issued to Solar Future?"

"As far as I know."

"And is it fair to say that Mr Calderon has benefitted personally from his relationship with Solar Future?"

An uncomfortable sigh. "Mr Calderon is now a director of the company."

"So your company employed him after his bank lent you money?"

Now a deep breath, the irritable reaction of a man unaccustomed to being pulled and pushed around like this. "That is one way of looking at it."

"Do you know Alfonso Ramirez?"

A moment of confusion. "He is the general secretary of Spain's largest mining union."

"Is he a member of the Laguna Club?" A ripple of laughter around room, and even Senderos is suppressing a smile as he strikes a couple of blows with the gavel.

"Not that I'm aware of."

"So the current head of NBS is your creditor, your employee and a long-term acquaintance, yet when you came to consider the relative merits of Castilian mining and NBS, you maintain you were entirely neutral?"

He hesitates, and when he speaks again it is with the restraint and the effort of a man desperately trying to cling on to whatever dignity he can. "Ms Gonzalez, I can only repeat that I have only ever taken decisions which I believed to be in the best interest of my country."

"No further questions."

★

Miriam just smiles at him, and he smiles back at her. She first sat down in the court room with a storm of mixed emotions. She felt stained by somehow aligning herself with the legal team he had found. As they waited outside the chamber on the first morning, she watched all three of the lawyers whom she first saw in Madrid, as others rushed up to them to deliver papers and issue advice that Gonzalez appeared to internalise with careful precision. These are the people who ultimately benefit from the same system that is destroying her friends, highly paid lawyers who generally serve the corporations that close down their local companies and build on their land. But then the rush of hope and excitement as she sees Ramos twisting on the stand, the crude pleasure of watching him deal with a world which is dragging him down and which he is no longer able to control. There was a delicious satisfaction in realising that when he said he had done what he considered to be the right thing he was telling the truth. It was satisfying because she knew that his torment would be that much worse if he believed himself to be innocent, and that would give him an understanding of what it was like to suffer in the way his victims did, people who had done nothing wrong but lost a job, a home, a feeling of self-respect.

She also finds herself increasingly uncomfortable about Mat's wealth and his proficiency at hiding money offshore. She senses her own hypocrisy in campaigning for left-wing causes and then going out in the evening for a meal he would take care of with an Amex card. Was the stylish food ultimately paid for with money squeezed out of schools and universities? Perhaps it was spirited away to some former British colony and brought back to pay for any excess he found enticing. But now he seems to throw himself into the dispute with an energy far beyond what she has seen from many of her unionised colleagues. She spends hours emailing her members with updates about the dispute, details of events, newsletters. Yet protests only seem to attract the same, small group of die-hards from her university who always attend. And here he was marching with her, and supporting everything she did, and now funding the trial. She initially thought of it as little more than a costly stunt, but then underwent the astonished recognition that this would actually happen, and when it did she was in the same room as Ramos, and there he was being examined in the way every trade unionist in Spain had hitherto merely dreamed of. And all this was because Mat decided that he would use his money to make it happen, and for all her dislike of the obscene aesthetic of the law firm he found, she knows that only they could have achieved what she has seen today. Gonzalez fired questions relying on information that could only have come from sordid, private investigators digging and digging until they found the filth they were after.

Many of these thoughts sit uneasily with the searing affection she now feels for him. She likes the fact that he has thrown himself into learning Spanish, such a stark contrast with the British and the Germans who had flocked in such numbers to certain parts of the country that they had been able to take over local government without picking up more words than they needed to order a beer. She likes coming home to find him immersed in a book she has recommended, keen to discuss it with her. He likes taking her to some of the local jazz clubs, and hunts out obscure venues where local musicians play in a steamy room on the floor above a music shop or in the cellar of a tiny club open only on weekends. Yet there are still those days when they remain in bed, rising only for food, watching films on Netflix, indifferent to what is happening outside her apartment. For all her reservations about his money, she knows she is closer to someone than she was at any point in her marriage, and she avoids any serious conflict over his finances that might endanger what they have. She knows he cares for her in a way Richard never did, and she wants him to be with her, wants nothing to separate them. So when they enter the bar after Ramos' interrogation, her deepest feelings are ones of immense satisfaction that he has brought this about, that he has created some sort of light, and that she is with him. They order some wine and review the day's events in excited disbelief. Mat has rented a cheap Airbnb for the week, the maximum period the case is expected to last. Miriam sometimes stays with him, but must return to León on the evenings when she is due to teach the following day. He wishes to go with her across town to take her to the station, but she insists he stay, avoiding the irritating trip on the rush hour metro.

So he sits down again and watches her disappear out of the bar, experiencing the same irrational thought that he did as he saw her off from Stansted five months earlier. It suddenly strikes him this is the last time he will ever see her, knowing how improbable it is. He texts her to get in touch as soon as she is on the train so they can skype, and he is still pondering the absurdity of the thought when a man asks him in an unusual accent if he can take the empty seat. After a moment he realises the man is looking at him, and Mat looks back. "I'm sorry, can I help you?"

"Your accent is excellent," he says in English

"Thank you." And he looks out of the café window, thinking perhaps Miriam may have come back and might stay with him, missing tomorrow's lectures as he suggested. The man is still looking at him. "Fieldings, right?"

The words cut through him, and his first thought is that someone has taken the trouble to find out where the money is coming from to fund the case. This impression is heightened when the man speaks again. "Or is it Chapelle?"

"I'm sorry, do we know each other?" Mat's tone is defensive.

"I should be offended, given all I did for you."

Mat is still utterly at a loss, thrown off guard by how much this man knows about him. "Who are you?"

"Let me help you out. A confident British banker arrives at a

conference where he is on the verge of committing millions of his
bank's assets on some junk that might have lost them everything if
he hadn't been impressed by a small-time hedge fund manager who
talks him out of it. Instead, British banker puts his bank's money
into the new hedge fund, but only after he puts some of his own
money in. Bank makes close to eighty million, banker makes over
two. Some years later, banker gets involved in very nasty industrial
dispute in Spain. Hedge fund manager sees a picture of him standing behind a group of miners, then another as a group of expensive
lawyers walk into Spain's highest court to file a law suit. Care to fill
in the gaps for me?"

"Ricardo Gomez."

"The very same, although I'm still hurt that you didn't recognise
me straight up."

"You look rather different to the last time I saw you."

"Twenty pounds lighter, you mean?" In fact, the weight loss
is not as impressive as the natural looking hair implants that now
cover his head. He is dressed head to toe in casual Ralph Lauren,
and has a pair of Beckham-advertised Police sunglasses sticking
out of the breast pocket of the sports jacket. The transformation of
the man's appearance simply adds to Mat's confusion at seeing him
here. "Seems like a long way to travel to find someone you saw in a
couple of photos. Are you in love with me?"

"I was for a while. Yours was the only institution I could get to
bite, and aside from you I only found three other private investors.
I made ninety-five mill, and just had to make sure my secret benefactor was all right."

"Things are good. The case went well for us today."

"I know."

"You watched?"

"I was in there. Paid an usher two hundred euros to find a seat
for me."

"You could understand it all?"

"For a smart guy like you I would hope a name like Gomez
might be a giveaway. Who would have thought having a Puerto
Rican father might help me get ahead in the world?"

"Spanish as your mother tongue. Lucky you. Some of us have to learn it the hard way. I'm still not clear why you came."

He sighs. "If you're really curious, I just had to know why."

And you flew half-way across the world to find out?"

"Partly. I got out a couple of years ago, and I'm ashamed to say I get a certain pleasure from sitting in first class when the dicks who wouldn't believe me are still in business."

Mat hesitates, still reluctant to reveal details that might be hidden and may make it out into the open if he talks about them. "You say you got out. What are you doing?"

"A few things. Would you believe I got a book deal?"

"What?"

"Three-hundred-thousand-dollar advance for explaining how the crisis happened and how some of us came out ahead. Thinking of calling it *Bet Shorty*. Seems like the right mix of references to finance and organised crime, with a little humour thrown in. What do you think?"

"I wouldn't have taken you for an author."

"Oh fuck, I'm not writing it. The publisher brought in some ghost, and I sit down with him once a week for a couple of hours. They just want to advertise it as written by the guy who made a fortune in the crash."

Mat suddenly grasps that he is a potential character in the book, and that the trial would be an attractive part of the narrative. Ricardo smiles at him, clearly discerning the fear in his face. "Relax, if I wanted you as my leading man I would have hired some of the private dicks you've been using to look into Ramos, I wouldn't have taken the trouble to follow you myself after you came out of the court today."

"How reassuring that you do your own stalking."

"Listen, the contracts you signed with Devon Capital guarantee you anonymity. The publishers' lawyers would never allow me to reveal you as one of the investors, and if I ever let it out the damages would be twice what I paid you after the crash."

"I just don't believe you flew over here on a whim because you were curious about what I'm doing."

The smile leaves Ricardo's face. He leans forward, now lowering his voice. "Look, I told you I got out, and I'll tell you what did it for me. My fourteen-year-old comes home one day and tells me this joke. A guy's driving along the freeway and has to pull up because there's a massive traffic jam. The guy rolls down his window and asks a cop what's going on. The cop shouts back that the president of Bank of America has stopped his car and is blocking all three lanes. He's standing on the roof of the car and is shouting he can't take it anymore. Says he can't live without his bonus, and he's going to pour petrol over himself and set himself alight unless people help out. There's a collection going on. The guy asks how much it's up to, and the cop says they've got around two thousand gallons and it's still pouring in."

"It's probably a lot tamer than most of the jokes you hear from a teenager."

"Once you get past the semi-amusing punch line you have to ask how much someone has to hate a particular profession to think it's funny to imagine folks banding together to help others self-immolate. Then you wonder if your son knows that you're one of the people he thinks it would be funny to burn. And when you realise you could literally throw ten million dollars into the ocean and still never have to work again … well, you see what I mean. So now you're looking at the chief finance officer of a housing charity. Took home almost thirty thousand bucks last year and never enjoyed a job as much in my life. Makes it easier to feel good about the brownstone on the Upper West Side, and I don't worry about my kids asking me what I do for a living."

Mat smiles at him. "For me what did it was when I found out a teacher I used to know lost his job."

"And the woman?"

"That's how I ended up here."

Ricardo nods. "When I saw you I hoped it might be something like that. I don't want to get into some bullshit speech about innocence, but even though I worked through all the calculations about what might happen, I never really understood how it might play out. Just assumed that some big institutions would fall, but I never realised the government might just step in and save them all, make everyone else pay for it. And Obama just goes right ahead and appoints half the guys who did it."

"If you're looking to feel even better about yourself I know a fighting fund you can contribute to."

He shakes his head. "Black and Willens. Do your union buddies know about them?"

"Only that they're a corporate law firm, but as the union isn't paying they haven't asked too many questions."

"Their US office has the reputation for being the best in the country for advice on tax arrangements. Their London office represented Pinochet when your government was inconsiderate enough to arrest him while he was there on holiday." He hesitates. "How much have they taken you for so far?"

Mat's initial reaction had been to maintain at least a degree of confidentiality, but this comes to seem pointless in light of how much Ricardo already knows. In an odd way, he also feels a sort of intimacy with the man who let him into the secret that has made him his millions. "Three hundred thousand euros up front. Another two hundred thousand just before the trial started and they estimate a further half a million if it goes to the end of the week."

"You must really love this woman."

"Would you believe me if I said I am a genuine sympathiser to the cause?"

"Probably not, but I can tell you that the best move is to get out now."

"After today?"

"You can't win. There's too much at stake for them. The euro dropped two cents against the dollar after Ramos shit himself on the stand. If the case goes the way of the little people, the whole austerity programme goes with it, and maybe the euro, the markets and everything else will follow. There are too many powerful people with too much to lose. You could win the case and the government would probably just change the law and carry on fucking everyone like before. You think you're fighting for justice? You're not, you're basically shorting the market again."

"I seem to remember being a sceptic myself once and someone talking me out of it."

"That sort of thing comes along once in a lifetime. I just found a field no one understood. Here, everyone understands exactly what's at stake and you've taken on too much. They can't let you win."

Mat looks down. It is a fast fall from the optimism he felt only an hour ago when everything seemed to be moving their way, yet there is something in what he's heard that he had already sensed. He draws a deep breath and looks up again. "Set aside the terrible cliché, but I would prefer to fight and lose rather than just watch everyone being ground into the dust."

"Only someone who'd never been poor would talk like that. You think you can stop Ramos and his pals with an appeal to justice. If they fall it'll be because they fuck each other to death, not because anyone thinks that human rights are a serious concern when you're worried about the bottom line."

"Is that what you tell the homeless people who walk into your charity?"

"All I ever do is find the money to build a shelter. I'm not trying to bring down a government or buy into any dream about trying to make the whole world a fairer place." He reaches across the table and lays a hand on top of Mat's. "Listen, I spent years sweating away to break even until you came along. Now I'm so fucking rich I can afford a conscience, and I'm grateful to you for that. You want to know the real reason I'm here? I figured I owed you a fuck of a lot more than a transatlantic flight, so here I am returning the favour. I'm telling you, get out now."

Before Mat can respond his phone begins buzzing. He looks down to see that Miriam is calling, and his first reaction is a deep discomfort at the abstract proximity of her to Ricardo, of the intrusion into his new life from the one he left behind. He declines the call and looks back at Ricardo, who already knows he has failed to convince him. Mat smiles. "I'm flattered you would make the trip, really. But I don't share your pessimism." He reflects for a moment. "There's no way back now. Not for either of us." He stands. "Good luck with your housing charity. I have to go now."

He leaves and decides to walk around before he makes his way back to the apartment, consumed with doubt over what he is doing. They have already scored a public victory and maybe that is all they can hope for. How would it help if he really did drop half of everything he has if the case really is unwinnable? He wonders if he can find some dignified way of ending it without disappointing her. It is after nine by the time he sits down in the apartment and pulls out his phone in order to call her back, having reached no clear decision about what he will do. He sees there are four missed calls, and when he returns the most recent one she answers instantly. "Where the fuck have you been?"

"I bumped into someone I used to know. What's up?"

"Turn on the TV. Ramos has resigned."

Chapter Eighteen

He spends the next four hours moving back and forth between three different news channels, frustrated that he missed the start of the show. By midnight the story has been pieced together by combining the off-the-record comments of ministers and their staffers. Ramos arrives back at the ministry at around four, white as a sheet. Opposition leaders are already tweeting that he has to go, and there is now an avalanche of questions about his other business interests and whether those companies owe anything to NBS. The finance ministry puts out a statement around six saying that Ramos has done nothing illegal and repeating the line that he has always acted in the best interest of Spain, but the journalists focus exclusively on the failure of the prime minister to offer full support. The reason for this is probably because Rajoy is too busy fielding calls from half his representatives in parliament, people who were feeling less than confident over their chances of re-election even before Ramos started talking about his dinner dates. By seven, the PM's press office is still refusing to make any comment about the matter, but having spent two hours locked away with his personal advisors, Rajoy calls Ramos and tells him he'd like a personal chat. Ramos turns up expecting a strategy meeting and hears instead that he's disappointed forty million Spaniards, but rather more importantly he's now made it difficult for ministers to run the line that they are suffering along with everyone else, and they're doing everything they can to relieve this universal pain by taking those tough decisions that will work in the long run. So just before eight Ramos walks out of Rajoy's residence, with the deathly pallor of the late afternoon now replaced with a scowling refusal to speak to any journalists. Rajoy issues a statement thanking him for all his good work and announces that the minister of foreign affairs will be moving to finance. Ramos eventually issues a statement of his own to the effect that he is standing down for the good of the country, as he doesn't wish to distract the government in its quest for economic recovery. His replacement immediately announces that all future appointments to senior posts will be made in a manner that is scrupulously beyond doubt. Just before midnight there is the result of a snap telephone poll that places Rajoy below the communist party leader as the person best suited to lead the country, and where sixty-eight per cent of respondents say they think the decision to cut mining subsidies was probably illegal.

By the time he goes to sleep Mat is convinced the government may look for a way out that will bring the case to a premature close. There are two more days of hearings scheduled, and it is scarcely plausible that the remaining witnesses can have the sort of impact that might reverse the momentum created by Ramos' testimony. If they settle now, they can buy off the miners without risking a legal defeat that may force them to call an election they cannot win. So when he sits down with Gonzalez in a café near the court the next morning, he is hopeful she will confirm an offer has been made. He finds himself uncomfortable with her, intimidated after seeing the flawless composure in her dissection of Ramos the previous day, the beauty of the smooth, continuous beat of the questions, always pointed but never aggressive. Watching her in the courtroom, he was reminded of an earlier event which it took hours to recall, but which seemed perfectly analogous when it finally came to him. He had taken some clients to centre court for the men's semis one year, and they saw Federer pulling Safin around, apparently untroubled by the enormous power of his opponent. So now when he arrives, he hopes she will indicate there will be a settlement and he can escape back to León. She greets him formally when he sits. "The government appears to have changed tack."

"They've offered a deal," he says enthusiastically.

"No, I'm afraid they seem to have taken the decision that they need to take what we believe to be a more combative approach."

"What do you mean?"

"When the court offices opened an hour ago, Martinez submitted a list of nine further expert witnesses they wish to call in order to demonstrate that there is a purely economic justification for government policies. Our initial assumption was that they wish to dilute the impact of what happened to Ramos by boring people into submission. The witnesses are academic economists, professors of government, this sort of thing. The decision on whether to accept this lies with the court, but the case has become so important that we suspect the judges are bound to allow additional time."

Mat is still lost as to how this might constitute a viable strategy. "Surely prolonging the case can't be in their interests. If the witnesses are as colourless as they sound, then they still risk losing the case without making any political headway."

She sighs deeply, and when she speaks the voice reveals for the first time a sense of sympathy. "The defence lawyers have also demanded a surety."

"I'm sorry, I ..."

"They have demanded that Justice for Castile should depose enough money to ensure that all potential costs will be covered if the case goes the government's way. By asking for so many witnesses they guarantee the case will go into a second week."

"I'm sorry, I still don't grasp what they're up to."

"We believe their aim is to make it so expensive to continue that you will give up. They still have the impression this is a case brought by a grass roots movement which depends entirely on small donations from large numbers of people." She hesitates before telling him what he already knows is coming. "I'm afraid that my firm will also need a further payment to cover our anticipated costs for what could be the whole of a second week. I ... I'm genuinely sorry. I promise we had no idea that matters might run on like this. We expected that the hearings would be two or three days at most. If Ramos had not been so vulnerable, then today or tomorrow would probably have been the final day. Now, I'm afraid you must decide if you have the funds to continue fighting and if you wish to take on the risk involved in pursuing the case till the end."

"How much do you want?"

"A further eight hundred thousand euros."

"And the government?"

"One million."

The calculations are complicated by the fact that he must factor in two exchange rates. The money in the BVI account is in sterling, which is then converted into dollars when he moves it to Wyoming, and he must pay his Spanish costs in euros. He cannot be entirely sure of the final figure, but even his rough accounting is enough to confirm what he already feared. When he looks back at her, she realises that he doesn't have enough. "I can apply for the court to reduce the amount demanded by the government since there is no history of non-payment, which would be grounds for requiring such a high sum at this stage." She hesitates once again. "You need to understand that if we lose, there is every chance you would have to pay their costs, and the final figure may well exceed the one I gave you."

He sits back in the chair and turns to look out of the window, the hope of a swift end now utterly extinguished. He knew from the start that it may go to court, but assumed that even a defeat could cost him no more than a million pounds. This would have still left him with over one and a half million. If he'd spent half on property in London, maybe office space or a large house, the rental would have set him up for life. He would make a thousand a week at current rates, which could only increase. Not real fuck-off money, but he no longer craves that anyway. Yet now he sees everything slipping away, and a wholly uncharted future stands before him. He watches the endless flow of people walking or running to work, and how he wishes he was one of them. Instead, he sits in this café with a woman he barely knows, listening as he pays her over a thousand euros an hour to break this to him. All he wants is to melt into the crowd on the other side of the glass, to just ease back into wealthy obscurity and leave the battles to others. He has a fleeting image of driving south in his Porsche, taking in the Moorish cities as he and Miriam stay in traditional hotels and amble around medieval ruins. And the image is all the more painful because he feels he could so easily have made it happen, but now it is fading away due to the arrogance of his thinking he could simply spray his money around to determine the outcome of a struggle like this. He might spend hours mulling how he could have done things differently, but the towering sense of regret is accompanied by a rising nausea. He drinks some water and tries to steady himself before speaking again. He turns back to Gonzalez and looks her directly in the eye. "Fuck 'em. I'll pay."

"Are you …"

"How many lawyers do you have working on this?"

"Six. We …"

"I want to cut costs. Go down to three. It sounds like a lot of this will just be a lot of bullshit economic theory anyway, and I don't need to pay a lawyer to research that. Also, get rid of the PR company."

"As you wish." He turns away from her again, and she stands up to leave, apparently indifferent to the abrasive tone. But he quickly turns back to her. "Wait, there's one more thing. I want the chief exec of NBS on the stand."

"Excuse me? You want Calderon to testify?"

"The constitutional court has the power to subpoena witnesses, and he's a potentially key witness in establishing the government has failed to act impartially. I want him on the stand."

For the first time she appears unsure of herself. "We can issue the request, but the decision to issue a subpoena will fall to the court."

"Well, you'd better phrase the request convincingly."

"I'll have my legal team draft it immediately, and we'll reduce the team as you've requested. This will mean I may also be able to reduce the amount we are asking you to pay at this stage." She is still standing, waiting there for any further demands. He's aware of exercising the power his money gives him, but the sheer immensity of what he is facing leaves him unconcerned at the humiliation of having her stand there until he decides she may leave. "Thank you. I'll see you in court." And he turns once again to look out of the window.

When she leaves he dwells a little longer on what has happened but then decides to take some precautionary steps to limit the scope of the potential disaster. He calls Felipe and explains the situation. The three miners who are the public face of the organisation need to be warned about what may happen and reassured that as their roles have no legal status, they are not liable. If the case is lost, it will also help if they simply stick to the line that Justice for Castile has ceased to exist and there is nothing more to say. In the unlikely event that they are questioned formally, they can give the contact details of the Wyoming shell company, where he knows the trail will end. Once he finishes speaking with Felipe, he phones the organisation's office in León to talk to Clara. He tells her that he is transferring three months' pay into her account and that of her colleague, and that if the verdict goes against them they should stand up, walk out of the office and not return. If anyone gets in touch, it would be best to simply say they used to work for an organisation that no longer exists. There is a moment's silence which Mat eventually breaks. "Keep the laptops, but probably better not to mention where they came from."

★

The next two days are composed of unimaginable tedium. After the theatre of Ramos' public disintegration, there is an appetite for seeing more aristocratic heads roll, but the reality is endless testimony from experts stressing the right of an elected government to push through unpopular policies. The earlier excitement is dimmed by the detailed, technical contributions of these witnesses, and their arguments are so steeped in legal and philosophical complexity that even Mat finds himself doubting the case put forward by his own team. The danger is that the judges may ultimately find there to be so much uncertainty that they will be unable to conclude that any law has been broken.

The court goes into recess at midday on the Friday and by the time Mat steps onto the train, he is confronting not only the loss of the case but also the unthinkable financial implications. There is a feeling of uncertainty he has never experienced, with the prospect of never having to work again suddenly replaced by the potential need to go back to working in a field he thought he had left behind.

Yet even this seems more complicated than it would have been a few months earlier, after moving to a city with virtually no financial services sector to speak of and without his having sufficient mastery of Spanish. It strikes him with shuddering force that he will be unable to find a job even in a sphere where he no longer wants to work. He tries reading, but passages drift through him without his taking anything in, his mind always returning to the uneasy issue of what he will do if they lose.

By the time the train pulls into León, he is thinking only of Miriam, wishing only to be with her, hoping that she can somehow make this go away. As he passes through the ticket barriers, she is standing there, and she's smiling, and everything seems possible again. He holds her, and then she leads him out to the car park where she's left the used Polo she picked up for five hundred euros so they could get around more easily. When they sit in the car, she goes to start the engine, but he asks her to stop. She has heard the case will run into the next week, but when he explains what is going on she shakes her head in angry disbelief. "So their response to the possibility of having breached their citizens' human rights is to spend so much that they can't be beaten." She sneers as she looks out over the steering wheel. "I don't know why it should come as such a surprise." There is then a recollection of his having left out one of the key details. "I know that you generally don't like talking about money, but can you tell me how much this could cost?"

He hesitates, struggling to force out the words. "More than I have."

She is silent, unsure how she can possibly respond to this. After a few moments, she feels the need to say whatever she can to reassure him. "It means that if we win, you'll get back everything you've spent."

"Right now, it just feels like they are too powerful. They just have too much they can throw against anyone who challenges them. I feel like an idiot for having thought this made sense."

"Don't say that. Think of what it has meant to the people here to finally see these bastards in a court of law. When I went back to work on Wednesday, my boss told me they showed Ramos' testi-

mony live during the law lectures, and so many students turned up
they had to close the doors. I went out with a couple of the philosophers, and we were in a bar when the resignation was announced.
Everyone cheered, and you made this possible."

"If we lose, it will all be pointless."

"No, it won't. It's better to stand up and do something rather
than just let these fuckers walk over you, and that's what you're doing. It's what all of us are doing. Anyway, we might actually win."

He smiles, the thought of victory having receded so far in his
mind that it is odd to hear someone speak of it as a realistic prospect.
"Let's get a drink. It may be my last chance to buy you one."

"Actually, we're going out. Some friends have invited us over
for dinner." They drive out of the city on one of the minor roads,
and he tells her about Ricardo. She looks increasingly surprised by
the anecdote. "He flew over just because he wanted to save you?"

"It was bizarre, although it makes rather more sense in light of
what's happened since. I think he had this burst of nostalgia because
he thinks I performed a sort of miracle for him, and he wanted to
stop me screwing up and finishing in the sort of life he used to have
before I came along."

"The problem with this line that there's no justice in the world
is that it's always open to such obvious counterexamples. Lots of
people do get educated, receive health care, and get a reasonable
deal at work. If none of that happened, then probably no one would
bother fighting for it. The fact that someone like Ramos can be
brought down means that you have just enough hope to think you
can actually win some of these battles."

By the time they reach their destination, he is feeling better
merely in virtue of being with her, but also because she gives him
a sense that perhaps they could win. As they walk up the driveway
to the house, he realises he has forgotten to ask anything about the
people they are seeing, and he is curious as to which of Miriam's
friends it will be. Their initial outings to meet others were complicated by his poor Spanish. He didn't like relying on her to constantly translate for him and also felt uncomfortable at the obvious
impression of his being like the countless British expats who felt no

need to learn the language. It was easier when they went out with her colleagues in the English department, but even this left him embarrassed at half a dozen Spaniards all speaking in their second language so that he alone could speak his first.

She rings the bell, and the first shock is when the door opens and Alicia is beaming up at them. The second is when they walk into the hallway and Sofia emerges from the lounge with the distinctive bump pushing out against the line of her stylish, black dress. She smiles at the synchronised look of surprise that spreads across the face of each guest. "Well, someone has to ensure the future of the human race given all these selfish people who refuse to procreate."

Alicia raises her arms to indicate that Mat should pick her up, and when her face is close to his she whispers in his ear, "Mummy's having a baby. I'm going to have a little brother."

"No way."

"For real."

Tom then emerges from the lounge wiping his hands on an apron emblazoned with Lionel Messi curling a shot into the Real Madrid goal. "We got some good wine especially for you. Paid almost five euros for it."

The initial discussion is all about the case, with Mat and Miriam surprised at how extensively it is being covered in Britain. Ricardo had been right about a general nervousness in the markets that the wider impact of a government defeat was unknowable and therefore unattractive. But this effect had heightened a wider level of repulsion at the thought of the world being run in such a way that calming the frayed nerves of bankers was the highest priority of those in power. The populist appeal of the case therefore made more or less anyone involved in the promotion of austerity feel rather more vulnerable because they feared that similar cases might be brought in any country where the human rights act was in force. It is Mat who tries to divert the conversation, increasingly exhausted by the detail of it, which he has followed day after day. There is also now that ever-present anxiety of what it will mean if they lose. He is aware that such an outcome would have far greater consequences for the miners, but it is nevertheless his own future which preoccupies him, and he must struggle constantly to lift himself. "So who's going to sleep downstairs when the new baby comes?"

Sofia smiles again. "No one. We're moving back."

Once again, Mat and Miriam are taken aback, Miriam staring in disbelief. "When?"

"January. Part of the reason for coming over this week was that Tom had an interview. The University of Valencia is opening up a study abroad programme aimed at American students, and he's going to be teaching on that. So he has to bring in the money for once, and I get to stay at home for a couple of years."

"You're giving up your academic position?"

She shrugs. "Enough is enough. I'm tired of spending all summer working on articles or a book while Tom is out in the garden with Alicia. I'm tired of students emailing me to demand more detailed comments on an essay, or asking when they can have a mark for some work they sent in only a couple of days before. I used to love teaching literature, but now I spend more time quantifying the financial value of my courses and writing research proposals designed to attract money for the kind of work the funding bodies think we need to be doing. I feel I used to work in a university that needed money, but now it's more like a service industry that happens to offer university courses."

Miriam shakes her head. "I'm sorry it's come to this."

"Don't be. I can't wait to come back. Tom's job has a reasonable salary, and we'll get enough money for the flat to buy somewhere decent. I really just want to take a break from it all and be with the children."

The reference to selling the flat is entirely neutral, and the fact that nothing has ever been said about it leaves Mat somewhat puzzled. They can't seriously doubt that he's the one who paid off the mortgage, but he finds it unlikely they would simply treat this as something so trivial there was no need to mention it. His best guess is they are planning some more personal and spectacular means of thanking him a little later. At any rate, the conversation drifts onto matters related to their move back, and he excuses himself to wander out into the garden. The house is a sort of shrunken version of a hacienda, with each room around half the size it ought to be. The raised veranda runs the entire perimeter of the house and supports a series of arches that suggest something much grander. The dirty, white paint is peeling in places, and the red roof tiles are discoloured with fungus, yet there is a fading beauty to it. There are palm trees on either side of the driveway, which the original owner must have had planted when it was first built. At the back, there is a series of conifers so densely packed they have prevented any grass from growing but left a floor of pine needles reminiscent of a forest. Between two of the trees there is hammock that has been put up by carving notches into the trunks, and despite the cool air he sits on it, straightens and then slowly rotates so he can lie back and gently swing. Thoughts of the case immediately return to him, and he fights to suppress them by focusing on what he has just seen. Tom and Sofia are radiant, happier than at any time when he was with them just a few months earlier during that perfect summer. He considers the fact that this transformation in their apparent mood comes despite their never having had the money he has enjoyed for decades, yet he wonders also if it is not partly due to his having lifted all of the financial burden they were carrying. Isn't it easier to feel like that when money needn't concern you, and doesn't Mat himself now face the possibility of having all his money taken from him and being left with only a few thousand in his current account?

It is this point he has reached when he feels something pressure against this thigh, and for one terrifying moment he fears another snake has found him. He turns slowly to see Alicia grabbing for his jacket in order to pull herself up. He reaches down and pulls her up onto the hammock with him. She lays her head flat on his chest and they wrap their arms around one another, swinging gently, nothing said. After a while she mumbles something he doesn't understand, and he must ask her to repeat it. "Are you sad, Mathew?"

"A little bit."

"Why?"

"Not everything is going the way I want it to."

"Is it because of Miriam?"

"No, no. Miriam is wonderful."

"Is it because you want Charlie?"

"Yes, and do you think you could get me some?" he is tempted to say, but has learned the pitfalls of pursuing this type of conversation. "No, it's just …" And then he has no idea what to say. It's not simply a question of being unable to discuss constitutional law with a four-year-old but more that he does not want to stain her existence by referring to those he has been dealing with in Madrid. It strikes him that he doesn't want her to grow up in a world where such people accomplish so much, but he has already come to see it is beyond him to change this, even with the millions he is throwing at it. And so he says nothing, and they sway there in silence as light filters through the thick branches above them.

It is late evening when they get in the car to drive home. Miriam has drunk nothing so that Mat could taste some of the semi-decent Rioja they have been served. She sees that he has returned to the morose state he has been in over the last couple of days and eventually gives up trying to talk things through with him. This is in large part because there is now such a loss of control over what will happen, with lawyers and judges determining everything. No discussion between them can produce a conclusion that will tell him what to do, and she is reduced to simply stating that the case can still be won, and in the worst-case scenario they will find a way to get by on her salary. They climb the steps to her apartment at just before ten, and he slumps down on the sofa. She goes to get some wine from the fridge but swears as she opens the door.

"What's up?"

"No milk for breakfast tomorrow." She looks at her watch. "I'm going to walk over to the all-night supermarket. I'll be back in twenty minutes. Do we need anything else?"

"Not for me."

She puts her jacket back on, kisses him on the head, and makes it down to the street before she realises her wallet is in the handbag she decided not to take. She takes the steps back up to the apartment two at a time and flies through the door to find him sitting at the dining table in front of his laptop. He slowly closes it in a way obviously intended to be inconspicuous. She looks directly at him, and his clear discomfort confirms that she is not supposed to know what he is doing. She walks slowly over to the table. "Do you mind if I just see what you were looking at?"

He draws in a deep breath, and responds falteringly. "Actually, I think that's an opportunity you should turn down."

"Actually, I think that's an opportunity I'd like to turn *up*."

There follow a few moments of uncomfortable silence before she speaks again. "I'm serious. I want to see what you were looking at." After a few more seconds, he reluctantly slides over the laptop and lifts the screen. The webpage flickers back into life, and she takes in the image of a girl, staring at it incredulously for several seconds. His head is lowered when she turns to him. "You're fucking kidding me."

Chapter Nineteen

"Adopt a child refugee! Are you fucking mad? Anyway, where did you find out about this?" Her tone is one of stunned disbelief.

"There are always lots of people selling newspapers or handing out material outside the court, and I just accepted a flyer without knowing what it was."

"And you just thought you'd visit the site out of curiosity? I assumed you were looking at porn like every other middle-aged man."

"Frankly, I think that conversation might have been a little easier."

"You said you didn't want children."

"No I didn't. I just said I didn't want them with Jo."

"Well maybe you should get in touch with Jocasta to say you're ready now."

"Actually, I looked her up on Facebook the other day. She married the CFO of Pepsi UK, and they have twin boys."

"Jocasta has twins. How lovely for those lucky children to grow up with a mother with the world's stupidest name. And did she give them those idiotic names?"

"She must have changed her mind."

"Go on."

He smiles. "Phobos and Hilarion."

She cannot help but laugh, and the tension is momentarily broken. She eventually looks back at him, but when she speaks the tone is now one of confusion rather than shock. "I still don't get it. You never said anything about this."

"It's not something I've concealed, I just vaguely thought about it from time to time, and then … Well …"

"Well what? What happened?"

"It's just after seeing Tom and Sofia earlier. It just seemed … it just seemed like they were …"

"Try to articulate something for fuck's sake."

He sighs. "All right, at one point Alicia came outside and climbed up onto the hammock with me, and it just felt nice to be with her. Later I watched her holding you while you read a book to her, and it struck me that it would be … that there was a sort of beauty in it. I'm just saying that they're like people I've known. They're not banging any parental drum, they just seem to be really happy despite all the shit they've had to go through."

"What about that argument we heard them having? Is that how you want to live?"

"Even that seems to be the kind of thing they just deal with. I saw Sofia the next day, and she was embarrassed, but I knew from the way she spoke to me that she would not have swapped her life for ours. Look, I'm sorry this came out now, I honestly hadn't reached the stage where I wanted to raise it."

"Well it's too late now." She then hesitates, uncertain if she dare ask the question at the forefront of her mind. "You don't think you may be undergoing some reaction to the possibility of losing all your money. You know, like maybe having some kids will make you feel better."

He rolls his eyes and scowls at her. "Fuck off with your patronising, amateur psychology. I'm sorry you find it so unlikely I may have an authentic desire to have a child with you."

Now silence. Both are taken by surprise at what he has said, and she looks down. "I'm sorry … it was such a stupid thing to say. I …"

He interrupts her, weary at having fallen into such a discussion by accident after so many other upheavals in recent days. He tries for the calmest voice he can, hoping this may dispel the feeling of confrontation. "Forget it. I understand this seems like it came out of nowhere, and if it's something you are against, then of course we will never do it and there are a million other things we can do instead. If you want to understand why I'm thinking about it, then the best I can do is say that it's something I feel very strongly I want to do with you, and I don't know if there is anything more I can tell you. I can promise you it's not some infantile need to compensate for the loss of my money."

"Look, I'm sorry … I didn't mean…" But he raises his hands. "Please. Look, maybe there is something else. It's not what you said, but … It's easier for you to just carry on with your life than it is for me."

"What the hell does that mean?"

His voice is quieter now, revealing the effort required to force out what he is trying to say despite not having chosen the time to do it, nor even having fully thought through what it is he is trying to express. "You've actually done something with your life. You can look back at students who entered a lecture theatre and left an hour later knowing something they didn't know when they came in. All I've ever done is buy and sell money."

She moves closer to him, takes his face in her hands. "That's not true. Even if we lose this case it's encouraged millions in the belief that these people aren't invulnerable. The government is fifteen points down in the polls. You could lose in court and still win the bigger battle."

"No, I can't. All I've done is pay someone else to do it. What have I done?"

"You found these lawyers, you marched with us, you helped give an entire region the sense that they can't just be pushed aside. How many people have done that?"

He shakes his head. "Let's not exaggerate here. I paid some money to a bunch of corporate lawyers, I'm not Ché Guevara."

She sits down in one of the armchairs and has the absurd thought that she will still have to go out to buy some milk. She realises that there needs to be some sort of resolution, and she is still annoyed at the insensitivity of her earlier comments. For all his rejection of the world he gave up, she sees there is still a sense of security his money gives him and she understands the rising fear he must be experiencing at the thought of it all disappearing. She appreciates also the contradiction in her own sentiments, disgusted by the world he was a part of, yet concerned at the damage this may do to him, and she has an odd feeling of protectiveness towards him. He is here because she asked him to be with her and to help. She doesn't like his money, but she doesn't want him to lose everything, doesn't want to see him defeated even if the loss is one which would do no more than leave him in the same world as virtually everyone else. "Do you wish you hadn't brought this case?"

He smiles at her. "When I was travelling back in the train, I went over that question in my head. At first I couldn't really understand why I felt the way I did, but then it all fell into place. When Jo and I got married, I had to plan the honeymoon. At first I started looking into the sort of exotic destinations popular at the time. Treetop bungalow on a private African island. Secluded hotel in Vietnam, that sort of thing. But she had quite traditional taste, so the one I eventually settled on was in France. We flew first class to Nice and were picked up by a chauffeur who drove us out to a château on a hilltop an hour down the coast from the city. We had the entire place to ourselves except for the staff who lived in a cottage in the grounds. Each morning we had breakfast served on the veranda overlooking the Med, and we had to choose from the four-course menu for the evening meal. We had a convertible Mercedes for our own use, or the chauffeur if we wanted to go out drinking and have him pick us up afterwards. Every meal, every wine, was exquisite. I paid twelve thousand pounds for ten days, and I am happier sitting here in your poorly decorated one-bedroom place drinking this rather ordinary Rioja than I was at any point then. For all the beauty, there was a horrifying emptiness to the sort of life I had with Jo. She wasn't malicious, but everything seemed like we had to spend our money on the appearance of fulfilment. Everything had to be an image of perfection, but there was so little depth. We would have dinner parties where the content of what was said always boiled down to how best to spend money on objects that conveyed a sense of taste, and there was often the feeling that we were trying to justify our wealth by concocting ever more exotic ways of spending it. Even when I was in that château, I knew there was something wrong, and when I saw Gonzalez tearing Ramos apart on the stand last week, I knew there was something right about seeing him exposed for what he is. So I wouldn't go back, and if we lose then I don't know what I'll do, but I know I don't want to go back to what I was."

She draws a deep breath. "OK, I'll ask the landlord to repaint this place."

"Thank God for that."

They laugh, but the humour cannot conceal the uneasiness of all that has been said. She is on the verge of saying to him that he cannot consider adoption simply because he wants to feel he is doing something worthwhile, that the only reason one could ever have a child is because you want one. But he has already hinted that this is precisely his motive, and she doesn't dare run the risk of saying something else he will find patronising. So she leaves it, and the conversation drifts artificially away from a subject that makes both of them so uncomfortable.

By the time they wake up the next morning each of them is thinking only of the conversation from the night before, but they have both resolved not to raise it because neither has been able to come to terms with the implications.

It is a perverse relief to be able to think about the case, and by the time Mat sets off back to Madrid early on the Monday morning, nothing more has been said. Yet still it is on his mind as he sits through the relentless tedium of the expert witnesses called by the government on the Monday and Tuesday. This cycle is momentarily broken when it is announced that Calderon has agreed to appear on the Wednesday, doubtless having anticipated that it may look slightly better than the country's highest court telling him he'd be dragged up there if necessary. At the end of the day's proceedings, Gonzalez asks to approach the bank of judges, and Mat is on the verge of rising to leave when he sees the look of shock on the face of Senderos, the presiding judge, as he fires some questions at her. When she returns to her seat, she is ashen.

Senderos briefly consults the senior judges on either side of him, each of whom appear non-plussed by whatever has been said, but after a few more moments the gavel comes down and he leans forward to speak into the microphone in front of him. "Counsel representing the plaintiff has requested a delay in order to prepare more fully for the next witness. In light of the importance of the case it is our view that both sides are entitled to some latitude, and we have therefore granted the request. The court will therefore be in recess tomorrow and proceedings will resume at ten o'clock on Thursday morning, when Mr Calderon will be take the stand."

Mat listens on in disbelief, wondering if he has misunderstood. But the sense of surprise is tangible throughout the chamber, with people turning to their neighbours in obvious confusion. He follows the legal team out of the chamber and catches up with Gonzalez when she stops in a hallway to make a call. She looks up when she sees him and raises a hand to silence him so she can finish. Mat grows increasingly tense as the conversation drags on, and by the time she snaps the phone shut he is infuriated. "What is going on? It looks like fucking amateur hour. How can you not be prepared?"

She says something under her breath that is initially unclear to him, but after a second he realises he had heard her say 'puta madre'. She takes him by the arm and guides him into a window recess where it is less likely they will be seen or heard. "Listen to me very carefully. I have been working fourteen hours every day of the week for the last month. You have told me to cut down my legal team by a half, and we're bringing a case for which there is no legal precedent and where we may be talking about reversing years of economic policy and bringing down the government that has pushed it through. If you don't like my judgment, then fucking fire me."

She spits out these words with such venom that he recognises that one false move now and she may walk away. It simply had not occurred to him how much she may have personally invested in it, having thought of her as no more than an expensive service he could exploit as he wished because he was paying so much. He slips into the most contrite voice he can. "All right, I'm sorry. I hadn't realised how much effort you were having to put in. The work you've done has been excellent, and I wouldn't want anyone else." He pauses, unsure if he can proceed without antagonising her further. "Could I ask nevertheless why you asked for a delay?"

The look of seething anger diminishes a little, her normal composure returns, and to his utter shock she smiles at him for the first time since they've known each other. He is at a loss to understand this and is about to ask her what is going on when he suddenly grasps it. "You've got something."

Chapter Twenty

Calderon strides to the stand. When he walks in there is no hint of nervousness, no trace of concern that millions would love to see him go the same way as Ramos, publicly shamed and reduced to the level of others who have not enjoyed his immunity from the economic plague that has struck everywhere. The tailored suit is immaculate, and Mat experiences a flicker of envy at the style and cut of the sumptuous material. When he sits and takes the oath he does so with the confidence of someone entirely at ease with his power. He conveys a relaxed, self-assurance that is doubtless the result of hours spent with PR consultants who have trained him in tone and appearance. But despite the flawless aesthetic there is also an ugliness to this act, a perceptible feeling of superiority that is visible through the mask. Mat's heart rate accelerates at the thought of his fall.

When Gonzalez rises, she opens with the questions everyone had predicted, and there is a sense of disappointment that Calderon begins by delivering answers that have surely been prepared by his own legal team.

"We heard from Mr Ramos that the two of you have been close acquaintances for many years."

"Correct."

"And you both loaned him money and accepted a position with the company to whom the loan was made."

"The bank for which I worked made a loan to a company in which Mr Ramos is a shareholder. I did not take the decision personally. All such loans go through a formal process, and the loan for Solar Future was no different."

"So you had no role in deciding whether or not the loan should go ahead?"

"As I have said, I do not deal with this sort of administrative matter."

"How much money have you made as a result of your appointment to the former minister's company?"

Martinez is on his feet immediately. "Objection. This is a personal matter. How can it be relevant to the Spanish constitution for us to know how much money this man earns?"

Senderos looks over at Gonzalez. "Do you have an answer Ms Gonzalez?"

"We have argued that our clients have been disadvantaged as a result of not enjoying the same access to senior government figures as people such as the witness. I wish only to demonstrate the extent to which he has benefitted."

Before Senderos can speak, it is Calderon who breaks in. "I have no objection to answering the question. It is in any case recorded in the company's accounts, and I am happy to make my personal affairs as transparent as possible in order to assist in the case. My earnings as a company director at Solar Future are two hundred thousand euros a year, all of which is declared in Spain, and on which I pay full taxes."

Gonzalez briefly looks down at a piece of paper in front of her that presumably has the same information. "Thank you for your openness. Do you accept that your relationship with Mr Ramos may well have contributed to your appointment to your current post as chief executive of NBS?"

Martinez leaps up again. "Objection. Calls for speculation."

"Sustained. Please confine yourself to the quest for information which is clearly factual."

Gonzalez looks down, and visibly gathers herself. The initial sparring has done no more than confirm what everyone already knew, and there is a growing sense that she is simply rehashing the information she used against Ramos the previous week. The moment of silence strengthens this feeling, but she then raises her head, looking directly into his eyes. "You say that as chief executive of your bank you don't deal with administrative matters, but you are fully involved with the management of the *galacticos* account. Is that correct?"

There is no facial movement or shuffling in his seat. He doesn't splutter or emit any other sound. There is no explicit sign of being placed fully on the defensive, but there is nonetheless a universal recognition that this man has just understood he is about to be eviscerated. Gonzalez just stands and watches. At first Mat is impatient that she is not repeating the question in order to force an answer, but the longer the silence goes on the more exquisite it becomes. It is impossible to tell how long they all wait, but it is eventually Senderos who must intervene. "Mr Calderon, you have been asked about a specific account. Are you familiar with it?"

His head rotates slowly towards the judges. There is a further moment of silence during which thoughts appear to be crossing his mind in such a way that they are accessible to anyone watching. "Can I get away with lying? Can I say something that doesn't offer a direct answer? Lying means the risk of perjury and prison. The question is too simple for there to be any obvious way of evading it." So he raises his head, gulps and turns back to Gonzalez. "I am familiar with this account."

"This is an account held in a Swiss subsidiary of NBS?"

"It is."

"Can you explain how it came to be called by this name?"

He hesitates, doubtless realising that his answer will embarrass him still further. "There was a time when Real Madrid had a policy of signing the world's most glamorous players, and they were called the *galacticos*."

"And why was this considered an appropriate name for the account?"

Silence again, and again Gonzalez simply waits. Mat has the bizarre thought that each pause is one which may be costing him hundreds of euros as the legal teams on both sides have to be paid to sit and wait for an answer. At last Calderon composes himself enough to speak. "Those who paid into the account were regarded as the stars of the Spanish business world." There is muffled laughter around the gallery at the analogy between the rippling muscle of leading footballers and the waddling hippos of the business community.

"Can you state the names of the wealthiest contributors?"

Martinez instantly rises. "Objection. This is confidential information pertaining the private affairs of people who are not accused of committing any crime."

Gonzalez turns to her right and accepts a laptop from the lawyer sitting beside her. "This information is no longer confidential. The names of those making the twelve largest transfers into this account were published on the website of *El Pais* at the moment Mr Calderon took the stand. I am simply asking the witness to confirm the accuracy of information which is already in the public domain."

Mat is stunned. His first thought is that Black and Willens must have been passing highly controversial material to journalists, which may well be unlawful. But it suddenly dawns on him that this must have worked the other way round. The newspaper must have approached the lawyers with what they had and Gonzalez requested the stay in proceedings because they weren't yet ready to publish. So now the lawyers repay the journalists with some product placement on the country's hottest show.

Martinez doesn't miss a beat. "If confidential information has been leaked to a national newspaper, then a crime has been committed and it is inadmissible to use such evidence in court." Senderos raises a hand to stop him. "Objection sustained. Ms Gonzalez, you may not require the witness to discuss the personal, financial details of any individual regardless of whether a national newspaper claims to have evidence of the payments you are asking about. I will, however, permit further general questions concerning this account, but I need to hear very quickly that this is linked in some way to constitutional matters."

She turns back to Calderon. "What was the money in the account used for?"

He hesitates. "To make payments."

"To whom?"

"I don't recall the precise list of individuals. I deal with many different matters."

Now she's had enough. "Was the money in the *galacticos* account paid to leading members of the governing party to fund their campaigns?"

"It may have been."

"Did you personally authorise the payments?"

"It's possible."

"Did you authorise a payment of one hundred and thirty thousand euros to the campaign of Mr Ramos during the last election?"

"I don't recall."

"Did he appoint you to your current post four months after you authorised that payment?"

"I don't recall all of the payments made from that account, so I'm not in a position to answer."

"Did you ever withdraw cash from the account and hand it to Leonardo Alvarez, the former treasurer of the Popular Party?"

"I believe so."

"And Mr Alvarez is currently awaiting trial for tax evasion?"

"I understand he is, although I hope for his sake you will not be asked to prosecute the case." Peals of laughter around the gallery, but she is unmoved.

"Are you aware of any transfers of money into this account from organisations associated with Spanish mining communities?"

He is thrown off guard for a moment before seeing through her strategy. "No."

"And when you met with Mr Ramos and other members of the PP to discuss help for NBS would you say that you were received sympathetically?"

"I found the government listened carefully to the arguments we presented."

"And would you agree your treatment was partially a result of your organising secret payments that may well have contravened Spanish electoral laws?"

Martinez is on his feet, but Senderos speaks even before he can object. "Ms Gonzalez, no illegality has been established and the witness is not qualified to comment on such an issue."

She turns back to Calderon. "My clients represent five thousand miners who face losing their jobs and the economic destruction of their region. Do you believe your friends in the PP listened as carefully to their case as they did to yours?"

"I have no doubt the government acted fairly at all times." From the upper tier of seats there is a shout of 'pendejo'. Senderos pounds the gavel on the sound block, "Silence in court." Mat turns to the left-wing journalist with imperfect English who has sat beside him for much of the case. "What exactly does 'pendejo' mean?" he whispers. The journalist ponders for a moment, looking for the best translation. "Something like 'hole of the ass'."

Gonzalez looks at Calderon, and there is an extended silence before she speaks again in a quieter, more restrained tone than the one she has been using hitherto. "You have been quoted as saying you may consider running for public office, and you believe you would be capable of restoring a sense of integrity to Spanish politics. Would you bring the same sense of integrity you have demonstrated in your banking career?"

"Objection. Irrelevant."

"Sustained."

"No further questions."

He sighs deeply, knowing that what awaits him is an equally ferocious assault from the journalists who will pursue him to his car as soon as he emerges from the building. After that, there is the prospect of a criminal trial related to the breaking of laws on party funding. Mat watches him as he walks out of court, the smart suit now more reminiscent of some beautiful decoration at an expensive funeral.

Senderos clears his throat and leans into the microphone. "There are no further witnesses, which means the judges will now commence their deliberation. The court usher will give thirty minutes' notice when we are ready to reconvene."

Mat makes his way forward to Gonzalez, who is engaged in an intense discussion with the more junior lawyer who has been at her side throughout. She smiles half-heartedly when she sees him. "It's impossible to know how long it will take. Given that they have already extended the length of the hearings so far beyond what is normal, I assume they will feel the need to work through the issues at length, but who knows? Could be an hour, could be two days."

"Look, I … you could not have done anything more. Thank you, and I'm sorry about Monday."

She nods. "Well, let's see what happens."

★

When he comes out, he is initially reluctant to stray too far in case the decision is announced before he can race back. But after standing for twenty minutes in the soulless corridors of the court, he approaches one of the miners who agrees to call him as soon as anything happens. He goes back to the same café where he met Ricardo, half-expecting to see him again, wondering what he would have made of it. When he sits, he pulls out his phone and calls Miriam. "I missed it. I was in a seminar, but the story is everywhere. *El Pais* printed a special afternoon edition and it sold out. They're saying Rajoy may have to resign."

His heart is pounding. "Have you seen any lawyers commenting on it? Is anyone saying how the decision is likely to go?"

"They're still divided, and the truth is no one really knows. They just keep saying that it's difficult to be sure if what happened went as far as being unconstitutional."

Everything she says corresponds to what he has already seen when flicking through the news websites on his phone. "Are you coming? I'd really like you to be here either way."

"I finish teaching at midday tomorrow. If there's still no decision by then, I'll get the first train I can." She pauses. "I said this to you before, but you need to understand what this means. Even if we lose, it's the first time anyone has had the impression that these people actually have to answer for anything. If we win … Jesus, it will be like a revolution."

"If."

"I know, but the mere possibility is priceless."

When they finish the call, he picks up his book but finds it impossible to focus, thinking through all he has seen in court, but also drifting periodically back into thoughts about the previous weekend's discussion of adoption. He hadn't even been sure that he would raise it with her, and he certainly didn't want to enter such a discussion without thinking through how he would approach it. Yet the image returns of her sitting with Alicia, the girl so fully engaged with the story being read to her, and the feeling that this was something he wished to see over and over again. The other unmentionable thought is the extent to which Miriam's aversion to having children is truly independent of her being unable to conceive. Would she really have been so adamant if the option were available? What if she were able to maintain her career while he looked after their children? What if he hired in an army of full-time nannies and Miriam selected the Victorian option of seeing her offspring for an hour each evening before they'd be spirited off to bed? He would even give them above the going rate and pay into some sort of nanny pension scheme for them. He is amused by his own fantasy, but even this inevitably brings him back to the reality of potentially being just hours away from financial ruin.

He has the sudden urge to discuss it once again with her. He wants to say that he wishes above all to stay with her and he would never do anything to pressure her. He picks up the phone again, but before he can call her back he sees he has received two texts in the last few minutes. The judges have announced that they are reconvening.

Chapter Twenty-One

It is mid-afternoon, yet still she decides it is time to open a bottle, selecting one of the larger glasses and filling it. She drinks, allows her head to fall back, and looks up at the ceiling. The immediate cause of her discomfort is a call from Tom earlier in the day, just before she went into her seminar. But she knows her concern is a mere symptom of the wider malaise she has felt since her conversation with Mat. There are two facts of which she is absolutely certain. She has never wanted children and has never regretted that she is unable to have them. Indeed, this has often seemed like a blessed release from the relentless pressure to reproduce she has seen heaped on her contemporaries. There are still the none-too-subtle forms of pity she must endure. The raised eyebrows as someone she meets for the first time processes the information that she doesn't have children, with the unspoken questions of whether this is due to bad luck or a selfish disposition. This sort of condescension is one to which she has simply become inured, an inevitable consequence of stepping off a beaten track followed by so many in the most uncritical fashion. There was a time when she would cite statistics about the number of relationships where the parents separate within three years of the first child being born. Or she would refer people to an article she once read where it was suggested that the number of occasions on which long-term couples have sex in the ten years after the birth of their first little screaming ball of joy, was roughly equivalent to the number of times they did it in the first four months of going out. Put the two stats together and this was enough to embarrass many evangelicals into at least a couple of moments reflecting on the fact they constantly argue and never fuck.

She doesn't dislike children and has always enjoyed the afternoons she has spent with Alicia or the offspring of other friends. It is perhaps the accusation of selfishness that most annoys her. She sees the prospect of loving one's children as the only acceptable motive for having them, and has listened in disbelief to those who suggest there is an obligation to start pushing out kids for the benefit of the wider community. Why not use the same argument to justify the reintroduction of slavery or gladiatorial combat? It's been years since she has seriously contemplated these issues, but what makes her so unhappy now is the way she responded to Mat. He had not lectured her or even raised the subject voluntarily. His motivation was the very one she felt to be appropriate, and far from presenting it as something that raised issues about their remaining together, he spoke of it because it was something he wished to do with her. She was so shocked at the whole subject having come up that she reacted far more insensitively than she would ever have wished, and now feels like a shit for what she said. What makes it more difficult is that she has seen the dewy-eyed look before in those who have decided the time is right, and for all his protests that he hadn't fully thought it through she was sure this desire wasn't going away any time soon.

So as she sits there, she confronts the simplicity of the incompatible desires they hold between them. He wants children and she doesn't. She is amused at how analysing the conflict does so little to help resolve it, yet there are other concerns that also start to bear down on her. She provoked him into reflecting on the myth of Gyges, and now he's here. He has done everything he could to help out in the struggle she asked him to take up. Whatever the source of his money, the fact is he has risked everything he has to help, and she bears a good degree of responsibility for his reaching this point. The obvious conclusion of such thinking is that she agrees to go along with it to make him happy, but that is against her deepest intuition about why one should have children in the first place. And what if it turns out that he doesn't find the routine of getting up nineteen times every night and changing the screaming monster quite as fulfilling as he thinks. Jesus, what if it's a girl? Then there will be the whole mother-daughter shit to deal with. "Where are you going dressed like that?" "Out." "You're fucking not." "I fucking am." Front door slams.

She picks up the glass again and quickly gulps back some more wine. Maybe it wouldn't be so bad. But before she can follow this line of thought any further her phone beeps. It's him. She opens the text. "Judges back."

Chapter Twenty-Two

Senderos is the first judge to enter and he remains standing until the other eleven have all taken a place behind their chairs. Everyone else in the court is also on their feet, and when the president sits, they all do. He clasps his hands in front of him and leans forward, drawing a deep breath before he speaks. "The case before us is one in which it is claimed that the government of Spain has breached the right to equal treatment of all citizens which it is required to observe under various provisions in the constitution. The case has been brought by an organisation representing a specific group of citizens, but it has been obvious from the outset that the implications are far wider, as the substance of the case is that one select group of citizens has received preferential treatment to the detriment of many citizens beyond those of the coalmining communities of Castile and León. The court has therefore been asked to determine whether or not the government's general economic policy is unlawful on the grounds that it has been applied in a way that runs counter to the rights of a large proportion of Spanish people. For its part, the government has argued that they came to power legitimately, and they have the legal right to implement the economic policies that are the subject of the case. It is not the role of this court to decide if the government's policies are economically wise, but to consider whether the policies comply with its obligation to respect the human rights of all Spaniards.

"It has become clear that the conduct of key members of the government and members of the business community with whom they have had contact, gives rise to deep concern over whether important decisions were taken for the appropriate reasons. Compelling evidence has been presented that these decisions were taken where there was a key, undeclared conflict of interest, and where there are serious questions over compliance with laws on electoral funding. The issue for the court is whether the questionable behaviour of certain individual members of the government and the business community amount to a breach of the constitution on the part of the government as a whole. We are of the view that this has not been established, and in the case of Justice for Castile versus the government of Spain, the court therefore rules in favour of the government of Spain."

Martinez turns to search out the civil servants who have been in court each day. His smile is that of an ecstatic teenager who has passed all his exams. The two other members of the team slap him on the shoulder, and it is clear they would be high-fiving but for a vague awareness of the formal setting. Gonzalez sits there, trying so hard to retain composure, but her shoulders are slightly hunched and she looks down. For the first time, Mat feels sorry for her, far more than he did after he had sworn at her two days earlier. The enormity of what has happened seems so much greater than the personal comments he had made, and he wonders if the vast sums she has taken from him will provide any real comfort. It strikes him that she fought the better case, she was in the right, and she was immaculately professional. Strange to think how little any of this counted.

As the judges rise and begin to file out a woman's voice screams out from the upper level at the back of the court. "Is this your justice? Is this what you call justice? None of them look at her, and the chamber begins to empty as if it were the end of a football match. When he reaches the main hallway, Mat can see journalists already interviewing some of the legal experts who have been ever-present, and other groups are gathered in tight circles speaking intensely about what they have just seen. He sees Felipe pushing through the crowd, scowling at a journalist who asks for a comment. Mat follows him as he marches out of court and over the road into the park where many of the miners who arrived in the city eleven days earlier are still encamped. They are aware of the decision, and there is already an ugly atmosphere. Felipe shouts to some of them, perhaps the elected officials who have had a sort of informal authority over how the camp has been run. The miners instantly begin collapsing the tents and packing. Mat asks one of them what is happening. "The headquarters of the PP is in a square around ten blocks away. Time to let the fuckers know what we think of them."

It takes only around an hour for the camp to clear, with everything stuffed into backpacks and messenger bags. Then they begin the short walk to the square where they will find the stylish, modern glass-and-steel structure that houses the PP. They march down a bus lane in order to minimise disruption to traffic, but when they get there they see a building defended by row after row of police who have anticipated this move. The miners stop around forty yards away, their numbers now swelled by others who have picked up on what is happening through social media and the news channels.

When the last of protestors has entered the square, a senior police officer walks forward with a loudspeaker and begins shouting at them in what seems intended to be a neutral tone. "This protest is illegal. You have no right to be here, and we ask you to disperse peacefully." There is no movement on either side, and he raises the loudspeaker again. "You need to disperse peacefully, or we shall clear the square." Still there is no movement, and the officer stands there for seconds that seem to stretch into hours. He then turns, walks back towards his men, and speaks into a walkie-talkie. A moment later two trucks appear from a road to the left of the PP building, and they roll slowly towards the protestors. There is a water cannon on the top of each one, and when they are within around thirty yards they open up. The first jet of water catches a man at the front of the line full in the stomach, and he is propelled backwards into the crowd where others try to catch him. Both cannon then begin rotating to spray water over a wider radius, hitting more people, but with less force. A stone comes flying out of the crowd, one doubtless picked up from the neat, pebble paths crisscrossing the park in the centre of the square. It strikes the first of the impenetrable trucks on the windscreen. More water, and the protestors retreat until they are beyond the point where the water has any impact. The trucks advance towards them, but now protestors start to move to the side and more stones are hurled at the trucks from multiple angles. The cannon fire at more targets, but they are now so widely dispersed it is impossible to focus on any one group without allowing the others to move back in the direction of the building. The sense is that the trucks are being surrounded and cut off from the lines of police, and they reverse back towards them, with the protestors returning to the positions they were in before the trucks arrived.

Mat is standing towards the back of the crowd, and he is tapped on the arm by the man beside him. "Cover your face, especially the eyes." He has a handkerchief wrapped around the face and a pair of diving goggles. Mat looks around and sees that many others are also protected in the same way, and he understands with horror what is coming. His hands are shaking as he pulls out his own handkerchief and then puts on a pair of Ray-bans, laughing nervously at the absurdity of this last touch. By now, they are within no more than thirty yards of the first police, and he hears Felipe's voice shouting out from the front. "Comrades, what sort of a wanker thinks he can shit on us from a building made of glass? I think it's time for some redecoration." He then steps forward and hurls a stone over the heads of the police. It strikes a first floor window, with shards of glass spraying down onto the police below. Several other stones fly out from the crowd, but then an order is shouted out, and several police emerge from behind the first rank and fire hissing canisters into the ground just in front of the first protestors. The gas explodes over them and there is an instant, mass retreat. But this time, they are pursued. A man falls as he runs away, and the two police who catch up with him first club him several times each with their batons before dragging him away. Others are also caught, sometimes to be beaten, and sometimes simply to be dragged or marched away.

Mat knows only that he is running. Not where, not how far, not if he should have stayed with the others. He catches up with a woman who is also fleeing. She turns into a narrow alley, the smallness suggesting it is a better place to hide. As Mat passes her, she looks at him, and then he hears her fall. He looks back, and the policeman is standing over her with his back to Mat. He then begins rhythmically striking her, focusing exclusively on her midriff, bringing down the baton over and over again on the foetal shape at his feet. Mat's deepest instinct is to turn and keep running. He doesn't know this woman, so she could never pick him out as the man who ran away and left her. But just as he is about to go, he sees she is looking at him, tears filling eyes that plead with him as she shields herself from the endless blows with the stick. And without thinking he sprints towards them, takes off, and stretches out his right leg to fly kick the policemen in the middle of his back. The man goes sprawling, dropping the baton, which Mat picks up. He lies on the ground, eyes hidden behind the dark visor, but Mat knows he is afraid, sensing that he faces the same beating he had been administering only seconds before. Instead Mat pulls up the woman, who can barely rise. Still the policeman remains static, and Mat watches him as he supports the woman while they move further and further down the alley. When they turn a corner, he drops the baton and tells the woman she must stand for a moment. He turns to the wall, throws up horribly, then tries to steady himself. Even in the midst of the extreme fear there is an understanding that the policeman may come after them, may even have been joined by others. He half carries and half drags the woman to the end of the alley, from where they emerge into a busy street that is in a different world to the one they just left. Perhaps only a few yards away, but a place filled with shoppers and tourists and parents pushing prams. The woman looks up at him, pulls the handkerchief from his face, and he understands they must try to look as normal as possible.

They slowly move in a direction he believes to be away from the square where the battle was fought, and after some steps she is able to walk better, limping heavily but now moving largely on her own. She looks up at him. "Do you have somewhere to go?"

"I need to get back to my apartment."

"Lucky you. I need to get to a hospital. Do me a favour and flag a taxi."

He knows he should offer to go with her but wishes only to be free from any trace of what he has just been through. They wait by the side of the road until a taxi comes along and the woman climbs gingerly into it, holding his hand for a while longer than she needs to when he tries to release her. "Thank you."

After she is gone, he stops another taxi and directs it to the apartment. On arriving, he looks down at himself, he realises his jacket is stained with his vomit, and he takes it off. It is six by the time he flops down on his bed. He simply stares at the ceiling for perhaps an hour, trying to process all he has seen, to compose himself by placing the various events into some sort of narrative he can make sense of. This reconstruction is interrupted by the ringing of his phone, and when he looks at he sees he has eight missed calls, all from Miriam. When he takes the call she cannot believe at first it is not his voicemail again. "Where are you? Are you all right?"

"I'm in the apartment and I think I'm all right. I was involved in a bit of trouble."

"You were at the PP headquarters? There are images everywhere of police charging demonstrators. Are you all right?"

"I'm all right, I'm all right. Just a little shaken by everything."

"Listen to me. You need to get out of the city. The police are still patrolling, looking for anyone they think may have been involved. Felipe was arrested. Dozens of others as well. Just get to the station and get a train home."

He is silent. He has attacked a policeman, and if he is picked up he fears arrest and prosecution will be the least of his worries. He finds it impossible to separate out the realistic danger from what is absurd overreaction. He was still wearing the handkerchief and the glasses when the man looked up at him, surely there could be no way of identifying him. "I'll get a train back as soon as I can. I'll text you when I'm on my way." Another moment of silence. "It was really bad, Miriam. Everything, I mean."

"I know, I know. Just get back here. I'm waiting for you."

He strips out of all the clothes he was wearing and stuffs them into the bin. Then he showers, changes into the most distinctly different clothes he can find, walks downstairs, and steels himself as he goes back out into the street. He takes a taxi to the station, and when he gets out there are dozens of police roaming around. They must have guessed that many of those from the square would be making their way back to León by train, and this is an easy chance to try to find some more people to arrest. He keeps his head down as he makes his way to the ticket office, where there are two policeman standing, each with a hand resting on his gun. He buys a ticket to a town a couple of stops before León, hoping that this makes it less likely he might be questioned by anyone. He'll pay a fine on the train if he has to but will do anything to avoid the police in Madrid. He walks nervously to the platform where once again there are police milling around looking at all those boarding the train. He sees them stop two men, fire questions at them and look at their identity cards. Whatever they see satisfies them, because the men are allowed to board. When Mat reaches a point where there are fewer police, he climbs into the train and finds a window seat on the side further away from the platform. He stares out of the window, willing the train to leave, feeling that if he gets out of here without being arrested, he'll be safe. He hears a voice beside him. "Signor?" He doesn't look round. "Signor?" He turns and sees the smiling face of an elderly man. "Do you mind?" He points to Mat's bag, which he has absentmindedly left on the seat beside him. "I'm so sorry." He clutches the bag to his chest, and the man sits. Still there is no movement, and he must force himself stop continuously checking his watch to avoid looking suspicious. After a period of time he cannot even begin to estimate, there is the distinctive sound of the immense wheels straining into motion, and the train eases out of the station.

Chapter Twenty-Three

It is just after midnight when the train pulls in. He has dozed off from time to time during the journey, but the sense of desolation after the decision was announced, followed by the intense anger and fear from later in the day, have left him exhausted. When he hears the announcement that León is the next stop, there is a wave of relief that he is now home. Home? Is that where he is now? For all that has occurred in the time since he moved there, it is still only six months since he was living in London, and less than a year since he was managing new investment at Fieldings. Yet there is a feeling of comfort at returning to a place where he will no longer deal with corporate lawyers, or attend trials, a place where he will be able to see Miriam again and where everything can be better because she will be there to help him.

When he steps onto the platform, there is a rising fear that he will find police waiting for him as he enters the ticket hall, the possibility of arrest and trial to follow his rapid movement from multimillionaire to unemployed dependent. He passes through the open-ticket barriers, no one staffing them at such a late hour. He looks for the sign to the taxi rank, but before he sees it he feels a hand grasp him firmly by the arm and spin him round. He has an immediate and powerful urge to flee, but instead of the dark uniform he anticipated it is her, and she's holding him and she's speaking to him, but he can't understand because it is suddenly too much for him and he's sobbing, scared, relieved, angry, elated all at once. So he clings to her, and when he begins to recover she guides him outside and into the car, and twenty minutes later they are in her apartment.

She sits in silence as he tells her about the events earlier in the day, and her eyes widen when he describes what happened with the policeman. When he finishes, she holds him again and confirms that the chances of his being identified seem utterly remote, and she's still holding him as he eventually drifts off to sleep.

The days and weeks that follow see the formal capitulation. The union ends its industrial action, deciding the miners are better off making what money they can before the majority face dismissal and start looking for other work. For many it will be the first time they have sought a job outside a mine, and few will find one. Those that can will fall back on the income of a spouse or family members whilst they try to calculate how they can keep their home from the banks who have repossessed so many of them in the previous few years. When set against this, Mat's own circumstances appear to be almost opulent, although he must also keep an eye on events. He has Justice for Castile declared insolvent, which results in the local court appointing administrators to find anything they can to pay off the creditors. In practice, this means they are looking to plug the gaping hole of several hundred thousand euros owed to the government-appointed lawyers. Mat has correctly calculated that they will give up once they realise they are dealing with a US-based company, and the furthest they ever get is the news that the company has ceased trading.

A few weeks after the end of the case, Miriam shows him a link she has been sent by a colleague that leads to an article buried on the inside pages of a right-wing paper. The piece talks about the liquidation of Justice for Castile, mentioning difficulties in understanding the organisation's financial arrangements because much of their money came from abroad. When Miriam asks him about it, she is obviously trying to hide the concern she feels. "A lot of people around here know how involved you were."

"I was an unpaid volunteer who helped to run an organisation owned by some people in the United States who I never met. If anyone has evidence that I was anything more, let's see it."

"What if they *are* able to work their way back to you?"

"The journalist has obviously been briefed by either the administrators or the government, but they don't seem to know that Wyoming is a tax haven. Even if they work out it's a shell company with dummy directors, hell will freeze before they find out any-thing about who really runs the BVI account. Pretty soon they'll work out that they would just be spending their own money to get nowhere."

He sees her sudden change of expression, and curses himself for being so careless. She looks at him quizzically. "What is the BVI account?"

For a second he imagines she will leave him when she discovers the full truth. He considers lying, but would rather risk the truth. He inhales deeply before speaking. "It's an offshore account where I hid money from a major deal in order to avoid tax."

She shakes her head and smiles. "Under the circumstances I don't really feel like giving you a lecture today. Seems ironic that a government got all of it in the end."

"If you really want to make me feel bad you can point out that they will probably hand it over to Ramos and Calderon in the form of tax cuts, because this country needs wealth creators like them to lead the economic recovery."

Conversation then drifts back to what he should now do, and he is ultimately relieved at having unburdened himself of the deepest of his financial secrets. The obvious way for him to get some in-come in the short term is to sell the flat in Streatham, the only thing he now owns. The other option is to rent it out so he can have some sort of stable income, and it is Miriam who insists that he do this so as to retain the sense of a safety net that is always there to catch him. She also points out that between them they will have more money than most, and they can still live a comfortable life. As the days slip by, so the fear of arrest diminishes, with no indication that the police are seriously pursuing any investigations into charges for assaults on their own officers. Given that the TV footage has been dominated by blood-stained protesters running from exploding canisters of teargas, it seems someone has taken a tactical decision that complaints by armoured riot police about their poor treatment at the hands of unarmed demonstrators may be ill-judged.

What also emerge are the details behind the decision of the con-stitutional court. There was an eight-four split, with all seven of the judges appointed by the Popular Party coming down on the side of the government. Mat and Miriam's initial reaction is a sense of the horrifying futility of having gone through the process in the belief they might receive a fair hearing. Yet it is also perversely reassuring that the intuitions they started with were not undermined by any complex considerations about justice that might have led them to shift their own views. In the end, the conservative judges simply backed the politicians who put them in office for life.

Three weeks after he returned to León, Miriam asks him if he'll come with her on a trip to the centre. She suggests they go for lunch, but she takes an odd route and when he looks at her she says she wishes to drop by the union office to pick up some of the flyers they are distributing about helping former miners to retrain. He is unhappy about going back there, feeling that he wishes to move on from the disaster of the recent past. He is surprised to see there are so many people there when they arrive, and assumes they are desperately seeking advice on finding new jobs. Miriam goes in first and as he enters everyone rises, turns towards him and begins clapping. After a few moments they stop, and Felipe steps forward, ushering him to an unoccupied side of the office. He has managed to plea-bargain his way down to a public order offence, and will face no more than a small fine.

"Firstly, we must apologise for asking Miriam to lure you here using such deception, but as you are now aware, Spanish unions must use a range of tactics to try to fight their cause." Restrained laughter. "When you are fighting a dispute such as the one we were involved in, it is easy to feel that the world is against you. Police, politicians, banks, businesses, journalists, they have all attacked us in different ways. It is therefore especially powerful when someone comes from a different country and does as much as you have to help us. You have stood with us at a time when many in our own country betrayed us, and even if we have lost, we have achieved more than we could ever have done without you. There is nothing we can do to thank you enough, but we can at least make good on our promise to you." A man steps forward, and Mat recognises him as one of those from the very first march he went on to the colliery where they had fired on the police using the improvised rocket launchers. He passes over a large box, which Mat opens. He pulls out a miner's helmet with the letters of his name stencilled on it. He studies the helmet, never having received anything like this before. When he looks up, he feels the need to steady himself and prays his language will hold up. "I find it very difficult to know how to thank you for this. I am proud that I could help in some way, and I'm sorry I was unable to do more. During the court case I saw just how deeply unfair and corrupt politics has become, but I am also grateful that I had the chance to fight with very decent people who stand up for something more than enriching themselves." He looks down at the helmet again, and then back at the others in the room. "In the past, there were people who paid me a fortune. When I look back I see how little it means, and I can honestly say that none of it ever had as much value as this. Thank you."

They begin clapping again, and he struggles to hold back the tears. After a while, Felipe breaks in. "I'm afraid that our official funds have been too stretched to provide food and drink for celebrating Mathew's entry into union folklore, but as luck would have it we have become the fortunate beneficiaries of a mysterious gift. A supply of excellent wine has fallen into our hands, and I wish to make it clear that I have no reason to believe it is in any way related to the disappearance of a similar supply of wine from the offices of the senior management at our region's largest mine. I am convinced that no secretary would ever have agreed to allow a couple of miners to slip into those offices after an evening shift in order to bring about a fairer distribution of Spain's natural resources."

There is general laughter, and a tray full of plastic wineglasses is brought out along with the impressive range of wines. When Mat tastes it, he realises it may be the last time he consumes something of this quality, and he is relieved to find that he doesn't care. They spend an hour there, and the prospect of unemployment confronting most of those in the room is less depressive than he would have assumed. In the time since the dispute came to an end, they have already begun to confront the world that stands before them and to consider how they will deal with it.

By the time they leave, he is stuffed with tapas and lightheaded with the combination of the wine and the atmosphere of the event. He is clutching the helmet and reflecting on all that has happened when he suddenly realises they are driving down streets in a part of the city he doesn't know. "Where are we going?"

"Another surprise visit."

"I won't have to make another speech, will I?"

"Given how good your last one was, I don't see the problem is. But no, no speeches this time."

They drive for a few more minutes and pull up outside a new-ish-looking house in one of the residential areas. As they walk up to the front door, Mat assumes that it is either one of Miriam's colleagues or more likely Tom and Sofia, given the secrecy of it all. When they go in, he finds himself in an empty house, engineered wood floors rather than the more common tiled ones, and immense glass bi-fold doors leading into a garden with what he first believes to be an immaculate lawn but which turns out to be a highly real-istic artificial grass.

She is leaning against a sidewall and smiling at him. "What do you think?"

"You said you could get your apartment redecorated. This seems a little extreme." He hesitates, but needs to ask her. "You … I mean we can afford this?"

"Not by a long way."

He shakes his head. "I'm not with you. I thought we were here because you wanted us to move in."

"Unless you have any great objection, I suggest that's exactly what we should do."

"We can afford to rent it?"

"No, but as we already own it, that's not really an issue."

"What?"

"Yes. A mysterious benefactor came forward and purchased it for us. Turns out the same thing happened to Tom and Sofia. I don't suppose you know anything about that?"

He smiles, feeling on the verge of tears for the second time that day. "They bought it for us?"

"They got so much for their place in Streatham they were able to buy somewhere in Valencia and then this place. Apparently the estate agent just about got down and kissed their feet when they said they were cash buyers, and offered them hundreds of places from all over the country. I'm not sure I can say why, but it feels like there is some sort of complex way in which everything came out right."

He looks through the glass doors into the garden, his mind already working through the implications of living without rental costs. He wants to find something to do, and the options increase immeasurably with reduced outgoings. When he glances over at her, she is staring back at him. "You're going through the calculations on how we'll live."

He smiles in embarrassment. "Just some preliminary thoughts."

"Better build in one more major expense."

"Which is?"

"Childcare."

He stares back blankly, unable to believe what this must mean. "You're serious? You want to do it?"

"Be a shame to waste a house this size on just the two of us."

He walks over to her and they embrace. He is the first to speak. "Why? What happened?"

"I think you're right. I just think it's something we should try. I'm sure it's going to be a lot harder than either of us realises, but given our bizarrely fortunate financial circumstances, this may be a way of re-employing the mining community when we need help."

"You know you're really starting to think like a capitalist."

"I wonder whose influence that would be."

He holds her again, experiencing a wholly unexpected sense of elation despite having lost so much. She is so pleased for him, seeing all that it means after he thought everything had gone. She knows that he can never be allowed to understand the truth.

Chapter Twenty-Four

It takes seven months of toil within a process that is understandably detailed. Background checks, proof of income, evidence of experience in caring for children, interviews to assess the stability of the relationship. Once they realise just how demanding the examination will be, they piece together the most authentic story they can. Mat is able to spend his time dealing at length with all administrative requirements, and they alter their lives to make them correspond to ones that seem appropriate. They travel regularly to Valencia to look after Alicia and Feliciano, her cherubic little brother, allowing Tom and Sofia to go away for weekends. They burn through books on raising children, adoption and the potential issues facing those who have emerged from areas of conflict.

A further change they judge will help their chances of success is that they marry. They are both uncomfortable about this, partially in light of the catastrophe each endured the first time around, but also because there is a shared dislike of the artificial display they must offer of the way they genuinely feel about one another. They are together because they want to be, and marrying for pragmatic purposes seems to add an element of dishonesty made all the worse for the fact that it is so public. Nevertheless, the research Mat does confirms that applications for adoption are statistically more likely to succeed if those applying are married, so they go through with it.

The approach they take is that if they're going to do it then they may as well throw in some style. They reject the option of major blowout for the simple reasons they don't have any money and there is always the danger of appearing naïve if you have a mass celebration for a second marriage. So they settle on a municipal office located in what had been a seventeenth century villa in a town in northern Castile. The building has the distinctive curvilinear complexity, but there isn't the florid excess and the inverted shells they have seen in some of the more extravagant, baroque churches in Madrid. Yet the prospect to which they are particularly attracted is that the ceremony can take place in the beautifully manicured gardens.

They resist compiling an endlessly increasing list of individuals they ought to invite, restricting themselves to only a few more than their respective parents. Mat asks a friend from his Cambridge days to be best man, and Miriam's maid of honour is a colleague from the university. Tom and Sofia are the only other adults there. At the meal in the local restaurant afterwards, Miriam smiles as she watches Mat patiently interpret for his parents when they communicate with her own. He has been here for ten months by now, and he is fluent. But for the days of the court case, he has maintained a rigid discipline of studying for four hours a day, dispensing with the formal lessons after the case because it was an expense he no longer needed. So he bought the course books his teacher had been using and worked through them on his own. She sees the result of the obsessive, long-hours culture to which he had become accustomed in the City. He would rise at eight, study on his own, and then move on to books intended to reduce the mystery of their potential child. He has also uncovered an occupation that combines an occasional, pitiful income with a sense of satisfaction. At Sofia's suggestion he started considering translation, and included some theory amongst the myriad of other texts he has recently made his way through. She was able to put him in touch with a small London-based independent publisher, and he will produce one translation a year of an emerging Spanish writer, for whom sales of a couple of thousand copies would be stellar. If they unearth someone of talent there is the prospect of breaking into the US market, but the likelihood is that he will spend months working for the few hundred pounds he would previously have earned in a day. He can't wait.

His parents have a rough idea of what he has lost, and apply the traditional English solution of saying nothing and demonstrating they have grasped what is going on by paying for a week in Venice as a honeymoon. By the time they return, they have now put in place all the information that will be required of them, and they wait for the marriage to be a couple of months old before they submit the application and enter the process of being assessed for their worthiness as parents.

When they receive official news that they are deemed suitable it feels analogous to having someone confirm one is genuinely a member of the human race. However valid the need for sifting out only those who are likely to succeed, there is something belittling about having others judge them in this way, and they experience an immense relief that they have passed a test they resented sitting the first place. At the same time, there is an increasing sense of nervousness. For Miriam, there is the satisfaction of evading pregnancy, bodily overstretch, birth, breastfeeding, sleeplessness, and the immediate post-natal surge of visits despite the mother's impossible levels of tiredness. But this is set against the fear of the unknown. When? What will the past be? How old?

In addition to the intellectual preparation, there is also a matter of acquiring the paraphernalia of parenthood, and this means immersion in the children industry. Not knowing either the age or gender of their future child makes this more difficult, yet still leaves open endless options for gender-neutral toys and furniture. Miriam tires of this more quickly than Mat, recognising the shared obligation of selecting essentials but still irritated that she must inspect five hundred objects in order to select one to meet their needs in a way that makes it superior to an infinitesimally small degree. She begins to crack when they agree to travel to IKEA to pick out bedroom furniture Mat has resigned himself to assembling when it gets delivered the following day. She will try to leave work early, but if she is not back by three then he will go alone and she will trust his judgement. She remains in the office to do some bureaucratic tasks she had simply ignored for the previous ten years, but decided that she should now carry out. This means she steps onto the bus around an hour after she was supposed to be home, and it is almost four-thirty by the time she prepares to get off at their stop. There is then a flash of recognition as she sees Mat's face on the other side of the road. "The fucker," she thinks. "He stayed in longer than we agreed," and she ducks down below the height of the window. At this point her mobile begins ringing, and her novel, purse and bottle of water spill from her bag as she fishes out the phone. His name is displayed, but she decides neither to take it nor direct it instantly through to voicemail. She remains hidden below the level visible from outside the bus for the next two stops, with those around her looking on curiously. She smiles up at the other passengers. "We just passed my lover's wife. Very jealous type. Better she doesn't see me."

When the bus turns the corner, she gets off and listens to the message. "Darling, I think I saw you on the bus. If so can you meet me at IKEA and we can take care of this together." She ponders this. There was a definite hint of doubt, surely enough to exploit when he gets home later. She waits a few more minutes to ensure he is clear, makes her way back to the house and pours a glass of wine that she drinks as she reads in the back garden. The pleasure of both the book and the wine is heightened in virtue of their being a replacement for the Scandinavian hell of flat-packed furniture. She waits around an hour before calling him. "Darling, I'm so sorry, I only just got your message … No, must have been someone else, I've only just got home. Should I come and join you now?... Oh dear, I'm really sorry. I really wanted to be there with you so we could pick out the cot together. Are you sure?... All right then, I'll cook a really nice meal for us tonight. Love you, bye." She then refills her glass and goes back to the excellent book.

The stress of waiting evaporates one Tuesday morning when Mat receives a call asking how quickly he and Miriam can travel to Madrid in order to meet their daughter. This comes towards the end of Miriam's summer break, so they are both free and decide to drive down the next day. There is a feeling of unreality that they are within hours of crossing from the abstract into the real, with theoretical discussion now to be replaced by the flesh and blood of a child they must care for. The drive takes several hours, and each of them is so nervous it is difficult to sustain a conversation. There is also the difficult association of returning to the city where the court case was decided and where they are so aware of all that happened after that. Mat struggles to suppress what he knows to be the irrational fear of being identified and arrested just as he is about to have precisely the life he wants.

They arrive at the children's home around midday, and they must each compose themselves before entering. After waiting for fifteen minutes they are shown into an office in which shelves sag with box folders, and ancient metal filing cabinets line two of the walls. Yet the woman who sits there rises and smiles in such a way that it lifts the general depression of the strip-lit room. She has a file open on the table, they can see photos of themselves clipped to the papers.

The woman takes a deep breath. "My name is Miranda, and I coordinate the placement of refugee children as part of the government's response to the current crisis. I wish to give you some background details about who it is you will be looking after." She looks down at the file hesitantly, and it is clear that she has probably flicked through it a few moments before they entered and is unsure of the details she is now looking for. "Yes, you're actually adopting."

Miriam decides it would be better to try to respond sympathetically to someone who is doubtless floundering in the midst of a situation beyond what any of them understand how to deal with. "Could you tell us her name?"

"Soraya. We believe she is about two-and-a-half, judging by her size and her linguistic and social development."

Mat is unclear what to make of this. "You don't know her exact age?"

"She survived when a boat went down off Ibiza. She was picked up with a group of others by the coastguard, but as far as we can tell whoever was traveling with her didn't make it. She was wearing a proper lifejacket, which probably saved her. Many of the traffickers provide fake ones. We assume she was with her parents who have been lost."

"Do we know where she's from?"

"The other survivors from the same boat are Libyan. They were smuggled through Algeria with the promise of passage to Spain.

The boat was fit for barely half the number of people on it, and they forced one of the other refugees to pilot it. They were hit by a large wave about four miles off the coast. The boat capsized and they were in the water for around two hours before they were picked up."

The thought comes to Miriam that they could simply get up and walk out, that this is too much, the horror too great. She tries to think through whether there is any way they could back out at this stage and looks over at Mat to see if she can detect any similar thoughts. He is fully focused on what they are being presented with.

"How much of all this does she understand?"

"In the short term, she will be unable to process what has happened. As she gets older there will be a need to address not only that you are adoptive parents but also what has occurred to her. We can recommend specialists who will be able to advise you on how to confront these sorts of issues, and when."

"How long ago did all this happen?"

"She has spent around ten days in a camp on the island. Children are a priority for resettlement because there is a greater danger of developing mental health problems if they remain there too long. We've done a preliminary analysis that suggests she is physically healthy, but you will need to bring her for weekly assessments for the first few months." She stops, evidently registering the concern. "Look, it may take years to establish how serious the impact is, but children can also be terribly resilient. If she is loved … Well it's astonishing how people can recover."

They are both silent, stunned by the recognition of what they are taking on. After a moment it is Miranda who speaks again. "Right, I think it's time you met Soraya. They walk down the main corridor until they reach a waiting room. A middle-aged woman sits there reading a magazine and next to her a diminutive figure leaning back in the thinly padded chair with cheap, plastic upholstery. Her legs swing back and forth, and there is a strange discrepancy between the traumatic nature of her recent history and her mundane boredom at sitting in a lifeless room. It's as if they expect the enormity of what she has been through means she should be beyond such trivial emotions, gripped by some sort of unendurable sense of suffering. She looks up at them when they come in, but the legs continue to swing, and she is wholly oblivious of her imminent transfer into a life utterly unrelated to the one she has experienced up until now.

Miriam kneels down in front of her and addresses her in a language they all know she doesn't understand. "Hello, Soraya. We have something for you." She passes over a teddy. The girl looks up at the woman beside her, who nods. She takes it, and there is the hint of a smile as she pulls it close to her face. "We want to take you home now. We want to take you to your new home." She must have become accustomed to not understanding over recent days, for there is no look of concern. Miriam stretches out one hand, and the girl simply looks at her. "We have a lovely home ready for you, and we can go there now." They know they must be careful not to try for physical intimacy before she feels comfortable with them, yet she must feel she is the object of their affection, so they each take a hand and walk to the car with her between them. Mat drives, with Miriam sitting beside the child seat, which takes up half of the second row of the Polo. She talks to her throughout the journey and passes over various toys that emit a series of children's songs and music.

The first few days are spent striving to ensure she feels comfortable. They have prepared a bedroom for her, but they decide that she will sleep with them at first, the hope being that if she is close to them she will come to see them more quickly as the parents they wish to be. After a while, the time comes when Miriam must return to work, and Mat will begin looking after Soraya on his own. They go through the routine they have planned to put her down each evening. Bath, story, lullaby. They do this together, and when they come down for a meal Miriam opens a bottle of wine.

"Are you sure you feel up to this? We could still see if there is a nursery that could take her."

"I think we have to do this on our own to begin with. She has to get used to us." He is suddenly silent, and she knows something is wrong.

"What is it?"

"I know it's ridiculous at this stage, but I was sort of hoping she would be more affectionate."

She smiles at him. "She will be. It's just a question of time. I'm relieved that she hasn't been screaming through the night." She leans over the dining table and puts her hands on top of his. "Look, she's beautiful and she'll have a home where she knows she's loved."

He nods, but she knows he's not reassured and she considers calling in sick the following day, but decides that such a strategy would simply be postponing what must happen at some stage. When she wakes the next morning, she realises she's alone. Soraya tends to be up before the two of them and Mat has fallen into the habit of getting up with her so that Miriam can sleep longer. When she comes downstairs to make herself breakfast, she sees they are in the garden sitting beside one another, Mat reading a book. Neither sees she is there. The girl's head is motionless, the face a study of intense concentration as she focuses on the pictures while Mat reads to her, periodically stopping to embellish some of the characters.

The beauty of this makes her want to cry, and it leaves her feeling more optimistic than she has since she decided they should go through with it. She never wanted it, and she still struggles to come to terms with how she has got here. She initially felt at ease with the knowledge that he was in Spain because of her, involved in a fight not his own. This endured through the early shock of running from the police after they fired the rockets, and when the case went before the constitutional court. But then it became clear that he might lose so much, and she suddenly lost confidence in her instinct that it was all right for her to have demanded the sacrifices he was making. She hadn't anticipated it could go this far, that the cost of loving her would be so high. Her thoughtless reaction towards him when she discovered him looking at the website for helping refugees was largely a reflection of her own growing discomfort at the responsibility she was now feeling, and this simply grew worse when she recalled her stupidity in accusing him of looking for some replacement for his money in the form of a child. Then she took a call from Tom on the day the court's decision was due to be announced. They had accepted an offer on their flat a few weeks earlier and had been over to pick out a place in Valencia. He had been unsure whether or not he should reveal to Miriam that Mat had paid off their mortgage, but he knew that if the case went the wrong way, there was the possibility they would need some help. He thought it was better that she knew of what had happened so she understood that there was every reason for them to accept their money. She cannot believe it when Tom reveals how much they have received for the flat and just what this could buy in Spain. And then they lose the case and she is with this man who has given everything for her, who loves her and wants to have a child with her. And she loves him, and she wants to be with him, and she knows that if they don't do this, then it may always hang over them that he did all she ever asked of him and she denied him something so fundamental. And so she agrees to it, lying that this is what she wants.

Yet as she looks at the two of them through the window, she feels more hopeful than she did. Maybe there would, after all, be something for her in the dream of the happy family, something she has only ever glimpsed and never wished to try for. She considers going out to sit with them, but quickly decides she doesn't wish to ruin the sublime image of the two of them together. So she finishes her breakfast in the kitchen and quietly leaves.

*

Mat is speaking to her in English, the strategy being that if Miriam speaks Spanish then this will ensure she grows up to be perfectly bilingual. When he reads to her, she appears gripped by the stories despite understanding so little, but after only a few days she has remembered the names of characters in the books she likes, so he reads them to her as often as she wants and buys any others he can find in the same series, arranging for them to be shipped overnight so they have them as soon as possible.

When she sleeps with them, she seems more relaxed about being held than when she is awake. They dare not try to move too

STEPHEN GRANT

quickly, the fear being that they may revive some nightmare she may have experienced in the camp or elsewhere. They must also live in the knowledge that they may lose her. A family member may succeed in tracing her through one of the aid organisations tomorrow, or next week or next year, and it may be decided that she is better off with someone else. That is just the way it is, so they get on with things.

When he finishes reading the book, he goes inside and sees the breakfast bowl and coffee cup in the sink. She must have chosen to disappear unnoticed so as not to risk upsetting the girl. He goes back outside with some suntan lotion and a plastic ball he picked up at the supermarket the previous day. She sits surprisingly still as he applies the lotion, eyes fixed on the ball. When he gets up he walks over to the ball and she rises to her feet. He kicks it to her and she grabs it at the second attempt. He asks her to kick it back to him, but she won't let go. He sees she is smiling at him provocatively. He crouches, arms stretched out before him as he moves forward like a predator and she turns her back and races to the far end of the garden. He follows slowly. She dodges from side to side, but he is able to box her into a corner and she begins squealing and speaking in Arabic. He grabs at the ball, allowing her enough time to pull it away from him, and then she laughs at this success. He then rugby tackles her to the ground, ensuring she falls gently, and slowly pulls the ball away as she struggles to hold on to it. When it rolls free, she tries to race after it, but he grabs a leg to pull her back, and she laughs even harder. He then jumps up and races past her to the ball, trapping it under his right foot. She runs towards it and reaches out, but he guides the ball away from her just as she lunges forward, clutching comically at thin air. She instantly recovers and once again runs for the ball, which he taps back past her into the space she has just come from, and he then runs the other side of her. She turns quickly, races towards him again and throws herself on top of the ball, unconcerned by the prospect that he may try to kick it away and catch her. She then lies on it, clinging to it with all her force. He lies down beside her and begins once again to wrestle it from her, laughing himself now as she resists. Just as he is about pull the ball clear of her, she wriggles violently and unintentionally strikes him in the face with her elbow. He screeches in surprise, releases her and lies on the ground, holding his hand against the spot on his cheek where she caught him. Then he realises she is lying on him and holding him. Yes, she's holding him, and he knows he's home.

Acknowledgements

The world of financial services is often so complex that even those immersed in it seemed to have had little idea of what was going on in the years leading up to the 2008 financial crisis. Fortunately, a series of books have since been published explaining the intricacies of what occurred in such a way that the uninitiated can gain some grasp of it. *Whoops! Why Everyone Owes Everyone and No One Can Pay* by John Lanchester is an account of the background and the unfolding events of the crisis more gripping than any thriller. *The Big Short: Inside the Doomsday Machine* by Michael Lewis is an equally compelling account of how a small number of traders worked out what was about to happen and cashed in. *Eight Days: the Battle to Save the American Financial System* by James B. Stewart is an extended essay printed in *The New Yorker* in September of 2009, which describes in riveting detail the eye of the storm at the end of September 2008. *Bad Banks* by Alex Brummer covers not only the events described in these other works, but also many of the banking scandals which occurred after the sector 'reformed itself' in the wake of the crisis. This novel draws loosely on three sets of events that occurred in Spain between 2011 and 2013. There is no single book in the English language covering in detail the strike fought by the Castilian miners, the various scandals that befell the Spanish banks, or the accusations of funding irregularities in the Popular Party. The BBC and Guardian websites do however contain many pieces on all three topics. The workings of Spain's constitutional court are doubtless the subject of many different essays and books, but if there is any correlation between what you have read here and what goes on there it is purely coincidental. As the passages in this book set in the court were merely a device for exploring the obvious injustices imposed upon people who came out on the wrong side of the 2008 crisis, I had no wish to be obstructed by any inconvenient facts when writing these scenes.

Available & Forthcoming from UWSP

- *On Language & Poetry* by L. P. Yakubinsky
- *Philosophical Truffles* by Michael Eskin
- *Potentially Harmless: A Philosopher's Manhattan* by Kathrin Stengel